Please return/renew this item by the last date shown

**Herefordshire
Libraries**

 **Herefordshire
Council**

Kate McQuaile is a graduate of Faber Academy's 'Writing a Novel' course. She lives in London and works as a journalist, but is originally from Drogheda in Ireland.

WHAT SHE NEVER TOLD ME

Louise Redmond left Ireland for London before she was twenty. Now, two decades later, her heart already breaking from a failing marriage, she is summoned home. Her mother Marjorie is on her deathbed, and it is Louise's last chance to learn the whereabouts of the father she never knew. Stubborn to the end, however, Marjorie refuses to fill in the pieces of her daughter's fragmented past. Then Louise unexpectedly finds a lead: a man called David Prescott — but is he really the father she's been trying to find? And who is the mysterious little girl who appears so often in her dreams? As each new discovery leads to another question, Louise begins to suspect that the memories she most treasures could be a delicate web of lies . . .

KATE McQUAILE

WHAT SHE NEVER TOLD ME

Complete and Unabridged

CHARNWOOD
Leicester

First published in Great Britain in 2016 by
Quercus Editions Ltd
London

First Charnwood Edition
published 2017
by arrangement with
Quercus Editions Ltd
An Hachette UK company
London

The moral right of the author has been asserted

A catalogue record for this book is available from the British Library.

ISBN 978–1–4448–3175–7

Published by
F. A. Thorpe (Publishing)
Anstey, Leicestershire

Set by Words & Graphics Ltd.
Anstey, Leicestershire
Printed and bound in Great Britain by
T. J. International Ltd., Padstow, Cornwall

This book is printed on acid-free paper

In memory of my aunt, Frances Purcell

In memory of my aunt, Frances Tidball

Prologue

The little girl is underdressed for the cold night. No coat, just a jumper and pleated skirt, and knee socks that struggle to stay up as she canters along the pavement towards the green postbox, clutching the letter she has written to an old man with a white beard in a snowy, distant land without borders.

Around the square, curtains are closed against the cold and the dark. The street lights cast their beams as far as they can, but between each wooden pole there is a dark space that momentarily eclipses the child, causing your heart to miss a beat each time she disappears from view.

She's at the postbox now, looking up at the slot that she can only reach by standing on tiptoe. She stretches and strains to push the envelope towards the oblong mouth of the box. You watch. And wait.

1

Outside, the light is fading across the stretch of the extended town, past the estates towards the farmland and low hills beyond. My mother, no longer conscious, is also fading. The nurses haven't spelled it out in so many words, but everything they say makes me think she is close to the end.

'Talk to her,' the nurses say. 'She'll hear you. The hearing is the last thing to go.'

So I talk to her in a low voice, mostly about long ago when I was a child because that was the time we were closest. I talk about our outings to the sea, the two of us walking down to Amiens Street Station and taking the train to Skerries, where we would change into our bathing costumes and run as fast as we could into the waves so that there was no time to change our minds. Sometimes we went further, taking the train all the way to Drogheda and then a bus to Clogherhead.

I remind her of how hungry we used to be after our dips in the cold water, so hungry that it didn't matter that somehow the sand always found its way into the sandwiches she had packed. She would point into the distance at the Mourne Mountains, miles away to the north. And always, before we went back home, we would walk to the harbour to watch the seals that followed the fishing boats in from the sea.

Those memories are real, as real as everything I see before me now, except that the colours are muted, old-fashioned. They almost have a smell to them, the way the dark green of the old double-decker buses that carried us about seemed to have a smell to it.

I talk on, hoping she can still hear, losing myself in those memories as I recall them, so that the sound my mother makes — a *ssshhh* sound, repeated over and over — comes as a shock. At first, I think she's saying, 'Shush,' telling me to be quiet. But there's distress in the sound, as if there's something more she's trying to get out but can't.

'What is it, Mamma? What are you trying to say?' I ask her gently, but there's no answer, only the *ssshhh*, again and again. Eventually, the effort of it is too great for her and she sighs and lapses back into silence. I watch and wait. She is so calm now that I don't even notice the point at which she finally stops breathing.

★   ★   ★

Hours later, morning is creeping through a gap in the curtains into the dark bedroom where I've lain awake through what was left of the night. I'm frantic, physically and mentally, my body trying to find a place in the bed that will bring some rest, my head trying to keep track of the thoughts that dart like arrows through it.

And, as if from a shell picked up on the beach and held to the ear, I keep hearing that sound she made before she died, the *ssshhh* sound. I

3

hear it over and over again, ebbing and flowing, relentless in its rhythm, haunting and tormenting.

I can't bear to think that something I said might have penetrated her unconscious state to hurt her. We had our moments, my mother and I, but even at those times when I thought I had come close to hating her I knew that there was no escaping the bond we had.

I talked to her about memories last night. I don't know whether she heard me or not. But there's another memory that I didn't bring up because it hurt her once, a memory that has punctuated most of my life and that I have never understood.

It surfaces now, unbidden, and I see a green postbox and a small hand stretching upwards to push an envelope into its oblong mouth. The edges of the image are blurred. It's as if someone has opened an old tarnished locket to reveal a silent film playing in slow motion inside. It's always the same. It plays over and over, the little hand never in any position but extending upwards, the envelope always held in those childish fingers, the mouth of the green postbox almost within reach.

And then, as strangely as it has appeared, the grainy image fades, leaving me puzzled and slightly disturbed, even a little afraid.

I am never sure whether that small hand is mine. But if not mine, whose?

★   ★   ★

My mother's coffin stands in front of the altar. It felt strange to leave her there through the night, alone in the locked church. The last time she was here was for Dermot's funeral. She wasn't religious. 'You don't need religion to be a good person,' she used to say. She didn't leave any instructions for her own funeral and probably wouldn't have been too bothered if we had told her we were going to put her body into a cardboard box and tip it from a boat into the sea. The funeral is for me, because I need something beautiful and soft and hopeful to take away the memory of that terrible last night in the hospital. So the choir sings Fauré's Requiem, because, with no *Dies Irae*, no day of judgement, it's the sweetest, gentlest requiem of all, and as we all shuffle to the altar for Communion the choir sings Duruflé's 'Ubi Caritas et Amor'.

We leave the church for the graveyard. It's cold and wet, a typical November day in Ireland, but when the undertaker indicates one of the funeral cars I shake my head. I want to walk behind my mother on her final journey. Ursula, my friend since childhood, walks beside me.

A couple of relatives have turned up: my mother's older brother and his middle-aged son. We haven't spoken yet. They weren't part of my life when I was growing up, though I had known of their existence. Now, I have only the mildest curiosity about them.

It's the Keaveneys, Dermot's people, I think of as my family, even though I'm not related to them, and they're out in force — Angela and her husband, Joe, and their daughters and grandchildren. I've kept my eyes on the coffin all through the prayers at the graveside, but when it's finally lowered I can barely see anything because rain and tears are blurring my sight.

Ronan, Angela's grandson, tugs at my sleeve and puts his little hand into mine.

'Don't cry, Auntie Lou,' he says, his big eyes looking up at me from a face filled with a kindness you don't expect from a five-year-old boy.

This makes me cry even more and his mother, Lizzie, squeezes my shoulder and tries to move Ronan away, but he keeps his grip of my hand and refuses to let it go.

'He's fine,' I tell Lizzie.

After the burial, there's a reception at one of the local hotels and, with the worst of the funeral over and having downed a large glass of wine, I begin to emerge from the fog that has enveloped me over the past few days, the fog that has softened the longing to call Sandy. Now, my mind clear but filled with pain and loss, I am desperate to hear his voice. I slip outside to a courtyard and dial his number.

'Louise.'

The lack of expression in his voice hurts me almost as much as the loss of my mother does. The end of a marriage is another kind of bereavement and I'm still in mourning for it.

'Sandy, I . . . my . . . ' I start choking. I can't finish what I'm trying to say.

'Louise, what's wrong?'

'My mother died.'

6

'When? What happened?'

'A few days ago. It was lung cancer but it was very fast. We had no idea anything was wrong. I should have told you. I'm sorry — I didn't know whether I was coming or going.'

'Oh, God, I'm sorry. I wish I'd known. Where are you now?'

'In Ireland. We buried her today.'

'Would you like me to come over? Is there anything I can do?'

'It's all right . . . it's over now. There's not a lot else to be done at the moment. I'm not going to stay much longer. I can come back another time to sort her stuff out.'

'Are you staying with Angela?'

'Yes. She's been great.'

'Will you let me know when you're back?'

'Okay. I think I'd better go now. There are lots of people . . . I have to talk to them.'

'Call me when you're back. Okay?'

'Okay.'

There's a faint thudding going on in my heart as I end the call. Talking to Sandy has brought no comfort. It has just reinforced my sense of having been cast adrift. I sit on one of the metal garden chairs and, to take my mind away from the nothingness of my marriage, I think about all the things I have to do.

My mother told me during her final days in the hospital that she was leaving everything to me, everything being the small house she moved into after Dermot died and whatever money she had in the bank. I'll have to go through her things and decide whether or not to sell the

7

house. But these are tasks I can put off for a while. I can go back to London in the next few days and, after a month or two, return to Ireland to sort everything out.

I don't know how long I've been sitting there when Ursula appears.

'Oh, Lou, what are you doing out here? You'll freeze to death without a coat.'

'I called Sandy.'

'And?'

'Nothing, really. He says to call him when I'm back in London.'

'Good. Now, let's get you inside and warmed up.'

My mother's brother, Richard, comes over to talk to me with his son, Peter, who has driven him down from Dublin. I have no recollection of ever having met either of them, but Richard tells me he remembers me as a very small child.

I'm not surprised when he tells me that he found out about my mother's death when he read the notice Angela placed in the paper; people of a certain age in Ireland tend to go straight to the death notices before they read the news. But I am surprised when he tells me they had been in occasional contact over the years. She had never mentioned it. His name rarely came up.

'The last time we talked was during the summer. I had no idea she was so ill,' he says.

'None of us did. She probably didn't, either, until it was too late.'

'Still, I wish I had known. I might have been able to help.'

Richard speaks in the light, refined tones of Dublin's more affluent southern suburbs, as my mother did. I see the physical resemblance between them, too. Like my mother, he's tall and, despite his age, moves lightly, fluidly. He's a handsome man.

'I'm very sorry you had to deal with Marjorie's death by yourself,' he says.

'I had Angela. Dermot's daughter. She was very good to my mother,' I say, making the point that the person I have leaned on most is not a blood relative.

He looks slightly uncomfortable, but I may be reading into his expression what I want to see. A quick calculation tells me that he must be close to eighty, but he wears his age well. Peter is a different type, shorter than his father and stockier. Probably a rugby player at whichever top boarding school he will have attended. His slightly florid complexion, bordered by dark hair that is flecked with grey, hints at future health issues. He won't age as gracefully as his father. I almost feel sorry for him; clearly, neither of us has inherited the Redmond genes.

As Richard and I talk, Peter smiles occasionally, his small and silent contribution to the short and difficult conversation. Perhaps he senses some hostility from me, or maybe he feels he has given enough of his time to the funeral of an aunt he didn't know, because before very long he looks at his watch and apologises, saying they have to leave.

Richard, looking somewhat relieved, says goodbye to me. But just as he starts to walk

9

towards the door, he turns around and takes my hand.

'Will you come and see me in Dalkey, Louise?' he says. 'I have some photographs you might like to see.'

I make a vague promise to visit him, but I have no intention of keeping it. He has never been part of my life. Why should I invite him into it now?

2

I'm a bag of nerves as I walk to the solicitor's office. Since the funeral, I've thought of little but this meeting and what I pray I'm going to hear.

The will itself is straightforward. My mother has left me her entire estate, which consists of her house and about eighty thousand euro in a bank account. When Dermot died a few years ago, she sold the lovely, spacious house he had built for her, insisted on giving Angela most of the proceeds of the sale and bought a small two-bedroom cottage just outside Drogheda, on the south side of the river. She paid a lot for it. The Celtic Tiger was still roaring, house prices were going through the roof and people joked that, if you didn't lock the gate behind you in the morning, you risked coming home in the evening to find that someone had built a new house in your garden.

The solicitor stands up and stretches out his hand, saying he has another appointment shortly.

'Well, Louise, again, you have my condolences. She was a fine woman, your mother, always a pleasure to deal with. She knew her own mind. And at least she didn't have a long-drawn-out illness. She didn't suffer for too long.'

'That's it? With the will, I mean? There's nothing else?' I ask.

'Were you expecting something else?' He looks surprised by my question.

'I thought she might have left something . . . like a letter.'

'No, nothing like that. Everything is laid out in the will.'

I want to weep with disappointment and frustration. I had hoped that, before she died, she would at least tell me the truth about the one thing I wanted and needed to know — how to find my father.

★ ★ ★

We were very self-contained, more like friends than parent and child, although she never really confided in me, never told me whether she was worried about anything. Before I started school, I wasn't exactly a lonely child, but I was desperate for a sister, someone who was just like me. I used to daydream about what life would be like if I had one. Would we look alike? Would she be older or younger? Where would she sleep? My room was just big enough to accommodate a small single bed, so we would have had bunk beds. I used to imagine the whispered conversations we would have in the dark before falling asleep, she in the top bunk, me in the bottom.

'Mamma, why can't I have a sister?' I used to plead, and my mother would ask me why I wanted one. Weren't we getting along very nicely as we were, just the two of us?

'I want someone to play with!'

There was no answer to that. She could take me to all sorts of places and events — the zoo, the seaside, the circus, pantomimes at the Gaiety — but she couldn't do anything to stop the envy I felt when I saw families laughing and playing together, parents and children calling out to each other as they climbed onto buses or spread out picnic rugs on the strand.

I wanted to know why we were different from other families, all of whom seemed to have fathers.

She explained that she hadn't been married to my father and that before I was born he had gone back to England, where he was from.

'Why?'

'Why what?'

'Why did he go to England?'

'He had to. I don't remember why.'

'Can we go to see him?'

'No,' she said. She didn't know where he lived and it would be impossible to find him because his name was David Prescott and there were hundreds, maybe even thousands of David Prescotts in England.

'Why don't you know where he lives?'

'I just don't.'

'Maybe he'll come to see us some day.'

'Oh, I don't think so, my darling, because he didn't know you were going to be born.'

I was easily fobbed off. The questions remained in my head, but over time I asked them less often because I knew what her response would be.

At the same time, as I became more aware of how other families operated, I became ashamed of not having a father I could talk about. I knew that acknowledging this would set me far apart from the other children at school, so I learned how to navigate around the issue. I became adept at dodging the kind of questions that might have put me on the spot. I never told lies. I just didn't tell the entire truth.

So if a classmate asked me something innocuous — like, 'Where does your father work?' — I would say I didn't know, and then I would change the subject or ask her something about herself or her family. It always worked, and I learned at a very young age how easy it was to shift attention away from myself. Only Ursula knew the truth in those early days at primary school.

We lived in a rented flat above a chemist's shop in Drumcondra. There was really only one proper bedroom — the one my mother used. What I had was little more than a box room. I can see it now, a tiny space that could just about accommodate my bed and a door that didn't open fully because the bed was in the way.

I can still see my mother's room in my mind's eye, a red bedspread providing startling colour against the dark floorboards and wardrobe. I see her dressing table, her Coty lipstick and Max Factor powder compact, her necklaces and bracelets, the silver cigarette holder that she was never without.

And if I close my eyes and lift my head just the tiniest bit, I can smell the perfume she wore, Calèche by Hermès. I wear it, too, but on me it smells different, powdery, not at all like the citrusy, woody scent that lingered in the air long after she had passed.

★ ★ ★

There was just one fisherman at Clogherhead's little harbour. He sat quietly immobile, like a statue in shadow under the setting sun.

We had been in the sea earlier, stepping carefully over the stones as the incoming tide washed around our ankles and then our knees, shrieking as the sea bed dropped away suddenly and we were beyond our depth, left momentarily flailing before we got the measure of the waves. We stayed long after all the other families, one by one, had gathered up their picnic blankets and baskets, disassembled their striped windbreakers and gone away, leaving the strand bare and quiet except for the sound of the waves.

'I think we've missed the last bus, so we're not going to get home tonight,' my mother said, looking at her watch. 'It looks like we'll have to stay here.'

My eyes widened with excitement. 'On the strand?'

'No, I don't think that would be a good idea. We'll find a bed and breakfast. Now, will we have a walk down to the harbour before we go back to the village?'

We walked along the pier, my mother and the lone fisherman exchanging silent nods of greeting as we passed him. I broke away from her to peer into the bucket beside him. It was empty.

'Did you not catch any fish?' I asked him.

'Louise! Don't be so bold,' she said. 'Don't

15

mind her,' she said to the fisherman. 'She gets overexcited when we get out of Dublin.'

'Louise,' he said, addressing me. 'That's a very nice name.'

A long time later, when the sun had stopped shining and the water had turned from sapphire blue to granite, the man and my mother were still talking and I was beginning to regret that I had started them off on this long conversation. Eventually, my mother said it was probably time for us to go.

'Off back to Dublin?' the man asked.

'Not until tomorrow. We missed the bus, so we thought we'd stay in a B & B tonight and have another day. It's not often you get days like this in Ireland, is it?'

'Indeed, it's not. We've been long due a good summer,' the fisherman said. 'Have you got a B & B arranged already or would you like me to recommend one?'

'It would be great if you could recommend one.'

I rolled my eyes upwards. I knew where this was leading. Men were always trying to talk to my mother, and she was always polite, always friendly, but gave them no real encouragement, told them nothing about herself. So I was a bit surprised when she let him drive us in his car to a farmhouse that he said took in guests. She had always told me not to talk to strangers and now here we were in a car with one.

They chatted on in the front of the car and I sat quietly in the back, looking out through the window at the change from coast to farmland, but keeping an ear on their conversation.

Eventually, the car stopped in front of a big farmhouse, whitewashed and thatched. A black-and-white collie raced around from the back of the house, barking excitedly as we got out of the car.

The front door of the house opened and a big, agricultural-looking woman wearing an apron came out.

'Dermot, how are you? You're looking well,' she said, before acknowledging my mother and me. She gave us a funny look, I thought.

'I'm grand, thanks, Delia. You're looking well yourself. Now, this is Mrs Redmond and her daughter, Louise, and I've told them you have the finest rooms in Clogherhead,' he said.

'He's full of *plámás*,' the woman said, but her face was beaming, basking in the flattery.

Inside, the floor was made of big stone slabs and we had to walk down a hallway to get to the stairs at the back of the house. I wasn't too impressed, but my mother said what a lovely old house it was and how marvellous that Delia hadn't covered up the stone with linoleum or carpet.

'You're not from around here, then?' Delia asked, picking up on my mother's tone and neutral accent.

'No,' my mother said. 'We live in Dublin.'

Another odd look from Delia. My mother didn't seem to notice, but I did.

The room had sloping ceilings, a wardrobe and one big bed. The windows were low and set deep into the walls, and when I looked out, my

17

heart leaped with delight at the sight of a donkey lazily cropping the grass in a small field at the back of the house.

'It's a lovely room,' my mother said, sitting on the bed. 'We'll be very comfortable here.'

Delia handed my mother some towels.

'Have you no bag with you?' she asked. It sounded like a reprimand.

My mother laughed. 'No. Actually, we just came for the day but missed the bus that would have got us back to Drogheda in time for the last train to Dublin.'

I could tell that Delia wasn't impressed.

'I'll leave you to it, so,' she said, turning to leave the room.

My mother took a comb out of her handbag and ran it first through her hair and then through mine. She stood in front of the mirror and put lipstick on. I wondered why she was doing that, but said nothing.

'Come on,' she said, taking my hand. 'Let's go.'

Delia was at the bottom of the stairs, waiting for us to come down. She rattled through the rules of the house. Guests were not admitted after ten at night, breakfast would be served at such and such a time and, as we were only staying one night, we would have to be out by eleven the following day.

'That's no problem,' my mother said, all smiles.

I was put out to see that Dermot was still there. He rose from the chair he was sitting in when he saw us.

'I'll have them back to you long before you close the door for the night, Delia,' he said.

He took us to a restaurant, stopping at a small shop on the way so that my mother could buy toothbrushes and toothpaste. The restaurant wasn't in the village. It was a big place, set back from what seemed to be a main road. It was full of people, some of them dressed up, others wearing ordinary clothes. My mother and Dermot ordered steak. I wanted steak, too, but my mother said it would be too much for me, so I had to have fish fingers and chips from the children's menu.

I spent the evening trying to ignore what I could see going on between them. They were drinking red wine and I noticed that her eyes were bright and dancing and that she and Dermot looked at each other a lot. I wondered what she saw in him. He looked a bit like her favourite film star, Paul Newman, and he was about the same age — old. He had a nice voice, though, and if I didn't look at him and his wrinkly old face, he sounded much younger.

He took us back to the farmhouse and I thought, Good, that's that. But then I heard him say he would pick us up in the morning and take us around the Boyne Valley, and I had a feeling that things were going to be different from now on.

3

It's my last night in Ireland and the family all turn up at Lizzie's for an early dinner. I shouldn't have favourites, but I can't help it. Brigid is adorable, the sweetest little three-year-old you could imagine, but Ronan cracks me up with his naughty little face and the things he says and does. He doesn't mean to be funny and gets cross when we all laugh. Now, he's tired and starting to become tetchy, and Lizzie says she'll put him to bed. She comes downstairs after a few minutes.

'He wants you to tell him a story, Louise,' she says. 'Do you mind?'

'Not at all. What's he into these days?'

'His current favourite is *Charlie and the Chocolate Factory*. It's on the top of the pile.'

Ronan is already tipping into sleep and struggling to stay awake for his story when I go into the room. I sit down on the side of the bed with the book. It won't take more than a couple of pages before he's out for the count. But he doesn't want *Charlie and the Chocolate Factory*.

'Tell me about the Sandman, Auntie Louise,' he says.

'Wow, Ronan, how do you know about the Sandman? I don't think I've told you about him before.'

'Mammy told me.'

'Well, let's see if I can do as well as your

mammy. Are you ready?'

He nods.

'Now, you know how sometimes you wake up and you rub your eyes?'

He nods his head as vigorously as he can. It's such an effort that I have to suppress an urge to laugh.

'That means that the Sandman has been to see you.'

'Why does he come?'

'Because sometimes little boys and girls are far too excited to sleep, so the Sandman comes and sprinkles the finest sand into their eyes and they can't help but fall asleep.'

'Will he come to see me tonight?'

'That will depend on whether you're asleep or not. He might.'

'Will the sand hurt my eyes?'

'Goodness, no. It's the finest sand you can imagine. It's made of gold and it's so fine you can't even see it. And once the Sandman sprinkles it into your eyes, you'll be asleep before you know it, and you'll have the most wonderful dreams. What would you like to dream about?'

He doesn't answer. He's already fast asleep.

'That was quick,' Lizzie says when I go back downstairs. 'He must have been really knackered. *Charlie* tends to keep him going a bit longer than other stories. I was afraid you might have been stuck up there with him for ages while he moidered you with questions.'

'He didn't want *Charlie*. He asked me to tell him about the Sandman. I was a bit surprised. I haven't thought about that story for years.'

21

'No, but I have,' Lizzie says. 'You used to tell it to us when you were babysitting for Ma and Da. It came into my head out of the blue a while ago and I've told it to him a couple of times. He's fascinated by it. It's the kind of story kids don't get told these days.'

Rosie pipes up with her own recollections of the times I had looked after them as children. 'Do you remember the time you took us to see Oliver Plunkett's head, down in St Peter's, and Ma was so pissed off? Weren't you, Ma?'

'I certainly was!' Angela says. 'Severed heads are no things to be showing small children, even if they belong to saints and are a few hundred years old.'

'But they begged me to take them to see it! It wasn't my idea.'

'Sure, didn't we all grow up lighting candles in front of it,' Joe says. 'And divil a bit of harm it did us, either. Did you have nightmares, girls? You did not.'

'I have to admit,' I say, 'that it was the first thing I showed Sandy when I brought him here to meet Mamma and Dermot! I told him to close his eyes as we walked up the side aisle and count to ten before opening them — by which time I'd snuck away.'

The girls shriek with laughter and I join in. It's a good feeling.

★   ★   ★

Angela drives me to the airport. It's a beautiful day, cold and bright, and the watery light of the winter sun brings out the colours of the fields and farmland, the deepest greens, the darkest yellows. It's the kind of day that makes you want to stay in Ireland forever.

As we pull up in front of the terminal, Angela leans across and hugs me and I disintegrate into tears. It feels like a severing.

She turns the engine back on. 'I'm not leaving you here like this. I'm going to put this thing in the car park and I'll come in with you,' she says.

I hate goodbyes. Maybe it's an Irish thing, the last-minute rush of emotion that never fails to hit as you realise you're leaving yet again. I like to jump out of the car with a quick wave and rush into the terminal without a backward glance. But, this time, I'm grateful that she's going to stay with me until it's time for me to walk through the barrier.

We sit at one of the cafés on the departures floor and reminisce about my mother.

'I have to admit it was a bit of a shock when my father called me in Liverpool to say he was getting married. I'd just come off a night shift at the hospital and I was exhausted, and there he was telling me he'd met a woman he was going to marry, and my own mother only a few years dead. I burst into tears,' Angela says.

I smile. I hadn't been too happy, either, when my mother told me she was going to marry Dermot and we were going to go and live with him.

'And when I met her for the first time, I thought she was a bit too full of herself, a bit too expensive-looking and far too young for my

23

father. There was a good fifteen years between them.'

I can't help laughing now. My mother was expensive-looking. I didn't know what style was when I was young, but she had it. She could buy a cheap scarf at Clerys or Arnotts and loop it around her neck in a way that made her look like a film star or one of those models you saw on the covers of magazines.

'I was convinced he was making a big mistake,' Angela says, encouraged by my laughter. 'And I don't think I was the only one. It was a lot for my father to take on, a single mother — we called them 'unmarried mothers' in those days — and a ten-year-old child. But they made a great go of it. He was floundering after my mother died and Marjorie turned out to be the best thing that happened to him.'

'He was good for her, too. He was lovely. I still miss him,' I say, and the tears come back into my eyes. 'Sorry, sorry, I'm such a mess at the moment.'

'That's not surprising,' she says softly. 'You've had a lot on your plate. First Sandy going and now your mother.'

'Yeah, I know. But it feels like more than that. It's as if I've lost everything that's been keeping me on an even keel and I have nothing left inside. And after I saw Mamma's brother the other day at the funeral, I kept thinking about all the things I should have asked her and won't be able to now.'

'Like what?'

'Like what her life was like before she had me,

for a start. Who her friends were. Whether she got on with her brother. And . . . well, you know . . . my father.'

Angela nods. 'It's a shame she never talked to you about all that.'

'I used to ask her to tell me what he was like, what he looked like, but she always managed to make me feel I was being a pest, asking too many questions. I used to ask her where he lived and she always said she didn't know.'

'Maybe she didn't.'

'Maybe. But I never really believed her. I think she knew exactly where he was and just didn't want me to have any contact with him. Anyway, you know how it is — you come up against a brick wall over and over again and eventually you give up. I just hoped she might have left something with the solicitor, a letter or even just a piece of paper with his address on it.'

'It's an awful pity my own father is gone. He might have been able to tell you a lot. I always had a feeling he knew much more than he let on. Of course, we all knew that your mother wasn't married to your father, but it just wasn't talked about. What about your uncle, though? Would you not think about talking to him?'

'I don't know . . . He did ask me to visit him, but I wasn't planning to. I hardly know him. Do you think I should?'

'I do. This has been on your mind for a long time, and now you have a chance to do something about it. Richard is your only blood relative and he's not getting any younger. Maybe he'll be able to fill in a few gaps for you. And you might even get to like him. He seems a nice man.'

'I might go to see him when I come back.'

'Good woman. Now, you'd better be getting yourself through the gate. God bless. And we'll see you at Christmas.'

I walk through security and turn around to wave at Angela. She waves back but doesn't move. I know she will stand there until I disappear from sight.

★ ★ ★

Back in London, it's lashing rain and the streets are dark and empty. Threatening. Only a few hours ago, I had been surrounded by Keaveneys. Angela and Joe, their daughters, Lizzie and Rosie, and their husbands and children. The flat feels cold, as if no one has lived in it for a long time. It looks cold, too, like one of those short-term rentals that you stay in for a while and walk away from without leaving anything of yourself behind. And yet everything Sandy and I put into it is still here. The paintings on the walls, the floorboards painted white, the big blue linen-covered sofas in the sitting room, the bed that's so huge we used to joke about inviting our friends over for a picnic in it. But there's nothing left of him, not even the smell of the old-fashioned aftershave he wears, Antaeus. It's as if there's nothing left of us.

I don't even take my coat off before I pick up the phone. He told me to call him when I got back. But his number just rings and rings and a feeling of desolation sweeps over me as I put the phone down. This is the way it's going to be, I tell myself. I have to get used to being without him. But I can't help wishing and hoping that something will change, that we'll somehow get back to how we used to be.

In just a few weeks, it will be my forty-third birthday.

4

The eleventh of December. My birthday. I have no great wish to celebrate my forty-three years. Trying to cope with the breakdown of my marriage and agonising over whether we can ever put it together again has been tough enough. Now, waking up every morning with the awful knowledge that I will never see my mother again, I feel as if I'm drowning. I haven't been able to work. Even if I was able to haul myself to the studios, I don't think I could cope if any of my singers turned up with something sad. They've been great. They send me texts saying they hope I'm all right and that they're looking forward to seeing me again soon. Ursula, though, says I can't just keep drawing down what I've got in the bank and the sooner I start working again the better. And, she keeps telling me, I mustn't cut people off for too long.

So she has insisted on getting a bunch of friends together at the Italian wine bar. All I have to do is turn up.

I lie in bed far longer than I should, feeling sorry for myself and wondering about the point of it all. London seems empty now that Sandy has taken himself out of my life. I hadn't even wanted to come here in the first place; I had done what my mother had told me I should do — as I had always done, whether her intentions were overt or hidden. Had I not met Sandy, I might not have stayed. But, then, where would I have gone?

I stay in the bed for most of the morning, but I don't sleep. If I don't get up, if I don't even speak, if I maintain silence and darkness, it will be as if time isn't allowed to move forward. I do a lot of that, these days. Ursula tells me it's a kind of depression and I should get help, talk to a bereavement counsellor or even a psychotherapist. I always tell her I'll think about it, but to myself I say, *No way.*

The light coming in through the chink in the curtains eventually becomes so bright that I push the covers away, drag myself out of the bed and into the bathroom to be shocked awake by the strong jet of the shower.

I make a plan of action for the day, although it's not much of a plan and there isn't much action involved. At some point, I'll wander down to the high-end boutiques on Westbourne Grove and treat myself to new clothes, something edgy, something to declare that I may be forty-three, but I look every bit as good as a thirty-year-old.

The flowers arrive around midday as I'm drinking my umpteenth cup of coffee — a big bunch of flowers. The colours are dramatic — dark red and pink and purple. I know they're not from Ursula. They must be from Angela and Joe. But when I look at the card that accompanies them and see that they're from Sandy, my heart leaps. And then I feel deflated when I remember that Sandy has always sent me roses on my birthday. I try to work out what these non-roses mean.

I think back to last year and the long-stemmed crimson roses. Twenty-four of them. So things must have been all right then, I think, throwing myself into yet another frenzied examination of my failed marriage, going over the same events, trying to remember the words that were said and the ones that weren't, the looks that were exchanged, the times he looked away. I want to be able to stick pins on to an imaginary graph charting the collapse that must have taken time but which seems to have happened almost overnight.

At what point did things start to go wrong and were there warning signs I ignored or just didn't notice? I analyse, deconstruct, hypothesise. If only I had done this. If I hadn't done that. I turn my attention to the card and try to contain the flicker of hope it lights, pinch it out before it becomes too strong. But it's too late. *Louise, with love, Sandy.*

I should take the words *with love* at face value: a warm message from my estranged husband on my birthday. We have, after all, seen each other since I came back from Ireland. He has been supportive, calling me every few days to make sure I'm all right. These enquiries — I stop short of calling them conversations — have a certain tone to them, a caring tone. But they make me feel like a patient talking to her doctor, rather than a wife, even a separated one, talking to her husband. So, when I read the words on the card, I fill them with meaning and hope, and when the phone rings an hour or so later, I'm on high doh.

It's Sandy, his Scottish burr like music to me

as he wishes me a happy birthday.

'Thanks for the flowers. They're lovely,' I tell him, now full of certainty that the flowers and the message accompanying them must signify some kind of turning point.

I wait to hear him say that he misses me, after all, and that maybe we can try to pick up the pieces of our broken marriage and put them together again. But he doesn't. So I start telling him about the party that Ursula has arranged and, buoyed by the arrival of the flowers and the message on the card, suggest that he might like to come, if he's not busy.

'I'm sorry, Lou, but I'm about to catch a plane.'

'Another conference?'

'Another conference. Well, happy birthday again. I hope you have a terrific party.'

Yeah, right. I put the phone down without saying goodbye.

★   ★   ★

The party is in full swing at the Italian wine bar when I get there and I feel I'm drowning in the sea of faces. And then I see Ursula among the crowd and I want to throw my arms around her, shower her with thanks for having always been there for me. Ursula, on the other hand, looks more than a little cross when she sees me saunter in, not only very late but also slightly the worse for wear after the half bottle of wine I've drunk to shore up my defences. I've never been a big drinker, but the twin catastrophe of losing my

31

husband and my mother has dealt my sobriety a blow and, as the evening goes on, I manage to down a few more drinks.

'I love the hair,' Ursula says. 'It suits you. Takes years off you. Fabulous jacket, too. I'm glad to see you've been treating yourself — for a change.'

In the afternoon, on a whim, I had walked into a hairdressing salon and asked the stylist to decide what kind of cut would work for me and to get on with it. I had nothing to lose. Hair grows and, over the past few months, mine had grown so much that I had taken to wearing it pulled back into a ponytail or scrunched into an unruly up-do. But I liked the cut the hairdresser gave me, short and spiky and gamine, nothing I would ever have imagined might suit me.

And, to celebrate the haircut, I had spent a small fortune on new clothes. A dark green leather jacket, a long and tight-fitting black cashmere jumper, black jeans and narrow ankle boots. The boots were almost flat, which was just as well, because any more of a heel and I would have had trouble staying upright.

'Let's drink to that!' I say, taking a bottle and filling up my glass.

'Do you not think you've had enough?'

'Oh, for God's sake, Ursula! That's a bit of a joke, coming from you. Pot? Kettle? Anyway, it's my birthday, and no, I don't think I've had nearly enough. Now, if you don't mind, I have to go to the loo.'

The Sandy lookalike I pass on the way to the loo stops me in my tracks, and for a moment I'm persuaded that my estranged husband has turned up, after all. But it's not Sandy. He's a lot younger and, as I discover when I examine him more closely, he doesn't really look like Sandy at all. But he's not unattractive. He'll do. I chat to him for a while, my confidence boosted sky high by the booze and by his telling me that I remind him of a short-haired Sandra Bullock, and then I go back to my party. But I know he'll be waiting for me when I leave. And he is.

With all the food I've eaten, I've sobered up enough to feel the disapproval of my friends as I wave goodbye to them and stagger back to my flat in Ladbroke Grove with my new friend. He, too, has had a lot to drink. He has waited for me, and now that we are inside my flat, he's eager for action. My enthusiasm has waned with tiredness. But I'm feeling confident. Here's someone who wants me, even if Sandy doesn't. And so I make all the moves I am supposed to make, all the usual sounds as we grind against each other. But when I pull away from him, I feel empty of everything but self-disgust.

I shunt him out of the flat, telling him my husband will be home any minute. He stares at me in drunken astonishment.

'You're . . . nuts,' he manages to say, struggling to get into his coat as I ease him out on to the steps and close the door behind him.

Tomorrow I'll make the phone calls to Ursula and the others. I'll apologise for abandoning them and walking off with a stranger.

I have an excuse; I've had to deal with too much loss all at once and alcohol has given me a temporary respite from it, but I'm all too aware that this has not been my finest hour.

★ ★ ★

'Sorry about last night. I didn't behave well,' I tell Ursula on the phone.

'So you bloody well should be. I hope you have the mother and father of all hangovers and that it lasts for a week.'

'I have a hangover and it's horrible. So am I forgiven now?'

'I'll think about it. But, really, Lou, how could you go off with a stranger? He could have been a serial killer.'

'But he wasn't, was he? I'm a good judge of character.'

'Yeah, and I'm sure a lot of women killed by charmers who turned out to be serial killers thought they were good judges of character, too,' she says drily.

'Well, I seem to recall that you've wandered off with a few strangers in your time,' I mutter.

'Lou, I know this is a hard time for you, but don't make it worse by doing stuff like that. Okay?'

'All right,' I say. 'Look, I'm starving. I haven't had anything to eat since breakfast. I don't suppose you fancy meeting up for lunch? My treat.'

We meet at one of the cafés on Westbourne Grove and order food. I start to ask for a bottle of white wine, but Ursula jumps in and tells the waiter we're going to have two glasses, small

34

ones. I protest, telling her that it's cheaper to order a bottle than to order four glasses.

'We're not having four glasses. We're having two, one each, and you're lucky I'm letting you have even one,' she says.

Ursula is bossy, but I give in. She's right. I've been drinking too much for too many weeks. It's time to cut back.

'Any word from Sandy?'

'Not since yesterday morning. He called to wish me a happy birthday. God, Ursula, don't ever let slip to him that I . . . '

'That you shagged some stranger? It's none of his business. But don't worry, I won't. So what's the latest? I suppose you're still hoping he'll come back?'

I shake my head at first. I try to keep telling myself that there's no hope of saving my marriage, that it's finished and that I have to move on. But that's not what I feel deep down. I would have him back in a trice.

'I still don't understand why he left, what I did to make him leave. I asked him if he'd met someone else and he said he hadn't,' I say.

She nods her head up and down. She has heard it all before, over and over.

'Oh, fuck, Ursula, I miss him so much.'

Ursula doesn't do soft. She either says what she thinks, which is most of the time, or she keeps quiet. You never have to wonder where you are with her.

'It really pisses me off when you keep talking about what you may have done to make him leave. I hate to upset you, Lou, but there

35

probably was a woman. There always is. 'Space' my arse — men make their own space all the time, no matter where they are, and women have to fit into it. They're all liars, even men like Sandy. They can't help it. It's just the way they are. And they can't bear to take the blame, so they learn how to make women feel guilty. Don't do this to yourself,' she says.

Easier said than done. It doesn't take much effort to recall the moods and silences that led up to the night Sandy told me he was moving out for a while. I had been tearing my hair out for weeks on end, wondering what was going on. Whenever I asked him if he was all right, I got a curt 'I'm fine' in response. Or he might say, 'I have a lot on at the moment.' It didn't occur to me that he was preparing to leave.

On what turned out to be his last night in our flat, he was monosyllabic and I was a bag of nerves, treading on eggshells around him. We were in the middle of supper when he told me he needed some space for a while.

'What do you mean, 'space'?' I stared at him.

'Just that . . . I need a bit of time by myself. It's not you,' he said, not looking directly at me.

'Sandy, for God's sake, we're married! We've been married for ten years and suddenly you're talking about needing space. You're not a child.'

I had raised my voice, but I wasn't shouting at that point. And then another thought struck me and I did shout.

'You're having an affair! That's it, isn't it?'

'There's no one else involved in this. I'm trying to tell you something and you're blowing it out of proportion.'

'*I'm* blowing it out of proportion? You're my husband and you're telling me you don't want to be around me. Jesus, Sandy, you've been like a month of wet Sundays for ages and I've stood back and worried but said nothing, and now you spring this on me. Don't play games with me. Just tell me the truth. Have you met someone else?'

He still didn't look at me directly, just sighed and shook his head.

'This isn't about anyone else. It's . . . hard to explain, but I need a bit of time by myself. I think we both need a break. We've needed one for a while.'

My head reeled in shock. I didn't need a break from him, but he had made the decision for both of us, so at that point there was nothing I could do but give in. I couldn't prevent him from leaving. So, defeated, I wept quietly and he held me for a few minutes. Contained for that short time in his arms, sobbing against his chest, I felt a tiny surge of hope that he would change his mind and stay. But he packed a few things in a holdall and left, saying he was going to stay at the flat of a colleague, Geoff, who was doing a stint abroad with a charity.

'The break will do us good,' he said, and for a moment I believed him. But as he walked out the door, I saw something in his face that looked like relief and I knew my marriage was over.

A shattering of glass brings me back to the present. Startled, I look around and see a child being dragged away from one of the nearby tables by a man I take to be his father, his high-pitched screams drowning out every other sound. Other diners are staring at the family, some in sympathy, most in disapproval.

'The little brat obviously wasn't getting enough attention, so he flung out his arm and sent everything flying. If I owned a restaurant, I'd ban children completely,' Ursula says. 'Now, aren't you glad you don't have one of those to deal with? At least you can start again without having to worry about how the kids are coping.'

When I was very young it had never occurred to me that I wouldn't have children of my own. That was what happened when girls grew up. They got married and had children, and that was the future I had assumed for myself. I had even thought about names for these children I would have, names that changed depending on which book I was reading at the time or which film I had seen.

I had watched Angela's girls grow up, fall in love and marry. When they became pregnant, I was thrilled. And when Ronan and Brigid came on the scene, I was filled with love for them.

But my own life hadn't turned out like theirs. And, now, childless and likely to stay that way, I think about what Ursula has said. *Glad?* I know what she means, but it's not necessarily the word I'd use.

5

I've been dreading the return to Ireland, but I feel my heart lift as the plane flies in towards the airport, with the wide sweep of Dublin Bay below and the Wicklow Mountains clear and blue in the distance. There has always been a reason to return. After this trip, there will be none, and I feel a small kick in my stomach because, even though I love the Keaveneys, without the anchor that my mother provided, there will be no chain pulling me back.

I haven't told Angela exactly when I'm arriving. I didn't want to give her a date and then renege on it, as I had reneged on my promise to spend Christmas with her and Joe. And now that I'm here, I want to spend this first night in my mother's house by myself.

Heavy rain begins to fall as I turn north on to the motorway, making it difficult to see beyond the space the little hired car occupies on the road. 'Welcome to bloody sopping wet Ireland,' I mutter to myself, gripping the steering wheel and slowing the car as much as I can without annoying the other drivers, who keep up their speed, unfazed by these treacherous conditions.

And then, as suddenly as it began, the rain stops, the sky is visible again and the sun throws a wet glow over everything. A double rainbow appears, and I want to believe that it's some kind of mystical sign telling me all will be well.

My mother's house is just outside the town, on the southern side of the river. The Keaveneys all live on the northern side. It's a small two-storey cottage, almost hidden by the trees and rhododendron bushes growing in the garden.

There are other houses along the road but, once you walk through the gate of my mother's property, you feel you're somewhere remote, contained within a world delineated by the dark, almost decadent crimson of the rhododendron. Another month or two and they'll be in bloom. I've often wondered what made her choose this house, shadowy and even a little bit mean, after living in a house that was washed through with the light that came flooding in off the estuary, even on the greyest of days.

She hadn't sought my advice, or even my opinion. When Dermot died, I spent two weeks with her, during which time she made no mention of her plan. Six months after that, she put their house on the market.

'I can't believe you did that without even talking to me,' I said when I phoned her, having heard from Angela about the plan to sell the house. 'It was my house, too.'

'It was never just your house, Louise, or mine. It's Angela's, too,' she said. 'And it's far too big for me now. I'm going to sell it and give Angela some of the money and buy something smaller.'

'But, Mamma, you could at least have asked me what I thought.'

'What difference would that have made?'

What difference indeed. My mother had never

sought my opinion about anything. Once she had made up her mind about something, anything at all, that was it. Even as a child I understood that.

I haven't been here since November, when she died. I couldn't face Christmas in Ireland, so I spent it by myself, with bread and cheese and a bottle of Pomerol. After that, I found several more excuses not to travel. But, before long, April had rolled in with its promise of spring and I knew I couldn't keep putting it off.

Now, the house feels damp and unfriendly after several months of neglect, but at least everything is working — the lights, the central heating, the kettle.

I close the curtains to keep the night outside at bay. I've always hated the dark. Even in London, walking in well-lit streets, I'm a little bit scared of the darkness that lies at the far end, beyond the lights, of the sense that nothing is quite safe.

I decide to light a fire, and find plenty of turf, coal and wood in the small shed in the yard, and an old pack of firelighters in the cupboard beside the fireplace. When the flames finally take hold, I pull up an armchair, the one my mother always sat in, and lean back into it, nursing my mug of tea and trying to make sense of all that has been happening, how and why my life has changed so much in just a few months. I still don't understand why my marriage broke down, but I suppose I must have been part of whatever was wrong. 'We both need a break,' Sandy had said, the night he left.

One thing I do know for certain is that my

mother, through her smoking, was responsible for her own illness. It was a habit I'd always hated, though her use of a cigarette holder gave a kind of sophistication to the way she would lift her fingers towards her mouth, inhale slowly as if she was thinking deeply about something, and then move them away, a thin trail of smoke wafting into the air in front of her as she exhaled silently.

Why, then, do I feel a weight of guilt about everything to do with her death? Is it because I left? But that can't be it, because it wasn't my idea that I should go to London, it was hers. And yet the thought that eats away at my heart is of my mother abandoned. By me.

The house still holds a faint smell of cigarettes, which had always been hard to banish, probably because of the suffocating foliage outside that limited the extent to which a breeze could sweep in through the narrow sash windows and around the rooms. The other house never smelled of cigarettes; the big windows, once opened, pulled air in and sent it swirling into every corner.

I go to the kitchen, find her supply of Silk Cut, just a few packets, and I fling them into the bin. It's my first administrative decision. But I hold on to the silver cigarette holder, whose provenance I have never asked. It must have been a present, but not one that Dermot had given her. She had it long before we met him.

★ ★ ★

42

Apart from the remains of the pizza I had delivered the night before, there's no food in the house. There's coffee and tea, but no milk. So I walk down the hill into the town for breakfast. New cafés have sprung up by the river and I choose one on the south side, called White Nights, on the assumption that its very name suggests the coffee will be strong. It is, and I have two big cups of it.

The river is the heart of the town. All sorts of small shops and businesses line the quays and there's constant movement across the small pedestrian bridge that runs parallel to the main St Mary's Bridge connecting the two sides of the town. I smile, thinking that, while Londoners talk about 'north of the river' or 'south of the river' and Dubliners talk about the 'northside' and 'southside', in Drogheda there was only ever the 'far side'. Whether you lived north or south of the river, anyone living on the opposite side was from the far side.

I look across to the nineteenth-century warehouses and mills on the north quay that have been turned into spacious open-plan apartments, the old brick exposed as a design feature. A few years ago, I suggested to Sandy that we should think about buying one of them.

'And do what with it? You wouldn't want to live in it, would you?'

'Well, no, but we could come here whenever we wanted. We could always rent it out.'

'Och, don't be ridiculous, Lou. It would be madness to buy a place we'd use only a couple of times a year. It makes no economic sense. And

43

two flats are equal to two sets of everything, problems included.'

He was right about the economics of it; had we bought the apartment, we would now be paying a mortgage that far exceeded the value of the place. But his real objection, I knew, was that he didn't want to have to see my mother any more than was absolutely necessary. Owning a place in Drogheda would draw us back too often for his liking. I hadn't told him about her initial opposition to him — in fact, when I first took him to meet her and Dermot, she was utterly charming to him — but he was good at picking things up. And whenever we did turn up together in Drogheda, he would throw out the odd remark about how controlling she could be, even to the extent of telling me where I should take him, whether we were heading out to visit the local tourist spots or just going out to dinner by ourselves. But, then, as the saying goes, it takes one to know one, and Sandy could be fairly controlling himself. The difference was that I was so besotted with him, I didn't mind allowing him to make the decisions.

Now, sitting with my coffee, I think how lovely it would be to stand at a big south-facing window and watch the river flow towards the sea, count the swans gliding on the fast water, feel the movement of the sun through the day and the passing of the hours. I play with the idea of selling my mother's house and buying one of those riverside apartments in which there are no memories lurking — a clean, new space with big windows that let in the sunlight and the starlight.

It's a pleasant daydream that lasts until I finish my coffee.

Back at the house, I consider embarking on a spring clean, but admit that this would really be an excuse to delay knuckling down to the real work. There's a lot to be done. It mystifies me that, for someone who was a perfectionist in so many ways, my mother kept so much stuff. She was almost a hoarder. Papers, photographs and documents that have been put away in no particular order over the years, now have to be gone through, separated into what needs to be acted upon, what should be kept and what can be thrown away.

But I start with her clothes. They're crammed into two wardrobes, one in her bedroom and one in the room that I used when I came over to see her, and also into a couple of old trunks stored under the beds. Her room, unused now for several months, smells of nothing in particular, but when I open the wardrobe I feel my eyes sting as I take in the smell of the clothes, the faint hint of Calèche.

I allow myself a minute or so of reflection and then collect myself. I work through the wardrobes steadily, taking the items out one by one, folding and placing them in the big black refuse sacks I bought earlier. Before long, I've filled a dozen black bags. I should ask Angela if she would like to look through them before I take them to the charity shop, in case there's anything she or her daughters would like.

My mother had good taste. I like to think that she passed some of it on to me. When I was in my early twenties, I became a slave to fashion, filling my wardrobe with things bought on impulse that did nothing for me. But by the time I was thirty, my mother's influence had won out and I learned how to dress well on very little money, although my style was very different from hers. For her, understated elegance had to be the main feature of any outfit. I like comfort above all else — no cinched waists for me, no high heels — but I can't help wishing I could wear these beautiful clothes.

After a couple of hours of steady work, I decide to take a break and drive the few miles out to Bettystown. The village has changed a lot over the years, the older houses and cottages sitting uneasily below the apartment buildings that shot up during the height of the property boom, but the strand is the same, stretching for miles. The day is so clear that I can see the mountains, soft blue and purple in the far distance. The tide is coming in, but I know I have plenty of time before it will cover the hard sand. I walk quickly, the dunes on my left and the sea on my right, until my legs ache, and then I face back the way I've come.

The dunes bring back memories, good ones. Ursula often came down from Dublin to stay with us at weekends and in the summer, and we used to cycle out to whichever strand took our fancy on a particular day. They were all within a few miles of Drogheda, and all had long stretches of silvery sand. But the beaches on the northern side of the estuary were quieter than those on the south and we were teenage girls

— we liked the buzz of crowds. Bettystown had the kind of buzz you got in a place with holiday chalets and amusement arcades, ice-cream vans and fish-and-chip shops.

I had my first kiss among those dunes. Ursula and I were with a few other girls from my class, all in our early teens, and we met a group of boys on the beach. We played spin-the-bottle, taking turns to spin an empty bottle we had found and kissing whomever it ended up pointing at. I don't remember much about any of the kisses, except that they weren't what I'd expected after the apprehension and excitement that had preceded them. They were all a disappointment.

I haven't thought about that game for years, but it seems to me now that everything that has happened in my life has had an element of a bottle being spun. And it has rarely been me spinning the bottle, just me going in whatever direction it ended up pointing, trusting it would be the right one. The only real decision I ever made on my own was to stop singing and start teaching. I'm not sure I even chose Sandy. Sure, I wanted him, but when it came to making the choice, making a move, it was Sandy who got us together, not me.

A dog's excited barking brings me out of my thoughts. I look towards the sound and see a big, rangy red setter bounding around the beach, jumping in and out of the water. Some distance behind is a man, walking fast in my direction. There's something familiar-looking about him, about the way he strides along by the edge of the water. But it's not until I hear his voice as he calls the dog to him that I realise who he is. My heart misses a beat. I hadn't expected to see him again after pushing him away so many years ago. He had left Drogheda a long time ago. It was unlikely that our paths would cross. And yet here he is now, walking towards me on Bettystown strand, although he shows no sign of having recognised me. He looks well. He has filled out.

I'm torn between whether I should talk to him or just walk on, but the decision is taken out of my hands. Soaking wet from the sea, the dog is keen to have a new playmate and jumps and dances around me so that my legs are covered in damp splodges of sand.

'Bran! I'm sorry, he's young and a bit . . . ' He breaks off, narrows his eyes to scrutinise me, and then says, 'Louise?'

'Declan. It's been a long time. You're looking great.'

'So are you,' he says. 'Are you back here now?'

I shake my head. 'No. I'm still in London. But my mother died, so I've been back and forth, sorting everything out.'

'I'm sorry about your mother,' he says. I can tell that he means it and I wonder why. My mother barely gave him the time of day.

He has the dog on a lead now and it's straining to pull away. 'Look, do you fancy a drink? I'll put this eejit in the car so he won't be jumping all over us.'

We walk to one of the older pubs — the kind of place frequented by old men who sit at the bar in silence, nursing pints of Guinness — and head for the snug. Declan's hair, once so dark it was almost black, is streaked with grey, and his face has a lived-in look about it. He's older, of course. But there's something else different about him.

'The glasses! You're not wearing any!' I exclaim, remembering the old black spectacle frames.

'Contact lenses. I'm ashamed to confess that vanity got the better of me a long time ago,' he says.

Now it's his turn to check how I have changed, and I sit back and allow him to look me up and down.

'You look the same. You haven't changed,' he says. 'So what's your life like these days?'

I tell him about my singing career that came to an end and about my move into teaching. I give him the short version of the Sandy saga.

'Children?' he asks.

'No,' I say, and quickly turn the focus on to him. 'Your turn now.'

He lives in Skerries, about fourteen or fifteen miles south of Drogheda on the coast, with his wife and two sons. He talks a lot about the boys. He's proud of them. One is at university in Galway, the other still at secondary school. His wife is called Áine and is a teacher.

'And what do you do? Did you become a vet?'

'I didn't, in the end. I went for medicine. I'm actually a psychiatrist now.'

I start laughing. I laugh so much that Declan begins to look worried.

'Oh, I'm sorry,' I splutter. 'It's just that Sandy is a psychiatrist, too. What a bizarre coincidence.

I really do pick them, don't I?'

He's lost for words and for a few seconds we look down at our drinks. But when we look up again, he lifts his hand to my face and puts his mouth on mine. And I kiss him back.

Time is playing tricks with me as I fall into the embrace. It takes me back nearly three decades as I feel the familiarity of the way he holds me, of the surprising softness of his mouth. But his arms are stronger than they used to be. They remind me of Sandy's. Every touch makes me think of Sandy. But Sandy is gone. He's a memory, I tell myself. Past tense. No future. Just this minute, Declan is the one who's real, and I lean into him, closing my eyes, losing myself in both the present and the past.

He pulls away.

'I'm sorry,' he says, but he's smiling in a slightly idiotic-looking way and his eyes are bright.

'I'm not sure I am.'

'I shouldn't have done that. I'm s — '

'Declan, if you say you're sorry again, I'll give you a thump! Forget it. It was a kiss. We kissed each other by mistake. Neither of us is going to go to hell for it.'

He looks stricken for a moment, but then he laughs.

'As mistakes go, that was a nice one, I have to admit,' he says.

He walks me to my car. He doesn't ask for my number and I don't ask for his.

'Goodbye, then,' he says.

I drive away, my eyes firmly fixed on the road

ahead. But I know that, if I look into the rear-view mirror, I'll see him standing in the same spot, looking after me.

The encounter has turned out to be nothing like the emotional car crash I might have expected. Maybe it's simply a matter of so much time having passed. What happened to us — to me — seems now to belong to a past so distant that it's almost irrelevant. Almost. I turn on the car radio that's tuned to Lyric FM and let the wall of sound that is Wagner expand into every corner of my mind so that there's no space for anything else.

★   ★   ★

Fortified by the visit to Bettystown, I tackle the first of the two trunks. My mother had allowed me, when I was a child, to use them for dressing-up games. There are old clothes going back to the early 1960s, dresses and skirts and blouses dating from before I was born. There are no trousers or jeans. She never wore them.

The clothes are beautiful and in pristine condition, but it puzzles me that she held on to so many things she no longer wore. Maybe she kept them to remind her of her youth. I slip on an ancient yellow sleeveless dress with a small waist and flared skirt, the kind of thing that became fashionable again a few years ago when *Mad Men* was so popular on television. The dress won't zip up at the back. I'm a different shape from my mother. Her bones were small, her limbs long and slender. Mine are bigger and

51

ger, although I, too, am tall. I recall her
ther at the funeral, thin and angular, a male
version of her. Perhaps my heavier bones come
from my English father. My almost-black hair is
coarser than my mother's. Does that come from
him, too?

I try on a few other things, but they neither fit
me nor suit me, and I'm about to close the lid on
the first trunk when I see something poking out
from a tear in the lining. At first glance, I think
it's an old cinema or concert ticket, but it's not.
It's a small blue envelope. I extract it carefully
from the lining and examine it. It's addressed in
pencil and in the hand of a child who has just
begun to learn to write in big block capitals.

> SANTA CLAUS
> LAPLAND
> NORTH POLE

I don't immediately give the envelope much
thought beyond assuming that this is something
my mother kept from her own childhood.
There's an old stamp on it and the envelope
looks as if it may once have been sealed, but
subsequently opened. Inside, I find a letter on a
folded sheet of lined paper, blue like the
envelope. The capitals fill the page.

> DEAR SANTY,
> PLEASE BRING ME A NEW DOLL FOR CHRIST-
> MAS.
> MY DOLL IS SICK.
> FROM AILISH

I feel an unease that prickles my skin, makes me shiver. *Ailish*. There's no Ailish that I know of in my mother's life and none that I can think of in my own. I don't recognise the writing — it could belong to any child in the early stages of learning to form letters and words.

But as I read the letter over and over again, read the address on the envelope, that strange old image comes back of the small arm reaching towards the slot of the green postbox. I try to look through my mind's eye at that small hand, try to read the address on the envelope held by the little chubby fingers.

Does the hand belong to me? And if it does, am I posting that letter to Santa Claus from a girl called Ailish? But why would I be posting a letter on behalf of a child whose name means nothing to me?

I concentrate, squeezing my eyes shut. But I can't make sense of anything. The image is too hazy, as if it has been captured through a Vaselined lens.

And then, with no warning, my stomach lurches and I think I'm going to vomit, so strong is the bile that rises to my mouth. I rush to the bathroom and kneel in front of the lavatory, my head resting on my arm, waiting for my stomach to erupt as pain builds in my head. But the nausea eventually subsides and I sit back on the floor against the wall with my eyes closed, willing the headache to retreat.

I haven't eaten very much today and maybe the two cups of strong coffee I had at White Nights were too hard on an empty stomach. I go

53

to the kitchen and eat a few cream crackers, and gradually my stomach settles and the pressure in my head lessens.

But I can't forget the sense of unease I felt as I read that letter.

There are so many things I've wanted to ask my mother, things I've been able to put aside on some shelf at the back of my mind since my return to London after the funeral. But now I'm back in Ireland and my head is full of anxiety. More than anything, I have wanted to know my father, or at least something about him. I can't understand why my mother chose not to let me have any contact with him. Now, in this letter to Santa Claus in Lapland, there's a new mystery, and I have a bad feeling about it.

Oh, Mamma, why couldn't you have told me more about your life, about all the things you kept from me?

6

Angela, laid back in her usual way, shows no annoyance at my not having told her in advance about my trip and immediately invites me round for dinner.

'I'll come and pick you up,' she says.

'You don't have to. I hired a car.'

'You won't be able to have a drink if you drive. We'll get you a taxi back, or you can stay here.'

When she arrives, I tell her what I've been doing and show her what I've found. The name Ailish doesn't ring any bells for her. She examines the envelope and the letter, but has no answers.

'They're a bit battered-looking, aren't they? And that stamp looks old,' she says. 'All I can imagine is that your mother was supposed to post it for someone and forgot. Can you think of any relatives or friends?'

'Not really. There was only her brother. There may have been cousins, but if there were, she never mentioned them. Both of her parents were only children. Anyway, there's no Ailish that I can think of. And there's no Keaveney called that, is there?'

She shakes her head. 'You still have a load of papers to go through. You might find something among them that will tell you a bit more. And if you don't, well, it won't have been all that important, will it?'

'I suppose not.'

But I'm not so sure.

My mother's cancer wasn't officially diag-
nosed until days before she died. When she told
me on the telephone that she wasn't feeling well,
I knew something was very wrong because she
was rarely ill and never acknowledged any kind
of physical weakness. I called Angela, who used
to be a nurse, and asked her to drop in on my
mother. I hoped she would be reassuring and tell
me there was nothing to worry about. But she
wasn't. 'I think you'd better come over,' she said.
I took the first available flight from Heathrow.
But, by the time I got to the house, the
ambulance men were taking her out on a
stretcher that looked a bit like a sled, and I
wanted to weep at the sight of her, swaddled in
blankets and looking like an elderly Snow
Queen.

How could I have asked her the questions I
wanted to ask after that? It would have been like
telling her I knew she was about to die. It would
have been cruel.

Joe is cooking steaks and he already has a
bottle of red wine open.

He's a builder and a good one. He has
survived the recession without having to lay
people off. When we are all sitting down and
eating, he asks me whether I'm any closer to a
decision on the house. I'm not.

'Well, if you want my advice, you should fix it
up, whether you decide to sell it or keep it. It
needs a lot doing to it,' he tells me.

This doesn't surprise me. It's not a warm

house, for a start. Nor is it a particularly comfortable one. It had started out, some time in the 1910s or 1920s, as a two-up, two-down with an outside lavatory and no bathroom. At some point, a one-storey extension was built to house a small bathroom and kitchen. No one is going to look twice at this house in its current state.

'That bathroom and kitchen should be knocked down and rebuilt. I told your mother that when she bought the place. Offered to do it for her for next to nothing, but she wasn't interested. All she wanted was central heating installed and the walls painted. She could have had a lovely little house,' Joe says.

'At least she asked you for your advice before she bought it. She certainly didn't ask for mine,' I said.

'She asked me for advice only in the sense that she wanted to know if it could be lived in straight away. I never understood it, moving there after the other house,' he says, shaking his head as if the disbelief that my mother had done such a foolish thing has never left him.

'So what needs doing to it now? And how much will it cost?' I ask.

'I'd have to take another look at it, but off the top of my head I'd say you're going to have to spend about 40,000 euro — and that's with me doing you a good deal. It's a lot, but if you do decide to sell the house, you'll get a better price than you'll get if you put it on the market as it is. And if you keep it, you'll have a grand little place. Now, that kitchen and bathroom have to go. They're crumbling away. And the two bedrooms are upstairs and there's no bathroom up there. So have a think about this. We could turn one of those bedrooms into a bathroom.'

'Okay.'

'We'd have another bedroom downstairs, with a shower and so on, in the new extension that we'd put up. And on the other side of the extension, we'd have a decent-sized kitchen. You'd still have enough yard space to have a little patio. And the other thing I'd do downstairs is take down that wall between the two front rooms.'

'Can I think about it? To be honest, I never understood myself what made her buy that place, but I can see that it could be transformed,' I say.

'Oh, and one more thing,' Joe adds. 'I'd think about cutting down some of those trees and bushes outside, or at least cut them back. They make that house like a morgue. You need a bit of light in there.'

As Joe talks, I find myself imagining how the house will look if I do what he's suggesting. Instead of the nondescript off-white paint on all the walls, I could use bold colour. I see my mother's bedroom upstairs, the internal wall moved back to increase the space, the walls painted a teal blue, the carpets removed and the floorboards covered in a dark brown varnish. I see the transformation that could be wrought by moving walls or taking them away and building new ones.

I've always loved rhododendron, but around

my mother's house it has something of the grave about it, something decaying. Cutting away some of the trees and dense foliage outside would enable the sun to penetrate far beyond the tall, narrow sash windows. I could grow roses in the garden at the front and have pots of flowering plants in the yard at the back. I could have a refuge from the emptiness that has been my life in London without Sandy.

'How long are you staying?' Joe asks.

'Maybe a month. Depends on how much I get done. Joe, I want to think about it a bit more, but if I do decide to take your advice and fix up the house, will you do the work for me?'

'I'd be delighted to. And in the meantime, why don't you start thinking about what you might like, maybe get yourself a notebook and write your ideas down. I can come around in the next few days, whenever suits you, and do a rough drawing for you, and then, if you do want to go ahead with it, we can get things moving.'

'Fantastic! Let's drink to that,' I say, and for a short while the letter from a child to Santa Claus in Lapland is far from my thoughts.

★   ★   ★

I have a dream that comes and goes. I am searching for my father. People tell me they've just seen him — waiting for a bus on Dame Street or walking along O'Connell Street. Time after time, I run to find him, but I'm always one step behind. He has moved on. I wake from this dream to find my face and pillow wet. And in that half-space between dreaming and being fully back in the world, I hear in my mind snatches of a tune sung in a high tenor voice by this imagined father, but muffled and coming as if from a distance, so that I can't identify the song or the words.

The last time the dream came was shortly after my mother's death. My father made an appearance in Drogheda this time, not Dublin. It was the same old routine. He had been seen on West Street, then at St Laurence's Gate, and then at the top of Barrack Lane. But I was too late every time. And then, as I stumbled back down the Pitcher Hill steps, I could see a man swimming in the river. I ran as fast as I could, my body almost taking wing as I took several steps at a time, and pushed through the crowds that were gathering to watch the swimmer. I saw him glide through the water, as if in slow motion, towards St Mary's Bridge. I ran to the other side and waited for him to emerge. But all that came from under the bridge was a swan, moving slowly upriver. I watched it until it drifted out of sight.

I've read somewhere that all the characters in our dreams represent aspects of ourselves. If that's the case, I still don't know which part of myself I'm seeking so desperately.

Maybe psychotherapy would be beneficial. I've lost count of the number of times and ways Sandy has hinted or said outright that I could do worse than give therapy a go.

'It doesn't have to be traumatic,' he would say.

'What's the point, then, if it isn't?' I would

answer in a glib way.

Sandy thinks I need to sort out my feelings about my mother. I don't need to go into therapy to understand that my relationship with my mother has been a complicated one. She was my entire world when I was a child. When I began to explore the world beyond her, she felt insecure and I felt guilty. Even when I married Sandy, I didn't really separate from her. I understand all that. What more can therapy do for me?

I'm thinking about all this as I lie in bed, unable to sleep. I'm thinking about my mother and Sandy, wishing the two people I loved most in the world had grown to love each other.

What have you got against him?

He's married.

He's divorced. Big difference.

So he's already left one woman. How do you know he won't leave you too?

She was right. He did leave me and I'm still crumbling away inside with the grief of it all. And maybe that's why rebuilding those crumbling walls of her house is becoming so important now. Maybe, by fixing the walls, turning that small, unattractive house into something warm and good, I can rebuild myself.

7

I wake up refreshed and positive and the sun is shining. After breakfast I walk around with the squared notepad Joe has given me, jotting down ideas and making rough drawings of how I would like things to be. I look at the ceilings in the bedrooms and wonder whether they can be removed to raise the height.

I haven't been inside the attic, but I can't imagine that it has been used to store anything very much. My mother would have had to put a stepladder on the small landing between the two bedrooms and then climb in through a fairly small trapdoor. Still, at some point I'm going to have to check what, if anything, is up there, beyond the horrible insulating material that irritates the skin, though I can probably leave that for Joe and his boys.

I look again at the letter to Santa, this time without experiencing that unpleasant physical sensation of the previous day, and I reckon I can blame my nausea on the strength of the White Nights coffee.

But even as I scan the letter for some kind of meaning, I see in my mind's eye the old image of the little arm stretching upwards. Am I making a link between these two things that doesn't really exist? Or can it be that I know what the link is, but have yet to make the connection? Maybe I once knew an Ailish but have forgotten all about her. But I don't want to think about that now. I want to keep it at a distance.

And, in any case, there's too much to do.

I've been through the wardrobes and trunks and put clothes, handbags and shoes into bags that I've labelled as things Angela or her daughters might like, things I can take to the charity shop and things that I might be able to sell because of their vintage and the fact that they are beautiful garments in good condition. I'm going to keep nothing except the jewellery, and there isn't much of that — her wedding ring and a few other pieces Dermot gave her over the years they were married. And the silver cigarette holder.

What I should do now is tackle the various papers, but I can't face what I know will be a nightmare of separating a jumbled mess into many different piles. My mother may have been elegant, but her approach to filing left a lot to be desired.

I think about her brother and about his invitation that I never meant to take up. But I've softened in the months since the funeral; I'm more willing to give him the benefit of all the doubts that have assembled in my head about the value of having any contact with my mother's family. At the very least, I tell myself, talking to him will help me to build up a picture of the life she lived before she had me, a life she told me nothing about.

I search through my purse for the piece of paper he wrote his number on, the day of the funeral, and find it folded in one of the pockets.

I pick up the phone and tap the number in.

'Richard, it's Louise. Marjorie's daughter. I'm back in Ireland,' I say when I hear his voice at the other end of the telephone. 'I wonder if you might have time to see me, maybe later this week?'

'This is a lovely surprise. I'm delighted to hear from you, Louise,' he says. 'What are you doing today? Why don't you come up now?'

I start making excuses. I hadn't expected to see him so quickly. I've had no time to prepare for a meeting.

'Please come,' he says. 'It would mean a great deal to me.'

So I tell him I'll set off shortly.

The drive takes the best part of two hours because I go wrong several times as I try to navigate the network of motorways that didn't exist when I still lived in Ireland. But I finally reach Dalkey. It was once just a pleasant little village south of Dublin; now it's an exclusive suburb where rock and film stars rub shoulders with the locals. Even after the crash, houses here are expensive. My uncle must be sitting on a goldmine.

His house is on a hill above the village and looks straight out over Dalkey Island and across Dublin Bay. It's one of those Victorian villas you see in the wealthier parts of Dublin. The front door isn't at ground-floor level, but stands grandly at the top of a set of granite steps with wrought-iron railings on either side. The cordyline palm trees in the garden that surrounds the house and the mountains in the distance give the place an air redolent of the Mediterranean in winter.

Richard leads me into the hallway and down a staircase to the kitchen, where he has put together a lunch of cold meats and cheeses. This was the house in which my mother grew up and which Richard inherited. I look around and think how different my own life might have been if my mother's family hadn't rejected her.

'I'm very sorry that we didn't really get to know each other. I just want to say that. It has always been a great sadness to me,' Richard says, as if he has read my mind.

I had never given much thought to my mother's family. They simply hadn't featured in my life. Now, though, I can feel myself becoming angry towards them, hating them for not having wanted to have me in theirs.

'I'm sorry, too, Richard. I look around this lovely place and this beautiful house, and I feel sad for my mother. I feel gutted that she lost all of this because she had me. She could have gone to England and had an abortion, but she didn't. She was a good mother, a terrific one. And your parents rejected her because of something that no one in Ireland blinks twice at these days.'

He winces and begins to say something, but stops.

'I'm sorry,' I say. 'I shouldn't have said that.'

'It's all right. You're entitled to say what you feel.'

But I don't say any more because he looks too uncomfortable. I've said enough.

Over lunch, he tells me about their childhood, his and my mother's, in this lovely house with its gravel drive and gently rolling lawns. He tells me about the games they played as children and the pets they had.

'Then I went off to boarding school. Only down the road. Ridiculous, really — I could have gone there as a day boy. But that's what you did in those days, if you had a bit of money — you sent your children away. We were, I suppose, what used to be called Castle Catholics. Marjorie refused to go away, though. They wanted to send her to some place down the country, but she threw a few tantrums and they gave in. She went to the local convent as a day girl.'

'And then what?'

He looks at me as if he's not sure what I am asking.

'I mean, what did she do after school. And — ' I falter, bracing myself to ask the question I've wanted to ask since I arrived here — 'how did she come to have me?'

'She did what most other girls who didn't want to become teachers or nurses or work in a bank did. She went to secretarial college and did shorthand and typing. And then she got a job as a secretary. She worked for years at the Tennyson brewery in Crumlin. And then she . . . well, she had you.'

'I never knew that. Where she worked, I mean. She told me nothing, really. And she never told me anything about my father. I was hoping you might be able to.'

'I'm sorry, but I have no idea. She didn't tell

our parents or me anything about him, either. It does surprise me, though, that she didn't talk to you about him. Didn't she tell you anything at all?'

'She told me he was called David Prescott and that he was English, and that he'd gone back to England before I was born. She told me nothing more than that. Does the name mean anything to you at all?'

'I'm afraid not.'

But even as disappointment wells up in me, I feel a tiny bubble of hope, because Richard has given me a piece of information I hadn't previously been aware of — where my mother had worked before she had me. That had been something else she had glossed over, telling me only that she had worked in an office and that it hadn't been very interesting.

'Is it possible that my father worked at the Tennyson brewery, too?' I ask. 'Maybe he was her boss. Was her boss English?'

'I really can't remember, Louise. He may have been English — almost certainly was, because it was an English company and only a few of the senior people were Irish. But even if the man she worked for was English, it doesn't necessarily mean he was your father. Marjorie was . . . vivacious, outgoing. She had friends. She knew a lot of people, a lot of men.'

'But if my father was English and she worked for an English company, surely the most likely place for her to have met him was there? At Tennyson's?'

'She could have met him somewhere else. She

hung around with a fashionable crowd. And there were a lot of English people at Trinity. He could have been one of them.'

'I could still go and talk to the brewery people. They would have a record of when she worked there, who she worked for, wouldn't they?'

'Ah. Well, now, I'm afraid Tennyson's doesn't exist any more. It closed down years ago. Look, Louise, it may be that your father is the man she worked for. Or it may be someone else who worked for the company. But if your mother refused to tell anyone — even you — anything about him, it's highly likely that he was already married. And it's very unlikely that he's still alive. He would probably have been a few years older than Marjorie. That would put him closer to ninety than eighty. I very much doubt that you're going to be able to find him, and my advice is not even to try.'

I want to argue, but everything he is saying makes sense. Trying to track down the father who never even knew I existed would be mission impossible. I feel my eyes becoming wet.

'I know I'm being a bit childish, but I had it in my head that you could tell me everything I needed to know.'

'If only I could. But there are other things I can tell you about your mother. I have things to give you, too.'

He takes me to a sitting room and gestures towards several ancient-looking photograph albums piled on top of a coffee table.

'I'll leave you to look through them. I don't think you'll have any trouble working out who's

68

who,' he says. 'I'll come back shortly.'

All the photographs are black and white. Cracked and grainy, they recreate the past in a way that's impossible to achieve with colour. Richard is right; I can easily work out who is who — the floppy-haired boy making faces at the camera or, oblivious to it, frolicking with a spaniel on the lawn; the little girl in her smocked dress, her attention focused on the doll she cradles in her arms.

My mother's mother and father — my grandparents — appear in some of the photos, and I study them, searching for hints of the attitudes that would lead them some day to reject their daughter and her child. But, in their formal clothes, their stiffly held poses, their expressionless faces, they give nothing away. They are of their time.

I turn the pages and move through those lives, see my mother and uncle in school uniform, see them as young adults — he, languid and handsome as he smokes a cigarette; she, arrestingly beautiful, elegant in a blouse and skirt. Later, there are photos of Richard with a young woman and a small boy, who must be his wife and son. My mother appears in some of them, playing with the child or chatting with the woman.

Richard comes back and sits down beside me on the sofa. He asks me whether I have any questions.

'Not really. Not for now, anyway. There's too much to think about. If it's all right, I think I need to get going now.'

He takes the photograph albums and holds them out to me.

'Would you like to keep these?'

I nod. At this moment, there's nothing I want more. I will take the albums back to Drogheda and look at those photos of my beautiful mother again and again.

'I hope you'll come again. I would very much like to get to know my niece,' Richard says as I leave.

I could tell him that he's left it a bit late, that he could have got to know me when having an uncle and a cousin would have been a good thing for a little girl living with her mother in a northside flat with no garden. But I promise to keep in touch, and I will, not only because he's my mother's brother, but also because he's a kind man. I've begun to like him.

He walks me to my car and, as I pull the seatbelt across me, he leans down to speak.

'Louise, I know it must be hard for you, losing your mother and not having any contact with your father. But Marjorie must have had a good reason for not telling you anything very much about him. You should keep that in mind,' he says.

I give him a weak smile and say nothing. My visit has given me a lot to think about, but I'm making no promises.

It's only when I'm back on the motorway that I remember I haven't asked Richard whether he knew anything about Ailish, the little girl whose letter to Santa Claus never made it to the snowy wastes of Lapland.

8

I get up early after a restless night during which I woke several times thinking about what Richard had told me — that, even if my father had worked at the brewery, he was almost certainly no longer alive and that there was little point even thinking about trying to find him.

I look again through the albums he has given me, poring over each grainy photograph, trying to imagine this early life of my mother that was so different from anything I had known.

She had never talked much about her childhood, brushing off my occasional questions with short responses and shifting to a different topic. I used to ask her about her parents, what they looked like, whether they were kind, whether I would have liked them. She told me they were nice enough and looked ordinary, like anyone's parents. Sometimes I persisted, asking question after question, but that was never a good idea because then she would snap at me. So I gradually came to understand during the years of my childhood that her own wasn't something she was happy to talk about. Some topics were out of bounds.

Until yesterday, I had never seen any photographs of her as a child or of her family. Now, I have several albums, and they keep me absorbed for much of the morning as I study these snapshots of her life as the daughter of a well-off family in an affluent southern suburb of Dublin. Her parents don't look ordinary at all. Her mother looks haughty, as if her eyes never look in any direction other than straight ahead or down. Her father, too, looks like someone who has never questioned his station in life. In some of the photographs, I catch shadowy glimpses of domestic staff.

And, as the day goes on, I become aware that this entrée into my mother's family life, through Richard and through the photographs, isn't lessening my need to find out more about my father. Far from it. It's true that she didn't want me to know anything about my father, but if I do manage to find him, how can it hurt her now?

Richard has given me one important piece of information that I hadn't previously been aware of — where Mamma had worked before I was born. I decide to walk into town and do some research into Tennyson's at the library.

The library is well endowed with computers and I quickly gain access to a terminal. There's quite a lot of online information about the brewery, and I learn that it was built in the mid-1930s by a family-run company with headquarters in Northampton. Like other philanthropic industrialists of the time, the Tennysons looked after their employees; in Dublin, the company built workers' houses laid out over several garden squares.

I key *Marjorie Redmond, Tennyson's Brewery* and *Dublin* into a Google search box, but there are no matches for my mother's name.

I make one positive discovery, though. I learn

that the company still exists, with one plant on the outskirts of Northampton, brewing a small range of real ales.

I check out Tennyson's website and find a contact email as well as a telephone number and an address. I sit, staring at the screen for a while. I have nothing to lose by contacting the company. But should I call or send an email? What should I say or write? I almost convince myself that I should wait, go back to the house and think about it for a few days. But I'm here now and there's no time like the present. I start typing.

I write that my mother, Marjorie Redmond, worked for the brewery in Dublin for several years during the 1960s, that she died recently and that I'm trying to get in touch with her former boss, an English manager whose name, unfortunately, I cannot recall, to tell him about her death. Perhaps the company can put me in touch with him.

I don't mention David Prescott. I don't know whether it would have been possible in those days, but I've often wondered whether my mother had simply made up a name to put on my birth certificate. Better to find out who she had worked for and then contact him in the hope that he can give me all or some of the information I need.

But how likely is it that the brewery will give out a name to someone writing out of the blue? And what if the man I'm seeking hadn't been her boss, but someone from another part of the company? No, I have to do this a different way, a more inventive way.

I delete what I've written and I set up a new email account in the name of Sandra Munro. It's not very imaginative, but I need something I'll remember, and Sandra Munro is as close to my husband's name as I can get. Then I write that I'm carrying out research for a book on the impact on local communities in the British Isles of philanthropic companies and their approach to employee welfare and housing. In particular, I say, I'm interested in talking to any former senior staff who worked in the Dublin plant in the 1960s and 1970s, before it closed down. I add my address, my mobile number and my London landline, read over the entire message several times and click *send*. I can feel my heart pounding against my chest.

It's unusually mild and dry for early April and, when I go to White Nights for something to eat, I sit at one of the tables outside so that I can listen to the fast flow of the water and the squawking of the gulls as they circle and swoop. It's a strange kind of music, discordant yet harmonious. It matches my mood. I have the *Irish Times* with me, but I can't concentrate on it; my nerves are strung too tightly.

What would my life have been like had I remained in Ireland? Apart from those years of being married to Sandy, when I was happier than I had ever thought I could be, would it have been so much less of a life than the one I have in London? Would it have been so very different? I might have ended up giving piano lessons to children who didn't want to learn and to adult beginners with little hope of ever becoming even competent, let alone good. But every now and then there might have been a child or adult whose delight in music made my efforts worthwhile.

I might have married Declan.

My nerves are jangled, too jangled to face the mess of papers that waits for me back at the house. A different plan forms in my head: I'll go to Crumlin. I know from my internet research that the brewery has been redeveloped into offices and film and recording studios. The building also houses a little museum devoted to the history of the company's operations in Dublin and its place in local history. I tell myself it's unlikely that I'll accomplish anything useful by going there, but at least I'll see the place where my mother worked and — maybe — met my father. There may even be someone in the museum, a former worker, who may have known her.

I could take the car, but I know that Dublin traffic is a nightmare, so I leave it outside the house and walk to the railway station. For a station on the main line between Dublin and Belfast, it looks pleasantly old-fashioned. I don't have long to wait for a train and, as it moves out of the station, I close my eyes and think back to those excursions my mother and I made all those years ago, in trains with compartments that we often had all to ourselves.

The train is one of those commuter trains with long open carriages, but at least it's not crowded. There's a flutter of excitement in my stomach as

75

we pass through the stations at Laytown, Balbriggan, Skerries, Rush and Lusk, Malahide, Portmarnock, the sea on our left, shimmering in the sunlight that refuses to stay behind the clouds for long. I have a good feeling. Finally, I am doing something that may or may not lead me to David Prescott, but at least I will have tried.

Leaving Amiens Street Station — I still think of it by that name because it's what my mother always called it, even though its official name is Connolly — I hail a taxi. Twenty minutes later, I'm standing outside the brewery, a low-level but striking redbrick building that dominates the surrounding area.

Inside, there's a central lobby with signposts indicating the way to the various studios and even a theatre. What I'm looking for is the museum that's housed on the top floor. It's tiny and crammed with photo boards showing the life of the brewery over the decades and the lives of the people who worked there.

I scrutinise the black-and-white photographs, in particular those that appear to be from the time my mother worked there, but I can't find her face among them. I approach the woman who seems to be in charge of the museum, telling her that my mother once worked here as a secretary and asking whether it might be possible to talk to anyone who had worked at the brewery in the 1960s.

'There are still a few old-timers who pop in, but we never know when they're coming. You can always leave me your name and a phone number and I may be able to get someone to call you. I'm not promising anything, though,' she says.

I write my name and number down on a piece of paper and hand it to her, but the disappointment I feel must be written all over my face because she then suggests that I might like to come back later in the day.

'That's when the oul' fellas tend to turn up. They can have a cup of tea and a biscuit and reminisce about the good old days,' she says. 'Though, if you ask me, I'm not sure what was that good about them.'

I wander outside and consider going back towards the centre of town, perhaps doing some clothes shopping around Grafton Street. But I don't want to be away from here for too long and I decide instead to walk around the neighbour-hood and explore the same streets my mother walked along every day for years.

I try to imagine her going to work in the mornings, perhaps smoothing her hair or having a last-minute check of her dress to make sure it wasn't creased. I think about her leaving the office in the evening, saying goodbye to her boss, making sure she didn't call him by his first name, being the perfect secretary so that nobody would suspect their relationship, and then waiting for him to turn up at her flat or room.

Was it romantic? Maybe it was in the beginning. And then, as time went by, maybe it became more frustrating than romantic. Maybe they had rows because he wouldn't leave his wife. Did she become pregnant with me because she wanted to force the issue? Was he the love of her life? And, if so, was Dermot some kind of consolation prize? When I think of Dermot, who became more of a father to me than I might have imagined when we first met him, I feel a twinge of guilt about having embarked on this search that may turn out to be, at best, a wild goose chase. At worst, it may bring the kind of heartache I'm not sure I can cope with. But what else can I do?

I don't know this part of the inner city, but I feel relaxed here. It has a small-town feel about it and there are children playing in the streets outside the houses. I find this reassuring, even in a fairly compact city like Dublin. My nerves have stopped jangling, probably because I'm actually doing something rather than just playing out imaginary scenarios in my head.

I wander into a square behind the brewery. According to the leaflets I've picked up at the museum, it was built to house some of the workers and their families. It's called Walter Square and it's typical of the other small estates built by Tennyson's, with four redbrick terraces laid out around a garden square. But the expensive-looking cars parked here suggest that previous generations of workers have long gone and have been replaced by bankers and doctors.

Oddly, there seems to be something familiar about the square and the houses, although I don't recognise anything in particular. It's possible, even likely, I think, that my mother brought me here as a small child and I have somehow retained a memory of it.

Lost in my thoughts, I don't notice the postbox until I'm in front of it, and all of a sudden I'm aware of that misted, shrouded image of the little arm clutching the envelope, reaching upward. The memory is so vivid and pushes so far forward that it's no longer just in my mind's eye. It has somehow moved beyond me so that it's almost in front of me.

And now I have two images and each one is as real to me as the other: the green postbox that is so much taller than the little girl who has to stretch to reach the slot and the green postbox that I am standing in front of. I look down and see that my arm is stretching out towards the slot, that my hand is touching it.

And I shiver, because I feel afraid.

I'm shaking now and I begin to run, away from the postbox, away from the square. I run until I'm exhausted, filled with dread and not knowing why. I have no idea where I'm going and I'm vaguely aware of people making way for me as I flee in panic. And when I can't run any more, I sink to the side of the pavement, curl up like a foetus and howl.

I have no recollection of being taken to the hospital or how many hours I've been there. I can't explain to the doctor what happened to me, what made me turn into an exhausted, shivering wreck on the pavement, but I tell him that I've been under a lot of stress because of the breakdown of my marriage and the death of my mother.

The hospital won't let me leave without an adult who can take care of me for a day or two, so I call Angela and ask her to come and fetch me.

Her face has an anxious look on it as she and the doctor move out of earshot to talk, but otherwise she's as calm as a ship in stormy seas. She settles me into the car and, as we leave the hospital, she tells me that if I want to talk about whatever happened, that's fine, but that if I don't want to talk about it for the time being, then that's fine, too.

'I don't think I can face talking about it right now,' I say. 'Maybe later.'

But when we get back to Angela's house, all I want to do is lie down and close my eyes. She puts me in one of the bedrooms, where I fall asleep in seconds. I sleep all evening and all through the night and late into the following morning without waking up. And if dreams have managed to invade my sleep, I don't remember them.

9

Angela is in the kitchen preparing lunch when I wander in from my long sleep, wrapped in one of her dressing gowns and feeling like death warmed up.

'How are you feeling?' she asks, putting down the vegetables she's chopping and wiping her hands on a piece of kitchen paper.

'Never felt better. Can't you tell?' I joke. But even as I laugh, the thought of what happened the previous day grips my mind and chills me. I've never felt as fragile and helpless as I do now and, before I even realise it, I'm shedding big wet tears and gasping between sobs.

Angela is beside me in a second, holding me tightly and telling me, 'There, there, just go with it, let it all out.' And I do. I cry and cry until I have no more tears, and then Angela loosens her grip on me and guides me to the big, comfortable sofa that has been relegated to the kitchen because it's so old and scruffy.

'Maybe it'll do you good to talk,' she says.

So I tell her everything in the order it all happened, about my visit to Dalkey, about the photographs, about Richard being unable to tell me anything about my father and advising me to put any thoughts of finding him out of my mind. I tell her about my trip to the library and discovering that the brewery still exists in England. She nods a lot, taking it all in but saying nothing.

And then I get to my trip to Crumlin and what happened there and I feel myself shaking again.

'I can't explain it, Angela. It was . . . terrifying. I've never been so afraid of anything in my life. Do you think I'm going mad?'

'Ah, no, not at all. You've had a desperate time of it these past few months, what with your mother and with Sandy. I wonder whether that's churning up an awful lot of things you've stayed away from before.'

'You mean you think I've been avoiding stuff?'

'Not intentionally, no. What I'm saying is . . . well, take your mother. I'm not surprised that you're feeling annoyed about the way her family treated her and you. Rejection is an awful thing and it doesn't matter how much you rationalise it. It's hurtful and damaging. I don't know what to make of what happened to you today in Crumlin, but there must be an explanation for it somewhere. Do you want to tell me about it again? Maybe we can try to make some sense of it.'

So I go back over it again, and the dread is still there, but it's manageable this time. I tell her about the memory that may not be a memory. But if it's not, what is it? I tell her about my initially pleasant walk around the square, the ordinary-looking but nicely built houses, the garden in the middle, and then the sight of the green postbox in front of me and the way the old memory suddenly came back, and how it was as if the two were the same, the real and the unreal merged together.

'Did you ever talk to your mother about that

memory that kept coming up?'

'Not really . . . no. There didn't seem to be much point. It was too indistinct. It used to be just something vague and a bit puzzling. Now, since my mother died, it's doing my head in. And what happened in Walter Square . . . Jesus! What was all that about?'

'There'll be an explanation somewhere. There always is. But it's not beyond the bounds of possibility that Marjorie took you there, is it? Maybe something happened that frightened you. I don't know what — maybe something as simple as a dog that you thought was going to bite you.'

'But wouldn't she have told me about something like that?'

'She mightn't have, especially if she didn't know how frightened you were at the time and had forgotten about it. Or she might even have told you and you forgot.'

'She didn't tell me very much about anything, really,' I say. 'And it's only now she's dead that I realise how little I know about everything. I didn't ask her too much, either. I don't know why I wasn't a bit more insistent. Well, I do know — she'd have gone into a mood and there would have been no point. And maybe I thought she'd be around forever and that there was plenty of time. I did ask about my father, but I knew she wasn't going to tell me any more than she was willing to.'

And then Angela tells me that she has a confession to make, that, because I was in such a state yesterday, she decided to call Sandy.

'Oh. What . . . what did he say?'

'He's on his way.'

'Here? Oh! And he . . . he's not pissed off?'

'Why would he be pissed off?'

'Oh, I don't know. It's just that so much has gone wrong between us. I'm not sure you should have called him. It's not as if we're together any more.'

'You're not divorced, Louise. He's still your husband. And when I told him what had happened, he didn't think twice about coming over. Now, why don't you go back upstairs and jump into the shower. He'll be here in a while, in time for lunch.'

I throw my arms around her. I can't speak because of the lump in my throat that threatens to make me burst into tears.

I hurry upstairs and, as I stand in the shower, all I can think about is the fact that Sandy has responded to my distress by jumping on to a plane. He cares, after all.

★   ★   ★

If I hadn't lost my voice, I wouldn't have taken up teaching, and I wouldn't have met Sandy. I still don't know what went wrong, whether I missed the warning signals — perhaps a break that happened once too often for comfort, tightness in my throat from lack of breath support. But I was never aware of any vocal problems. It was as if I had gone to sleep one night with a healthy voice and woken up the next morning unable to sing a note.

Shortly before it happened, I had a bout of flu that had kept me in bed for more than a week. Maybe the virus had stayed in my system, preventing me from getting my voice back.

Now, though, I have a vague memory of things not being quite right long before my voice stopped working. I would turn on the radio and become quite disturbed for the first few seconds because the music always sounded out of tune. Sometimes, the tunelessness extended beyond music. I often had to walk out of rooms because the light bulb or the fridge seemed out of tune with the other sounds in my head and in my ears.

It was one of the worst times of my life. I had come to define myself as a singer, and now I was a singer who couldn't sing. I kept up the old routines, opening the lid of the piano, pressing my fingers on to the keys, standing straight, breathing in, taking the air down as deep and low into my body as it would go. I was always hoping for the miracle, that when I began to sing there would be something of the old voice, but what came out was just a dull, closed sound that was more or less in tune, but not tuneful. I tried one well-known teacher after another, convinced that one of them would have the magic formula that would restore my voice. None of them did.

Eventually, I did get my voice back by dogged exploration of voice and body and with the help of a good teacher, and the work started to come back. But I was already moving in the direction of teaching. Giving up on my singing career wasn't a difficult decision. It wasn't just a question of knowing that I was never going to set the world on fire as a singer, that I was never going to be one of those globe-trotting divas with a diary bursting at the seams for years into the future. It was also the realisation that I had never really enjoyed performing. I could sing Carmen and Dalila — I could even look like a Carmen or a Dalila — but I lacked the confidence to be a seductress on stage. I was a very small fish in a big pond, and I think I had known that from my first weeks at the college, when I heard voices that were far better than mine.

I often think singing is a disease, an affliction rather than a gift. You start off having lessons, just for fun, and you enjoy them. They're something to look forward to. And then, one day, something happens. You produce a phrase, or just a single note that's better, richer than anything you've thought yourself capable of. After that, you're hooked. You're an addict and singing is the narcotic for which you're willing to give up everything, including even the milk you used to put in your tea and coffee, because dairy has bad press in the world of singing.

It took a while, but I kicked my addiction. Over time, I sang less and taught more, and I discovered that I was happier teaching. I loved working with young singers who were hoping for a career on the opera stage. I loved helping people with ordinary jobs and no ambitions for a singing career to discover what they were capable of. And then one day a big Scotsman walked into my studio.

I wait at the door, watching Sandy get out of the big car that looks too small for him. I'm nervous about what we will say to each other, worried about whether he's going to be distant, even though he has been concerned enough to dash over to Ireland. But there's no awkwardness. He comes towards me, arms outstretched, as if we haven't been apart, as if he hasn't walked out of our ten-year marriage.

'What have you been up to, you daft hen?' he says, exaggerating his Scottish accent and wrapping me in one of his old bear hugs.

I want to collude with him in this cheerfulness that he has probably decided is the best approach. If it will help to bring him back to me, I'll be as bright and cheerful as I need to be.

'I'll tell you later. Angela's anxious that you should be fed. She's worried that you might be fading away,' I say, and I'm pleased when he laughs and pats his slightly expanding girth. Maybe there's hope for us after all, I think, crossing the first and middle fingers of both hands behind my back.

'Sandy,' Angela says. 'It's lovely to see you. We've missed you.'

Lunch is simple — fresh vegetable soup, bread and cheese — and as we sit and eat and talk, the three of us, it's as if we were all meant to be around the table, as if I didn't have a breakdown yesterday and as if Sandy is here not because he has been summoned, but because he wants to be.

'How long are you staying, Sandy?' Angela wants to know.

'A couple of days.' He looks at me. 'Is that all right, Louise?'

Is it all right? It's the best thing that has happened to me in months. I nod my head, almost unable to speak because my heart is bursting with a feeling I can't quite put a name to. I feel like a small child who has been rescued from some terrible misfortune by kind grown-ups. But I feel anxious and afraid, too, because I'm not sure what Sandy's arrival means. Is he just being caring or is he ready to come back? I don't think I can bear it if he lets me down.

'It's fine,' I manage to mumble, torn between these conflicting feelings, but desperately wanting to believe that, finally, I will get my husband back.

We decide that Sandy and I will stay at my mother's house, and when we get there I tell him about my plans to renovate before making a decision on selling or keeping it. He nods his approval, even making suggestions as he reacquaints himself with its boxy rooms and layout.

I can hardly believe the change in him. If his upbeat mood is a pretence, he's making a good job of it. There's none of the moroseness that hung over every conversation we had leading up to and after his departure from our flat. The more recent, careful tone has also gone. I want to know what has brought about this change, and I speculate that, despite his previous denials, he had, after all, been having an affair that has now ended. But now is not the time to ask him about this. I'm too happy that he's here. I can try to put aside for now all the questions that have been plaguing me.

I know Sandy will want to talk about what happened in Dublin, but I know his way of doing things. He will leave it for a few hours, maybe even until tomorrow. He will let me get used to him being here first, won't start to push for information, won't force me to reveal what I can't or won't.

It's a long time since he's been here, so I suggest that he might like to go for a walk while there's still light in the sky.

'We could go to Bettystown, walk along the strand,' he says.

When he says *Bettystown*, Declan darts into my head. What if we bump into him? Will it be awkward? Maybe we should —

'Louise?'

'Oh, sorry! I was miles away for a second. I just remembered something. Yeah, Bettystown will be great.'

And it is.

What is it about walking that opens up the mind and calms it? Can it be something as simple as the rhythm of putting one foot in front of another, over and over again? That's what I do in London when I have something to sort out in my head. I put on a pair of trainers and walk fast for an hour or two and somehow — I don't know how, because I don't even try to think about anything but the business of walking — by the time I get back home, I have a solution of sorts.

Now, Sandy and I stride along the damp sand, the wind blowing in our faces and our hair, and, at one point, when I trip over a piece of driftwood that I've failed to see, he takes my hand and keeps hold of it. We don't talk much over the noise of the waves and the wind.

I sneak shy looks at him, at his thatch of hair that was once a reddish blonde, but is now, I see to my surprise, mostly grey. How did that happen without my noticing it?

He looks at me, too, and I wonder what he's thinking. Maybe he's also seeing things he hasn't noticed before, things that surprise him. Or maybe he's just wondering about how to deal with the consequences of my episode yesterday in Dublin, how to talk to me about it. But he's holding my hand and I feel the safest and happiest I've felt in a long time.

We talk about music in the way we used to, about the pieces that lift our hearts or crush them, Sandy intermittently booming out phrases that we love or hate.

I could have walked for hours like that, but there's rain on the wind and we dash back to the car, reaching it just as the skies open.

'Fucking Ireland!' Sandy gasps, collapsing into the car. 'You can't go five yards down the road in the sunshine before it starts pissing rain!'

'Yeah, yeah, and the sun never stops shining over Scotland. And, of course, it never, ever rains there.'

We stop at a supermarket and stock up on food, and, when we get back to the house, I light the fire while Sandy cooks — two sirloin steaks with big floury potatoes and salad. He loves cooking. No nouvelle stuff, though. He's a heart-attack-on-a-plate kind of cook. He opens a bottle of red wine and, as he hands me a glass, I ask him whether it's all right for me to drink. 'Of course, it's all right,' he says, and I'm relieved because it means he doesn't think I'm losing my sanity.

He still hasn't mentioned my breakdown and I wonder when it is going to come up. But it won't be tonight and I'm glad about that.

It's almost like old times as we chat over dinner. If anything, it's even better, and I feel myself daring to hope that we may be in sight of a new beginning. I ask him which of the two rooms he would like.

'I thought I might bunk in with you,' he says. 'If that's all right.'

'It's fine . . . but I thought . . . '

'Can I come back, Lou? Can we start again?'

'Yes,' I say, choking. 'But . . . '

'We're going to be all right,' he says.

Later, his big arm flung chastely across me, I lie awake for hours. I can't help tormenting myself with questions. Did he sleep like this with other women during the months we were apart? Was there one woman or were there several? But I chase these thoughts away, because I don't want to have them tonight. I don't want to sleep, either. I want to be awake, listening to Sandy's breathing and feeling what I haven't felt for a very long time. I want to feel the way I did all those years ago, when a singing lesson turned into a love affair.

I liked the sound of his voice when he rang me to book a consultation. It was low and soft, with a Scottish lilt that had a touch of roughened velvet to it. And when he turned up for his first lesson, I liked the look of him, too. You wouldn't call Sandy good looking in the traditional sense. But he's big and broad and protective, the kind of man you know you'll be safe with, even if you're seeing him for the first time. And when I saw him for the first time, filling the door frame, with a great big smile on his face and a load of music tucked underneath his arm, I couldn't help but be immediately charmed by him.

'So, tell me a bit about your singing. What are you looking for from lessons?' I asked. What I really wanted to know was whether he was married, whether he was available, what it would be like to lie beside him at night and feel him press into me.

'Well, I sing bass in a choir. We're going to be doing Beethoven Nine soon, and some of it lies a bit high for the basses. I want to work on the top of my voice, but I think I need to work on my voice in general, and you come well recommended by our chorus master, Michael Robinson.'

'Ah, you sing with Marylebone Voices? It's a very good choir. Yes, I know Michael well. Let's crack on then, shall we?'

Nothing happened for a long time. I fancied him in a gentle kind of way. There was something about him I couldn't put my finger on. It wasn't that he reminded me of anyone in particular; it was more a kind of recognition, as if

I had known him all along. But even that didn't explain it. When he first started coming for lessons, I had been wrapped up for a while in a long-distance romance with an American journalist I had met through Ursula and who was based in Dubai. It was high-octane stuff: the phone call from Chris saying he had a few days off and why didn't we meet up in Rome or Paris or wherever; the three or four days of intense emotional and physical activity; and then the weeks of hardly any contact. I was beginning to wonder whether I could be bothered with this lark for too much longer.

Sandy usually had his lessons in the early evening. Sometimes, if he wasn't rushing off and I didn't have anyone coming after him, we walked down to the pub on the corner for a drink. We talked about anything and everything — books, films, music and politics. He sometimes referred to the divorce he was going through, but didn't give me the impression he was suffering because of it.

'We probably got married for all the wrong reasons,' he said. 'You know, you get to thirty, you're working long hours, you look at the person you're with and you think it all adds up to the right timing. And a few years later, you're still working long hours and you realise that, if you ever had anything in common, you don't have it any more.'

'That's sad,' I said.

'Sad, but, in our case, true. Elizabeth isn't musical, either. It's not that she doesn't *like* music. She does, but she can take it or leave it.

It's probably towards the bottom of her top ten likes, behind books, films, trekking — '

'Trekking?'

'Aye. Peru, Nepal. She's very fit, very tough. You wouldn't catch me doing that stuff. I'm a delicate flower.'

I laughed. 'And now? Where is she? Do you see her?'

'She's in Exeter with another academic, who's more than delighted to head into the mountainy distance with her whenever they have the opportunity. I see her when it's necessary. It's what they call an amicable divorce. What about you?'

I could have told him about my American, but I didn't bother. I realised that there was nothing much to tell.

'Oh, I'm what you might call fancy free,' I said. And then, reddening at the lie, I jumped up and went to the bar to get more drinks.

Sandy had a way of making me laugh without saying anything that was downright funny. And he was so different from my idea of what a psychiatrist would be like. I could easily imagine him using no more than his charm to coax his patients into becoming well again.

The lessons were fun and he was a good student. His technique gradually improved to the extent that I hardly ever needed to check his breathing, but he still had his moments of confusion. On the day we got together, he was having one of those moments. So I got up from the piano, took his hand and guided it to my stomach, reminding him how I was able to take in a breath and begin to sing without tensing the muscles there. But even before I had finished the phrase, I became aware that his hand had slipped around my ribcage and was resting in the small of my back, and that his other hand had moved up to my shoulder and was pulling me gently towards him.

We spent hours in my bed, having sex, talking and laughing, having sex again, and when we eventually left the flat to go out for something to eat, Sandy suddenly turned to me in the middle of Ladbroke Grove and began singing 'Where'er You Walk'. I hardly noticed the litter, the discarded greasy remains of takeaway food, the drunks staggering along the pavement drinking lager from cans. And when Chris rang the following day from Dubai to ask whether I fancied a weekend in Paris, I told him I had met my future husband.

★ ★ ★

I wake to hear Sandy singing 'Ae Fond Kiss' at the top of his voice and the clatter of last night's pots and pans and dishes being washed. By the time I stagger downstairs, he has moved on to 'Bonnie Mary of Argyle' and is scrambling eggs and frying rashers.

It's over breakfast, as we tackle the business of eating, that he brings up my Dublin episode. I tell him about my visit to Richard in Dalkey and learning that my mother had worked as a secretary at a brewery in Crumlin. I don't have to tell him that I'd hoped to find something

95

there that would lead me to my father. He knows all about my obsession. It's when I tell him about what happened in front of the postbox that he begins to look worried.

'What do you think that's about?' he asks.

'Well, Angela wonders whether my mother might have taken me there at some point and something happened that gave me a fright,' I say. And then, with a laugh, I add, 'I suppose it would have had to be a very big fright.'

'You've never told me about that postbox memory before, the first one.'

He says this in a straightforward way, but I can feel a hint of accusation somewhere in his tone. What he's really saying is, *Why haven't you mentioned this before?*

'No. I haven't really talked about it to anyone. Maybe I didn't really think of it as being all that important. It was one of those things that flitted in and out. And . . . well, it wasn't so disturbing before. It was just . . . weird.'

'And it *has* become disturbing now?'

'Yes. I think it started to change and get worse after my mother died.'

'What do you think made it change?'

'I can't think of anything in particular. But it was hard, sitting there and watching her die. Maybe that was it.'

I wait for Sandy to speak again, but he stays silent, frowning now, wearing his analytical face.

'What are you thinking?' I ask.

'I'm thinking that it wouldn't be a great idea for you to go anywhere near Crumlin again. For the time being, anyway. What I'd really like is for you to come back to London,' he says.

'But what about everything I have to do here? I haven't even started properly on the papers.'

'They'll keep. You're the sole beneficiary. You can take your time.'

'But there are things I need to look for . . . There could be stuff that explains everything.'

He takes my hands in his, squeezes them and gives me a long look.

'Louise, you need a break from all this. I don't want you to be here on your own and, at the moment, I can't take time off to be with you. The papers can wait. We'll have a quick sift through them, check whether there's anything useful, and then we'll put them in a couple of big cardboard boxes until the house is finished and we can come back to them. I don't want to overstate the significance of what happened to you the other day, but I don't want to dismiss it, either. I think there's a lot of stuff in your childhood that you need to deal with. That's what your episode in Crumlin is telling me. And I think that's what it's telling you.'

I know where this is going. He wants me to consider psychotherapy. But he doesn't come straight out with it because of how I've reacted in the past. Once, after one of those conversations, I had a dream in which a man was riding a bicycle up and down Ladbroke Grove in front of the flat. He was standing on the handlebars, doing all sorts of strange contortions, making the bike do a bizarre series of jumps and wheelies. I felt disapproving. He shouldn't have been doing such dangerous manoeuvres in the middle of a main road. I mentioned it to Ursula the next day.

'Easy peasy,' she said. 'Trick cyclist.'

'Trick cyclist?'

'Slang for psychiatrist.'

'So the dream means that I disapprove of what Sandy does?'

'Nah, it's not about Sandy. It's about what he wants you to sign up to. Psychotherapy. You don't like it. You think it's dangerous.'

She was right. I didn't like the idea of it at all. Maybe it's an Irish thing, the idea that you just get on with whatever it is you need to get on with, that you don't dig too deep for fear of what you might disturb. And maybe some things shouldn't be disturbed. They lurk in dark places in our minds for a reason; we've banished them to the shadows because we don't want to be reminded of them. But my childhood was a happy one, even without a father. There was nothing that I wanted or needed to forget.

★   ★   ★

When Sandy goes to have his shower and I'm sitting, drinking another mug of coffee, my thoughts stray back to the postbox memory. I had told both him and Angela that I hadn't talked about it to anyone before.

But that's not strictly true. The memory had always been there, but after we moved to Drogheda it came more often and more strongly for a while. I told my mother about it once when she came into my room to say goodnight. I

98

thought she might be able to tell me what it was about, but she said nothing for a long time and, when I looked up at her, there was a look on her face that I didn't recognise or understand. It was as if she had turned into someone else. She sat on the edge of my bed without saying a word for so long that I became scared. And when I said, 'Mamma! Mamma! What's wrong?' she turned and walked out of the room without a word, leaving me to put out the light and turn on my night light by myself.

Hours later, I woke, the bang of the front door echoing around the house and in my ears. Then silence. I got out of bed and opened my bedroom door. All the lights were on, but there was no sound. Starting with the kitchen, I walked around the house, ending up in the bedroom my mother shared with Dermot. The lights were on there, too, but the bed was empty.

In a panic, I opened the front door and stared out into the night. It was pitch black, the kind of darkness that had always made me nervous, that made me think I would be swallowed up by it. But my fear for my mother was greater than my terror of being devoured by the dark, and I ran towards the gate.

The lane that passed our house stretched up the hill to join the main road into town, but it also continued in a half-hearted way down to the river, which was already widening as it made its way to the sea. I looked back at the house, where the lights burned bright, making the darkness seem blacker still, and turned down towards the river. I broke into a run, stumbling over potholes that I couldn't see. All I could think of was my mother and whether it was too late to save her.

When I got to the bottom of the hill, the reflection of the moonlight in the water created enough light for me to see the two figures ahead. My mother and Dermot were sitting on the low stone wall that ran along the river bank. He had one arm around her and his other hand held hers. They weren't speaking. They just sat quietly and, for a moment, I thought, There's nothing wrong; they just went out for a walk. Except that Mamma was wearing only her nightdress and no shoes or slippers, and Dermot was in his pyjamas.

'Are you all right, Mamma?'

She didn't answer, but looked through me with eyes that seemed more dead than alive.

'She's grand,' Dermot said. 'Nothing to be worried about. She'll be fine in the morning, when she's had a good sleep. We'll get her home now.'

They stood up and I saw how gentle Dermot was with her. He held one of her hands and I held the other, and we walked slowly back to the house. Dermot made hot milky drinks for the three of us and, once she had drunk hers, put Mamma to bed. She fell asleep straight away.

I looked at the clock. It was nearly four o'clock and there was a grey light in the sky.

Hours later, when I woke, my mother was in the kitchen making scrambled eggs and acting as if everything was normal. But I was already blaming myself for what had happened. I had upset her by talking about the postbox memory and, because of that, she had gone to the river. There was no other explanation. I made a silent vow never to bring it up again.

10

Back in London, we've fallen into something like our old lives. Sandy has moved back in, but is so much in demand at conferences that he's often away from home. He has even taken a break from the choir, a big wrench for him, especially with Elgar's *Dream of Gerontius* coming up.

We haven't talked about our several-months-long separation. It doesn't feel right to ignore it, to act as if it never happened, but I don't want to be the one to bring it up and push for answers that I may not want to hear. So I throw myself back into my teaching. Most of the time, I use a studio in central London, not far from Oxford Street. Sometimes, if all the studios are booked up I teach in the flat.

Before we got married, we thought about selling our flats and buying a house, maybe one of the Edwardian houses a bit further north, but still close to Ladbroke Grove. My flat wouldn't be big enough for children, Sandy said. I remember being struck by a strange feeling when he said that. We'd never seriously discussed children and his remark made me realise that he'd simply taken it for granted they would eventually materialise. I had assumed that, too, without really giving it any thought. But when he began talking about the children we would have to fit into our home I was terrified. I made all the right noises, but inside my head all I could hear was some inner voice whispering, *No, no, no.*

I remember, too, that when we first got together I woke up once to find him gazing down at me. I rubbed my eyes to get the sleep out of them and squinted up at him.

'That's a strange look you're giving me,' I said.

'I'm thinking that, if we have a child, I want it to have your eyes.'

'Well, I certainly don't,' I said. 'My eyes are far too small!'

'Ah, but that's why they sparkle so much!'

Foolishly, I had thought at the time that the conversation was about me, but even then he must have been thinking ahead to children that didn't yet exist. And never would.

We never did get around to buying a house. Sandy sold his flat in Fulham and moved in with me and, a year or so after we got married, we bought the basement flat and connected the two to make a maisonette. I stopped taking my birth-control pills, but secretly prayed I wouldn't get pregnant. Sandy didn't seem to anguish over it. Once or twice he suggested it might be good for both of us to get checked out. But we didn't do anything about it and, now, when I look back, I ask myself why Sandy didn't push more. I don't have an answer. In any case, I don't think I was the only one feeling ambivalent about having kids because Sandy eventually stopped talking about them, too. If he had been that keen, wouldn't he have made more of an issue of it?

I've started going to the gym with Ursula. I hated it at first, and tried to find excuses not to go, but Ursula wouldn't let me back out. Now, I look forward to the sessions. I feel good after them.

I've also started to see a psychotherapist, but the pressure to do so has come less from Sandy than from Ursula and Angela.

'Her name is Sheila Fitzgerald and she's good,' Ursula said, handing me a piece of paper with a name, address and telephone number. 'She's Irish, too, so she'll have a head start on understanding where you're coming from.'

'You went to her?'

'No, but one of my exes did. I rang him up and got her deets.'

I like Sheila. She's about the same age as Angela, around sixty. She even looks a bit like Angela — on the sturdy side and with once-fair hair, cut in a soft bob below the jawline. At our first session, just over a month ago, I sat facing her and told her about the Crumlin incident that had brought me to her. Now it's the beginning of June and I've been seeing her twice a week, but we haven't returned to the Crumlin episode yet.

Our sessions go like this: I lie on a couch and Sheila sits at the back of the room, where I can't see her, and I talk and talk. I talk about anything and everything, but not about Crumlin. I'm doing this reluctantly. I'm doing it because I know I have to do it if I'm going to get a grip back on my life.

So I talk about my mother. I could talk for hours about her, about what I loved about her and what I hated about her, too. Only I don't use the word *hated* to Sheila because she will read too much into it.

'She could be a bit overprotective,' I say. 'You know, not happy about the crowd I hung around with when I was in my teens.'

'What about Ursula?'

'Oh, she loved Ursula. We were like twins. We were inseparable from day one at school. No, it was more the new friends I was making that she was . . . wary of.'

It's Declan I'm thinking of, in particular, as I tell her this. And as I lie on the couch with my eyes half-closed, I can see us meeting after school, him taking my books from me and walking me most of the way home. At weekends, we go for long walks. Sometimes he brings his dog along. Bran. *All our dogs are called Bran. When one Bran dies, we get another.* He thinks he might want to be a vet. I'm not sure at this stage what I want to do, although I like history. It's my best subject. Declan is my secret. I haven't told Mamma about him. I don't want her to meet him because I know what she'll do. She'll invite him to our house so often that she'll suffocate him. She'll be nice to him, so nice. But when she and I are alone together in the kitchen, washing and drying the dishes, she'll say something about him that isn't exactly bad, but isn't quite good, either. And that will leave me feeling unsure about him. I know this is what will happen because it's what she always does.

I've never told Sandy about Declan; I would end up telling him things I'd rather he didn't know. And I'm not ready to tell Sheila about him, either. Not yet. So I tell her about meeting

Sandy, losing him and getting him back, and about my mother's death. But I keep it all at surface level. I'm not ready to dig too deep. She must be bored stiff.

I tell her about the house in Ireland and my plans for it. I like talking about that. I've given Joe the go-ahead to start the work. I'm still considering whether to sell it or keep it, but the more I talk and think about what it could look like, the more I think that I'm going to keep it.

We talk a lot about music, about how I came to the piano at the relatively late age of eleven and then discovered singing.

'It was thanks to Dermot, really. He sang in the local male-voice choir and there was a piano in the house. He had an old recording of Richard Tauber singing 'You Are My Heart's Delight' and he used to sing along with it. It was quite funny — sometimes he came in a bit the worse for wear after choir practice and all he had to do to soften my mother up was sing a few bars of that song.'

I tell her that music is probably the only thing that makes complete sense to me.

'People have their idiosyncrasies, haven't they? You just have to accept them. And all sorts of things go wrong and you have no control over them. But music is gloriously predictable. Most of the time, you know exactly where it's going and it's utterly satisfying when it gets there. And even when it does something you're not expecting, you still end up thinking that this was the only way it could have gone.'

106

I tell Sheila about my childhood in Drumcondra with my mother, how energetic and vivacious she was, how she filled my existence in those early days before I started school and met Ursula.

And then the Dolls' Hospital comes into my head, and, for some reason I can't explain, I start to cry. Why would talking about a good memory, a special one, bring tears? But it does — quiet torrents of them. It's the first time I've wept at one of our sessions and I have to use the box of tissues that Sheila keeps on a coffee table next to the low couch. And, despite my having wiped my eyes and blown my nose, the memories of that day are flooding back and it's as if I'm there, fiercely clutching Audrey to me, unwilling to let her be taken from me.

I kept my eyes down and fixed on the frilly hem of her pink dress.

'Do you not want her to get better?' the nurse asked, bending down so that her face was level with mine. She had soft brown eyes and there was something warm about the way she spoke.

I felt my grip on my doll loosening.

'Look,' the nurse said, making a sweeping move with her arm, and I lifted my eyes and looked around the room. There were dolls everywhere, on shelves, on tables. There were teddy bears, too.

'We have made all these lovely dolls better and now they are waiting for the little children who own them to take them home,' the nurse said.

'Can you really make her better?' I asked, not quite ready to believe that my doll, whose blue eyes I had pressed too hard when exploring their ability to open and close, could be restored to full health.

'Oh, yes,' she said. 'Now, you give her to me and the doctor will examine her.'

So I held out my doll and the nurse took her very carefully and laid her on a table, and a doctor in a white coat came and examined her. After what seemed like a very long time, he looked at me and gave me a big smile.

'I think we will give your doll a little operation and a good rest in a very nice bed, and after two weeks you can come and take her home,' the doctor said.

The strange thing is that, although I remember every detail of that visit to the Dolls' Hospital in Mary Street, I have no recollection at all of having returned to collect my doll. I don't remember her being part of my childhood after that.

I didn't think of that doll for years. Not until, just a couple of years ago, when I popped over to visit my mother for a few days, I read a story in the *Irish Times* about the Dolls' Hospital, and memories of our visit to Mary Street flooded my mind. She looked puzzled when I mentioned it, but after a moment said she had a very vague recollection of having taken me there.

'What became of the doll?' I asked. 'Did we ever go back for her?'

'Oh, I'm afraid it's all too long ago for me,' she said. 'But we must have gone back. Yes. Yes, I'm sure we did.'

I'm still thinking about that conversation with

my mother when Sheila's voice brings me back to the present.

'Are you all right?' she asks.

'Yes, it was just the shock of remembering it all so . . . so clearly. But what I can't remember at all is what happened after we left. I can't remember a thing!'

'Perhaps you can remember how you felt about leaving your doll behind?'

'I'm not sure, but I don't remember being upset or worried. I think I knew she'd be all right.'

'Maybe your mother reassured you that the doll would be fine?'

'I don't remember. I don't really remember her saying anything or even being there. I just remember the couple and how kind they were, and thinking that they would take care of Audrey — that was my doll's name. She was called after Audrey Hepburn.'

'Was that your mother's suggestion, to name her after Audrey Hepburn?'

'Probably. I don't remember.'

'I wonder whether you felt Audrey would be safe because there would be a couple — both a mother and a father — looking after her.'

'Maybe . . . I suppose I might have thought that. Two parents being better than one, and all that. But I can't remember. I always felt safe with my mother, though, if that's what you're getting at.'

'So what do you think happened to Audrey? Did your mother take you back to collect her?'

'It's weird, but I have no idea what happened

to her. That's a bit odd, isn't it, that I can't remember?'

Sheila throws the question back at me. 'Why do you think that?'

★ ★ ★

Back in the 1980s you could phone Aer Lingus, reserve a ticket and then pay for it at Heathrow. Or not. A few times, I got as far as the airport, but had to force myself to walk those last few yards to the ticket desk and take out my chequebook. What was I afraid of? Being swept into my mother's all-embracing, omnipotent orbit?

I loved my mother, even if it sometimes doesn't sound as if I did. I grieve for her now. But if I ask myself when I was happiest with her, my mind shoots straight back to those early years in Drumcondra, when it was just herself and myself in that small flat with no garden, but with Dublin at our feet. She was always organising things for us to do. In summer, there were those excursions out of town to the sea, the excitement of getting on to the train at Amiens Street, hoping we'd have a compartment all to ourselves.

In the winter, our pursuits were urban. She used to take me around Dublin, pointing out landmarks, telling me about their history, making them come alive for a small child entranced by the magic of a bustling city. She showed me where Nelson's Pillar had stood at one end of O'Connell Street until republicans blew it up in

1966. She took me to the GPO, the General Post Office, headquarters of the leaders of the 1916 Easter Rising. We went to St Patrick's Cathedral and she told me about Dean Swift, who had written a book called *Gulliver's Travels*. It was easy to absorb history without realising I was doing it.

These urban wanderings always ended with a trip to Bewley's Oriental Café on Grafton Street, where, she said, everyone in Ireland turned up at one point or another. I loved it — the old booths, the butter curls, the exotic smell of the coffee, the buns and the cakes. It was always full; there were students from Trinity, just down the road, people up from the country for a day's shopping, and people who couldn't walk past it without being drawn inside.

Around the time of my birthday, every year, my mother would take me on a trip far beyond Dublin, sometimes by bus, sometimes by train.

'Where are we going, Mamma?' I would ask.

'It's a surprise. You'll find out when we get there.'

We travelled all over the country, usually to cities or big towns — Cork, Galway or Killarney, even north across the border to Belfast or Derry — spending one or two nights in small hotels. After she married Dermot, she still insisted on taking me away on these short trips.

'It's good for her to have me to herself every now and again,' I heard her tell him once. And it was. I revelled in my mother's company as the two of us strolled around, hand in hand, or, when I was older and taller, arm in arm.

I started to move out from under her spell when I got to my mid-teens. Perhaps it was simply a matter of growing up and a need to pull away from her. Or perhaps, in some subconscious way, I was jealous that I was no longer the sole focus of her life, and so I retaliated by downgrading my dependence on her.

I talk about these things to Sheila, but in a rambling kind of way. She doesn't say much, but sometimes asks me questions. I can't fully explain those times when I almost didn't make the trip home, so she explores gently. Can I recall what thoughts were in my head as the battle raged between picking up the ticket and turning on my heels and going back into London? Was it Ireland that was the problem or was it my mother? Did I feel less close to her because she had expanded her life beyond me when she met Dermot? Or did I fear that I might be pulled back under her spell? I have no answers, but the questions stay in my head. I haven't consciously considered them until now.

The postbox image, the original one, is coming more often. Initially, I try to block it because I'm afraid that it will merge with what happened in Crumlin and turn me into a gibbering wreck. But it doesn't, and so I let it drift forward to the front of my mind. Sometimes it seems as if it's expanding beyond the original contours, the way a damp patch on a wall or ceiling appears to be spreading and you wish you had traced around the outline with a pencil when it first appeared so that you could keep a check on whether it was getting worse.

Most of the image is the same as before: the small arm, the envelope, the green postbox. But now I'm aware that it's dark around the image, and it feels like the darkness of night rather than some clouded background shade. There are other things that come to me — flit in and out so quickly that I can't give them any definition — fleeting sensations of cold, of excitement, of fear.

I've begun to talk to Sheila about Crumlin. I tell her that my mother worked in the brewery there and that I think my father may have been her boss.

Sheila says little, but takes in a lot. She never offers an opinion on anything I present to her, but throws out questions, encouraging me to find the answers myself to what's troubling me.

'I know you'll disapprove, but I've written to the brewery's headquarters,' I tell her. 'Maybe someone there will be able to tell me how to get in touch with him. Or maybe they won't bother to write back. It's been a while since I wrote to them.'

'Why do you think I'll disapprove?'

'Because . . . '

I let my answer trail off, because I don't want to tell her how dishonest I've been, lying in my email about the reason for contacting the brewery and using a false name. I stay silent for a while and then I come up with something for her.

'Because maybe you'll ask me if I'm ready to cope with what I may find out . . . or what I may not.'

11

I have a new singer. Her name is Julia Ross and she wants to go through some repertoire for a recital she's planning for later in the year.

'I'm so glad you can do this,' she said when she first called me. 'My regular teacher is taking a break for six months to visit her family in New Zealand. Your name came up a couple of times when I asked for recommendations.'

I was flattered. My card is among those pinned to the noticeboard at the studios, but it's always good when people recommend me.

I like to know who and what I'm working with and her name didn't ring any bells, so I looked her up on the internet and came up with a few amateur recitals in churches around London.

She arrives for our session at the studio a good fifteen minutes late; not the greatest start. But as she sweeps into the practice room, breathless with effusive apologies, I find myself being charmed by her. In some strange way, she reminds me of my mother, though there's no obvious physical resemblance.

A man might describe Julia as a bit of a stunner. But that's too banal a description for a face of pale porcelain beauty, framed by shoulder-length dark auburn hair. She's somewhere between thirty and thirty-five, but there's quite an old-fashioned look to her and she's wearing clothes that might even be described as prim — a little pink cashmere cardigan buttoned up the front and a string of pearls around her neck, a knee-length pencil skirt and pointy-toed kitten-heel shoes. It's an Audrey Hepburn kind of look.

I ask her to sing a couple of the pieces she's brought along, so that I can get an idea of her voice. She has a pretty, light soprano, but the songs and arias she has given me are far too heavy for it.

'You have a lovely voice, Julia, but I'm not convinced that this is the kind of thing you should be singing. I'd be very happy to work with you, but I think I'd want to take you away from this heavier repertoire — for a while, anyway — and try some lighter pieces,' I say.

I always chose my words carefully in this kind of situation. Someone who thinks of herself as a Wagnerian soprano is likely to be upset if she's told that her voice is more suited to light opera or musical theatre.

'Oh,' she says. 'But my previous teacher thought these pieces were perfect for me.'

'They might be at some point, but not now. You're pushing the sound out. That's because you're not using your breath properly.'

She looks taken aback, but says nothing, so I go on.

'I think you're concentrating too much on the sound you're making, when you should be using your body — your abdominal muscles, your intercostal muscles — to support your voice. Singing is physical. You have to *feel* it rather than hear it. As I said, I'm happy to take you on, but

115

I'd want to spend most of the time on technique at first. And I'd also want you to work on lighter stuff — at least for now. It's up to you.'

She thinks for a moment and then widens her mouth into a disarming smile.

'I'll give it a try.'

We do some work on technique and, by the end of the session, she's exhilarated and so enthusiastic about working with me that she books several lessons over the next few weeks.

She wants to know if I am married, what my husband does, what he's like. So I tell her a little bit about Sandy and me, omitting the bit about our months of separation.

'I'm so envious of people who are blissfully happy,' she says. 'I don't seem to have much luck in that department.'

Are Sandy and I blissfully happy? I wouldn't go that far. We were once, and I hope we will be again. But, of course, I don't say this to Julia.

'We rub along very nicely. We're a bit like two old socks — we get lost in the laundry basket every now and again, but we always seem to find our way back as a pair.'

'You don't make it sound very romantic,' she says with a laugh.

I want to jump up and say that my marriage *is* romantic, that it's the kind of marriage I had always dreamed of but never thought I would achieve. But I don't, because there's that gap of several months that Sandy and I don't talk about.

Julia's session ends with the arrival of Ben, one of my favourite students. I introduce them and

116

marvel at the immediacy of her effect on him. It's as if she's bestowing a blessing on him, and, in a way, she is. She gives him her full attention, looks at him as if he's the most interesting, attractive and important person she has ever met. I wonder whether she has worked at this or whether she's simply one of those women who can't help but reel men in. I can see that Ben is already in thrall to her. He beams all the way through his lesson and, when we finish and start discussing when to fix our next session, he can't resist mentioning her.

'Extraordinarily beautiful, that Julia,' he says. 'Is she going to be a regular?'

'Possibly,' I say, with some caution. One of the sessions Julia has booked is for the same time next week, but I don't say this to Ben. His wife stays at home looking after three small children and he has a low-paid teaching job in a tough inner-city school. I can tell from his reaction to Julia that he's already besotted with her — who wouldn't be? I almost am, too — and I don't want to facilitate anything that might increase the pressure on his already fractious marriage. So when he asks if he can have the same slot next week, I think about saying it's not available. But he has already seen the blank space in my diary and Julia's name in the slot above it. Next week it is.

When I next see Sheila, I tell her about the session with Julia and the way Ben reacted to her.

'It really was incredible. I've never seen anyone — apart from my mother, and even she couldn't compete with Julia — have such an effect on a man.'

'And how did that make you feel?'

'A little bit envious, I suppose.'

'Why?'

'Any woman would be envious of her. She's vivacious and she's unbelievably pretty.'

'And do you think you're neither of those things?'

'Oh, I know I'm not bad-looking. I scrub up well. But there's something so delicate about her. I can imagine men wanting to protect her.'

'And you can't imagine men wanting to protect you?'

'No, I can't. I think they see me as being strong and not needing to be protected.'

'Even Sandy?'

I say nothing.

'But Sandy turned up in Ireland, didn't he? Wasn't he being protective?'

'I suppose so. But . . . with regard to Julia, it's not just me being a bit envious of her looks. I felt a bit worried, too.'

'What were you worried about?'

'That something might happen between her and Ben. I don't want Ben to go all soppy over her and wreck his marriage.'

'I wonder why you're so convinced that he and Julia are going to become involved? And is it up to you to decide whether they become involved or not? Why do you feel you have to protect Ben? Could it be that there's a more personal reason for your anxiety about Julia and Ben?'

Sheila has struck deep. Of course, I realise,

there's a more personal reason. I want to protect Ben's marriage because I'm still trying to salvage and protect my own.

'Yes,' I say, now looking into my own soul. 'It's all about me, isn't it? I'm still terrified of losing Sandy again and I'm acting out my fears by projecting them on to Ben and Julia.'

'Shall we explore this a bit more on Thursday?' Sheila says, indicating that our fifty minutes are up. 'I'm afraid it's time.'

★   ★   ★

You don't make it sound very romantic. Julia's words stay in my head, annoying me, and I wish I had told her there and then just how romantic our marriage has been. Apart from those months of limbo.

I could have told her about our wedding day, which I can honestly say was the best and happiest day of my life. That's not to downgrade my Dublin childhood with my mother, but Sandy brought a different, grown-up kind of happiness that I hadn't experienced. Before Sandy, I had agonised too much over relationships, over things that seemed so crucial at the time but were, in retrospect, clear signs that I should have cut my losses and moved on.

Early on in our relationship, he told me he had a confession to make. I immediately thought he was going to tell me about an indiscretion, maybe a one-night stand, which he now regretted, during those first weeks together. But it was nothing like that.

119

'I fancied you before I met you,' he said.

'What? How? I don't remember my name being up in lights and my picture splashed all over the place.'

'It was a few years ago. You were singing Dido at one of those country-house festivals.'

'And was I good? Were you bowled over by my incredible singing?'

'I'm sure you were and I probably was, but I can't remember,' he said, chuckling. 'You were wearing some outrageously sexy costume and I just kept thinking how gorgeous and tragic you looked.'

'Why didn't you come and talk to me afterwards?'

'Well, I couldn't, could I? I was still married to Elizabeth. But when she and I finally went our separate ways, I have to admit that you did come into my mind. Took me a while to track you down, but here I am.'

You can't get any more romantic than that, can you? He had *tracked me down*. I wish I'd thought of telling that story to Julia, but it was too late. The moment had passed.

★   ★   ★

The work is progressing on the house in Ireland. Joe calls me regularly to give me updates or suggest minor adjustments here and there. He emails me photographs and videos. The extension is up, and now it's just a matter of doing the tiling in the bathroom and kitchen, and putting in the fixtures. I pore over the catalogues he

120

emails me and send him back my choices. We discuss them on the phone.

'Will you be over any time soon?' he wants to know. 'I only ask because we'll want to get going on the upstairs. We'll need to empty the attic so we can lift the ceiling. There's nothing to speak of up there, but you might want to come over anyway to see where we're at.'

'Oh, Joe, I don't think I can get away for a while. I have an awful lot of work on.'

The truth is that I can't face leaving London at the moment. Things are going well with Sandy. And it's true that I have a lot of work lined up. But I also have a faint dread of going back to my mother's things, even though I want to know the truth about my father, want to know everything my mother never told me about him.

'No problem,' Joe says. 'But you'll have to come over at some point.'

I will, but not for some time, and not unless Sandy comes with me. Or unless I'm so sure of him that I don't mind leaving him for a while. But I'm not sure of him. I'm trying hard to put our months apart at the back of my mind, trying not to torment myself over what made him leave and what made him come back. I look back over the years to when we first met and I try to remember what brought us together and kept us together for so long. For me, there had been that strange familiarity coupled with an attraction I had felt almost immediately and which got stronger the more I got to know him. He made me feel safe, too. But for him . . . ?

He used to joke that I was so clearly in need of

a big strong fellow like himself that he felt he had to make a sacrifice and take me on. Once, he looked at me as we lay in bed, drifting into sleep, and told me I was the most beautiful and precious thing in his life. How safe and strong that made me feel.

We had a lovely life, the kind of life I would never have had with Chris or any of the other men I had been involved with. We did gloriously simple things. On Sundays, Sandy went out to get the papers and we read them slowly over breakfast, as if the day was going to be endless, and then we might wander off to the Tate to look at some paintings, or even just meander around Holland Park. We had friends — his hospital friends, my music friends — and we mixed them all up together. It was great fun.

Now, I don't want to rock the boat by asking him too many questions. And there's something else that bothers me. The episode in Crumlin has led me to question the way I remember things, and now I can't help wondering whether I did something — *some thing* — that made Sandy leave me. Did something happen that I just cannot remember? Or is there a much more straightforward explanation? Has what he once felt — that I was precious and beautiful — simply disappeared? And is it ever going to come back?

12

Eventually, more than two months after I sent my email, the brewery contacts me.

'Am I speaking to Sandra Munro?'

'You are.'

'My name is Jill Tomlinson. I'm company secretary at Tennyson's. The brewery. You contacted us a little while ago.'

'Ah, yes, I did.'

'I'm sorry it's taken us so long to get back to you, but we don't often have requests like yours. Writers and journalists tend to be so much more interested in the Quaker companies. They don't seem to realise that some of the brewing companies also indulged in a great deal of philanthropy and looked after their employees very well indeed,' she says.

'Yes, it's a shame, really.' I can't think of anything else to say.

'Now, would you mind telling me a little bit more about your project? About your previous work in this area?'

I'm not prepared for this, but I'm good at thinking quickly. I know I can't lie. If I tell her I've had work published, she may check me out on the internet. So I tell her that I studied sociology at Birkbeck College in London as a mature student and, through my degree, became interested in corporate philanthropy. I tell her that this is my first major project and that it may eventually form the basis for a doctorate.

She seems to be happy with this.

'I don't know what your schedule is, but what I suggest is that you come and visit us and see our archives. You also asked if you might be able to talk to any former staff who worked in Dublin. I'm afraid there aren't many still alive, but there are a few. That's another reason we've taken a while to respond to you. We had to contact them and ask if they would be willing to talk to you. Happily, they are, so if you have a pen handy . . . '

My hand shakes as I begin to write. She gives me four names and a little bit of background on each, but only one of them was in Dublin during the 1960s, and his name is David Prescott. My heart is racing so fast that I feel it's going to burst. I can hardly speak. She gives me the addresses. David Prescott lives in a village near Northampton called Friars Ashby.

Jill Tomlinson has suggested that I visit the brewery's head office in Northampton, where she will give me access to the company archives and be available to answer any questions I may have. I agree, because even though I now have what I want, I don't want to raise any suspicion on her part that I have a different agenda. And maybe I'll discover some useful information in the archives, possibly even see my mother in a photograph. Down the phone line I can hear her flicking pages. When she speaks again, she suggests a date two weeks away.

'Actually, I wonder whether you might be able to fit me in this week. I'm afraid I have a full

124

schedule next week and for a few weeks after that.'

'Let me see . . . Yes, I think we can manage it. How does eleven o'clock on Thursday work for you?'

It's Tuesday now.

'That works perfectly for me,' I tell her. 'Thank you so much, Jill.'

★　★　★

I have a session with Julia, this time at the flat because the studios are booked up. She's embracing the lessons with a fervour bordering on the religious. Her singing is improving, her voice opening up, becoming freer. I'm delighted with her progress and she's happy, too.

'I can't believe my luck in having you as my teacher! I never imagined I could sing like this,' she says as the session ends.

There's no one coming after her, so I ask whether she'd like a cup of tea.

'I'd love one!'

Today she's wearing a close-fitting navy top with a sweetheart neckline, over a pair of white capri pants. Her perfect little feet are encased in expensive-looking pointy-toed flat shoes. I tend to wear loose, comfortable things when I'm teaching at home. An old T-shirt or jumper and slouchy pants. But when Julia is around, I take extra care with my clothes because I don't want to feel like a slob. Today, I'm wearing a white silk shirt over a pair of skinny jeans. It will be just my luck to spill tea over it.

As I fill the kettle and take out a couple of mugs, Julia continues in her enthusiastic way, admiring just about everything in the flat — the big windows overlooking the communal garden at the back, the wooden floorboards that we've painted white, the paintings on the walls.

'I painted them,' I say.

'They're yours? But they're marvellous!' she exclaims.

I know my paintings aren't bad. They're certainly big, and Sandy likes them because they provide striking colour against the white walls and floor. But they're not *marvellous*. They're abstract canvases on which I have let loose paintbrushes dipped in various shades of blue and green. Sometimes I throw in some streaks of red, purple, orange, yellow, but the dominant colours are always blue and green. I've never thought of my colour preferences as being psychologically significant, but seeing Sheila regularly has made me think about ordinary things a bit more. Maybe I should mention the paintings to her. What would she make of them?

Julia's voice interrupts my thoughts. She's looking at a photo collage in the kitchen.

'Is this you?'

She's pointing at an old Polaroid snap of me aged about twenty. I'm standing in a queue outside the Royal Albert Hall and I'm wearing jeans and a T-shirt. I've never thought of myself as particularly photogenic, but I like this photograph, taken when I was still a student. I look good in it. My hair is piled up on top of my head. I'm smiling and I look happy and attractive.

'That's me. My friends and I queued for hours for a prom. I got bad sunburn on the back of my neck.'

'You wouldn't catch me standing in a queue for hours,' she says, continuing to examine the collage.

'Is this your husband?' She's pointing to an old photograph of Sandy.

'Yes, but that was taken a long time ago.'

'He's rather attractive, isn't he?' she says. 'I bet he looks even more handsome now. Men often improve as they age, don't they?'

'Well, I don't know if that applies to too many of them, but I have to agree that Sandy still has whatever he had then. I'm not sure I can say the same about myself, though.'

I laugh as I say this, waiting for her to come out with something complimentary, to say that I still look good, but she says nothing, just smiles, bends her head and takes a long sip of her tea.

I feel as if I've been slighted. Admitting to myself that I'd hoped for a meaningless compliment from Julia makes me want to lash out at her, say something about her singing to take her down a peg or two. But, of course, I don't. Instead, I mention that Ben hasn't been to see me for a couple of weeks because of one family commitment or another. She and Ben are now overlapping regularly and, because they're so easy with each other, I'm convinced that they're meeting away from the studio as well.

'Yes, I know,' she says. 'He has rather a lot on

his plate. Difficult wife and all that.'

'Difficult?'

'She resents him having a singing lesson every week because it's time away from her and the children, and because it costs money. I can understand that, but I do feel sorry for him. He loves the sessions with you so much.'

I've met Ben's wife a few times — often enough to know that she doesn't resent him having singing lessons. That Ben is clearly discussing his marriage with Julia makes me worried that their friendship is progressing towards a boundary that it shouldn't cross.

'Julia, it's none of my business, but I do feel in some way responsible for . . . for anything that may be going on between you and Ben.'

I pause. Her expression tells me nothing. She stares at me, waiting for me to continue.

'I don't want to see him hurt or his marriage jeopardised. I just think you should be . . . well, careful.'

She sighs and smiles.

'Oh, Louise, I wouldn't dream of doing anything to threaten Ben's marriage. He and I are friends. Yes, I do know he's got an enormous crush on me and we meet up sometimes for a drink. But that's all it is. You can be sure there's nothing going on between him and me.'

I'm not convinced, but maybe that has less to do with her and more to do with me and the lack of security I feel in my own marriage. When she finally leaves, I wave her off with relief.

★   ★   ★

By the time Sandy comes home, I've put Julia and Ben out of my mind and I'm thinking, with a mixture of nervousness and excitement, about my trip to see David Prescott. Sandy picks up on my mood.

'You're looking pleased with yourself,' he says, holding out his hand for the glass of red wine I've just poured for him.

I've noticed that, since our reconciliation, he doesn't directly ask me to explain anything. Instead, he makes a comment that provides an opportunity for me to elaborate. He's still being careful with me.

'Am I? Well, I've had a few good sessions today.'

'Found a new Callas or Pavarotti?'

'I wouldn't go that far, but I'm seeing a lot of improvement in a couple of people. It's very gratifying. It's a nice feeling.'

I know I should tell him about my plan to drive to Northamptonshire on Thursday, but if I do that I'll end up telling him all about my elaborate deception, so I keep quiet.

After supper, we decide to watch a film, but, as usual, we can't make up our minds. So we open the box of DVDs and go to our default favourite, *Withnail and I*. We both love that film, although I'm no longer able to watch the last few minutes because I find them unbearably sad. But I notice that, even at the funniest moments, Sandy isn't entirely engaged with it and is even a bit fidgety. He checks his phone several times.

In the old days, I would have joked with him, asked him whether he was expecting a text from his lover. But tonight I say nothing. I pretend I haven't noticed anything, but I can't help being a little bit anxious.

'I could do without this bloody trip,' he says eventually, putting his phone down.

'Trip?'

'The Vienna one. Tomorrow.'

'Oh. That's a bit sudden.'

'No, it's been in the diary for ages.'

'First I've heard of it.'

'Shite, sorry, I must have forgotten to mention it.'

What he means is that it was arranged during our time apart.

'How long will you be there?'

'I'll be back on Tuesday.'

'Tuesday? That's a long conference.'

'It's two conferences, really. The one in Vienna is Thursday and Friday and a bit of Saturday, but I've been asked to stand in for a speaker who's had to drop out of a seminar in Prague on Monday. There's no point in coming back here for a day and then heading off again, is there?'

'No, I suppose not.'

'Don't look so glum, hen. I'll bring you back a Sachertorte.'

'Just what I've always wanted.'

It's hard pretending to be bright and confident. I have to keep reminding myself that Sandy has chosen to be with me. He left for a while and now he's back. I shouldn't concern myself with anything else. I shouldn't be suspicious, or jealous. I could ruin everything.

So I try to be enthusiastic about his trip,

130

suggesting that he might be able to get to the opera on Saturday evening.

'I've already thought of that,' he says, with a big grin. '*Der Rosenkavalier*. Managed to get a ticket.'

Rosenkavalier. Of all operas, the one I love best. Well, apart from *Butterfly* and *Otello* and . . .

'I'm green with envy,' I say.

And even as I say this, I hear in my head the heartbreaking strains of the final trio, in which the Marschallin accepts that she must give her lover, Oktavian, to the younger Sophie. I hope it's just my fatalistic streak breaking through and that my sense of foreboding has no foundation.

I lie awake long into the night. My thoughts are full of Sandy and the fear that he may still be seeing someone else, someone he's going to be with in Vienna. But they're also full of the trip I'm going to make to Northampton on Thursday to meet the man who may be my father.

Sandy leaves early the following morning and I do something despicable when I eventually get up. I go through his clothes, looking for evidence I hope I won't find. A hair that isn't mine on the shoulder of a jacket. A crumpled note from a woman whose name I don't recognise. A restaurant bill. But there's nothing incriminating. I have to give him the benefit of the doubt.

My mother once read my diary and challenged me about what I had written. Appalled and embarrassed, I promised myself then that I would never do what she had done. Yet here I am, examining my husband's clothes, taking things out of his pockets, even separating pairs of socks to check whether there's something hidden in them, some love token. I'm filled with shame.

I am afraid and excited at the same time.

I haven't told anyone yet, not even Mamma. I wonder what she will say, how she will react. We aren't getting along very well at the moment and that's probably my fault. I think she sees me growing up and growing away from her. I just wish she would be a little more patient and leave me to myself. I'm not going anywhere. All I want to do is be in charge of my own life and my own future.

I will probably have to tell her soon that I'm going to have a baby. I think that will mend things between us. She'll understand that we may have our differences but that underneath everything we are the same.

I don't know what I will say to Declan, or even if I will say anything at all. I look at him sometimes and wonder whether I really love him. I think I do. But Mamma keeps telling me I can do better, get a boyfriend who's better looking. If I really did love him, wouldn't I stand up for him and say I didn't want anyone else?

'What's this?' my mother demanded, holding up the green exercise book I used as my journal.

I wasn't sure what she meant. I turned to my journal first thing in the morning and last thing at night, and I often forgot the extent to which I recorded the mishmash of thoughts that flitted through my head.

'*I will probably have to tell her soon that I'm going to have a baby,*' she read, putting heavy emphasis on the final six words.

I said nothing at first, appalled that she had shown so little regard for my need to have some element of privacy.

Eventually, I said, 'You read my diary. You shouldn't have done that.'

'Don't tell me what I can and can't do. I'm your mother. Now, you're going to sit down and you're going to tell me everything.'

In writing my diary, I had been caught up in the romance of creating a child. It was the mid-1980s. Even Ireland was becoming more flexible, a little more liberal. But as I listened to my mother, I realised that having a baby wouldn't be as I had imagined. I had yet to start having singing lessons, but had long since passed my grade eight piano exam with distinction and was already thinking that I might concentrate on becoming a pianist.

But my mother had no idea at this stage that I was dreaming of a career in music. If I had a baby, she told me, I wouldn't be able to go to university and would end up in some unfulfilling job, dependent on her and Dermot for support. What kind of life was that for a young woman? What kind of legacy was that for a baby? She didn't even mention Declan.

'Are you telling me that you regret having me, that I was a mistake?' I asked.

'No, not at all,' she said. 'Look, Louise, times were different when I was young. There wasn't a great deal available to girls, even clever ones, in terms of a career. I could have been a teacher, or a nurse. I could have worked in a bank. Or I could have become a secretary, which is what I did. Times are different now. There's so much open to you. I won't let you tie yourself down with a baby.'

I began to cry. Everything she said made sense, but my heart was breaking. She sat beside me on the edge of my bed and put her arms around me, and for a few minutes it was as if we were back in the little flat in Drumcondra.

My mother arranged everything. She told the school we were going to a family funeral in England and that I would be away for a week. I presume she told Dermot the whole story, but he said nothing to me that indicated he knew what was going on. He was just his usual kind self.

My mother told me not to tell anyone, certainly not Declan, and not even Ursula. 'The fewer people who know, the better,' she said. 'Then we can forget all about it.' But I couldn't keep something like that from Ursula, the nearest thing to that sister I had always wished for.

'Your mother's right. You can't have a baby, Lou. It would be a disaster,' she said. 'But you're looking a bit . . . as if you're unsure?'

'No. No, I'm sure.'

And at that moment I was. Or at least I thought I was.

My mother and I flew to London. I don't remember much about the clinic, but I do remember feeling sad and empty when the procedure was over and I was allowed to leave.

We were staying in a good hotel and she did everything she could to make me feel cosseted and cared for. She even took me shopping to buy the kind of clothes that I loved and she hated. I knew she was right about everything. But I knew, too, that things had changed between us and I grieved for our relationship just as much as for the baby she had forced me to abort.

I saw Declan once after that. I was distant, offhand. He was hurt and puzzled. I maintained the lie of the family funeral. Then I came up with one excuse after another to avoid seeing him. And eventually he stopped calling me. He never knew about the baby. How could I have told him what I had done?

13

Northamptonshire is prettier than I expected it to be, and Friars Ashby is like a picture-postcard village, with houses made of golden-yellowish stone and a single pub looking out over the village green. 'Our villages are what you might call hidden gems,' Jill Tomlinson told me as we sat in her office earlier that morning in Northampton. I park the car outside the pub and go inside. I'm torn between the urge to go straight to David Prescott's house and the need to calm myself down before I knock on his door.

I look at the beer taps and see several marked Tennyson's.

'I'll have a half of that, please,' I tell the barman. 'It's local, isn't it?'

'Couldn't be more local if it tried,' he says, taking a glass and filling it. 'Are you passing through or stopping in the village?'

'I'm here to see someone, actually,' I say, pulling out the piece of paper on which I've written the address. 'Maybe you can tell me where Nene Cottage is.'

'Just over there; the other side of the green. Looking for David Prescott, then?'

'That's right. Do you know him well?'

'One of the regulars. Used to work for Tennyson's. You a relative?'

I'm tempted to say I am, but I shake my head.

'He was a friend of my family when he worked

in Ireland, years ago. They asked me to look him up,' I lie.

'That'll be a treat for him. He's been a bit lonely since the wife died a few years ago. Lovely lady, she was. They never had any kids. Pity. He'd have someone to take care of him now.'

I finish my beer quickly. I want to hear more about David Prescott, drink in every detail of his life that the barman can give me. But he's so close now, just a few hundred yards away, and the need to meet him is becoming overwhelming.

'I'd better get going,' I tell the barman. 'Maybe see you later.'

David Prescott's house is hung with wisteria, his front garden filled with old-fashioned flowers like lupins and peonies. My heart is beating so fast that I fear I am going to faint.

The elderly man who opens the door is much more sprightly than the barman had led me to expect. His face is attractive, despite the deep wrinkles engraved into it. He must have been handsome once.

'Mr Prescott? I'm Sandra Munro. Jill Tomlinson phoned ahead . . . '

'Ah, Miss Munro. Come in. You found your way here easily?'

'I did, yes. It's very good of you to see me at such short notice.'

'It's no trouble at all, Miss Munro. I have plenty of time.'

He leads me into a room with French doors giving on to another garden at the back of the house.

'It's such a pleasure to be asked to talk about Dublin. They were good years,' he says. Maybe it's my imagination, but I see a momentary look of sadness come into his eyes.

'Have you spoken to any other Tennyson's people for your research?' he asks.

I've rehearsed my spiel.

'Not yet. Apart from Mrs Tomlinson at the brewery. I spent the morning there. She suggested I see you first, because you live so close to Northampton. The other people whose names I've been given are rather spread out, in Leicestershire and Cambridgeshire. I'll have to visit them another time. I'm interested in the particular years you were in Dublin.'

'Yes, they were interesting years. They were certainly years of great change in this country. But in Ireland? Were the 1960s vastly different from the 1950s? I'm not so sure.'

As we talk, I search for something, some expression in his face that will make me recognise something of myself. But I look nothing like him.

He leaves me alone for a couple of minutes and I have a chance to look around the room, at the framed photographs of himself and a woman I presume to be his wife. They span several decades. His hair is white now, but I can see that it was dark when he was younger. And while he's thin now, he was slightly stockier then.

Returning with a tray laden with teapot, cups and saucers, and a plate of biscuits, he notices my interest in the photographs, but says nothing about them.

'Now, tell me more about this project of yours. Jill said you were writing a book.'

I talk about my fictitious project, telling him I'm particularly interested in talking to him because of the number of years he spent in Dublin, where the brewery had made such a positive impact on the lives of the people who worked for it. He nods enthusiastically.

'Yes, yes, I was proud to work for a company that looked after its workers so well,' he says. 'And the houses we built in Dublin were shining examples of the kind of things we did for our workers. Have you seen any of them?'

I tell him I've been to the old brewery in Crumlin and to Walter Square, but that I haven't been inside any of the houses.

'They were excellent houses. They were a good size and very pleasant and very functional. Designed by quite an eminent architect, whose name doesn't immediately spring to mind. I suspect they must be worth rather a lot, these days.'

As he continues to talk about his time in Dublin, I think about him and my mother together. They would have been an attractive couple. He's cultured; I can see that from his bookshelves. And several books of poetry are piled on a table. My mother would have liked that. She was happy with Dermot, but perhaps this man really was the love of her life.

He's talking away happily when I stop him in mid-flow. I like him. I don't want to deceive him for a moment longer.

'I haven't been entirely truthful about why I'm

139

here,' I say, and I have to pause for a few seconds because my voice is shaking as much as my body. He looks at me, puzzled.

'My name isn't Sandra Munro. It's Louise Redmond. Marjorie Redmond was my mother.'

There's no reaction at first and I start to wonder whether I've managed to get everything wrong. It's as if his face has frozen. And then it comes — an explosion of anger that I'm not prepared for.

'How dare you! Why have you come here? What do you want? This is monstrous! Monstrous!'

I beg him to let me explain why I've sought him out. But he won't listen. Every time I try to speak, he holds up his hands and stops me.

'Stay where you are. I'm going to show you something,' he says, turning his back on me and walking out of the room.

So I wait, bewildered and frightened by his initial rage, yet still daring to hope that what he's going to show me will somehow prove the link between us.

When he comes back, he's carrying a document of some sort.

'I don't know who you are, but I know that you're not my daughter. Yes, I did have a daughter, and her mother was Marjorie Redmond. But my daughter is dead.'

He hands me the document. It's a death certificate, and it's for Louise Redmond, born on 11 December 1969, died on 30 April 1973. I feel my vision blurring and my head spinning, and then I feel myself falling, falling.

* ★ *

I open my eyes and for a moment I'm confused by the elderly face I see peering anxiously at me. And then I remember what has happened and I hear myself emit a sound somewhere between a sob and groan, a sound that I've never made before, even during those first days without Sandy, even when I lay curled up and howling on a Dublin street. It's the kind of sound a wounded animal might make.

'You fainted,' David Prescott says. 'Just for a few seconds. Are you all right now?'

I ask to see the death certificate again and pore over its details. Louise Redmond died of meningitis at Northampton General Hospital. Marjorie Redmond registered the death.

'That's my date of birth, the eleventh of December, 1969,' I tell him. 'And I have a birth certificate. I don't have it with me, but I do have one and your name is on it. I *am* Louise Redmond. I'm your daughter!'

David Prescott lowers his head, shakes it, and when he looks at me again, his old eyes are glistening.

'You're not. You can't be,' he says, shaking his head. 'I was with her. I was at the hospital when she died. It broke my heart. She was the most beautiful child, with the sweetest nature. No, my dear, I don't know who you are, but you're not Louise.'

Through my tears, I listen to him tell his story — how he had fallen in love with the young woman who had worked as his secretary, how

141

they had maintained a secret affair for several years, how she had fallen pregnant.

'Marjorie was very beautiful, very vibrant. And so intelligent. We never meant it to happen,' he says. 'My wife and I had no children. Celia couldn't have them. It was a great sadness for both of us. You can imagine how overjoyed I was when I saw our daughter for the first time.'

'Why didn't you leave your wife?'

'Oh, I would have. There was nothing I wanted more than to be with Marjorie, to be open about our relationship and to marry her. But it was Marjorie who wanted to keep things as they were and it was Marjorie who ended our long affair.'

'But Northampton? Did my mother live here?'

'For a while. I was transferred back here and, after a few months, Marjorie came with Louise. I couldn't imagine not having them near. I found a house for them in Northampton. I saw them every day. And then Louise contracted meningitis and died. I was there, at the hospital, with her and Marjorie. All night. We waited all those hours, watching her slip away, praying there would be a miracle. Parents are supposed to be able to protect their children. But there was nothing we could do. It was the worst time of our lives. And Marjorie was broken. I was afraid of what might happen, that she might kill herself. We comforted each other, but everything had changed and, a few months later, she went back to Dublin. She asked me not to contact her and I never heard from her again.'

Every mention of Louise has made me wince,

as if she is someone else and not me. But, of course, this dead Louise is not me. I am alive. But if I'm not Louise, who am I? I am my mother's daughter, and I tell this to David Prescott again and again. I show him photographs of the two of us together over the years.

'Yes, this is Marjorie,' he says. 'But you're not Louise. You can't be. It's impossible.'

'I just don't understand this,' I say, and I hear how weak and uncertain my voice sounds.

'I'm feeling rather shaken by all this, too, and I can't think very clearly, but I have a question for you. Did Marjorie tell you that I was your father?'

'Yes,' I tell him. 'She told me my father's name was David Prescott and that he was English. She said she'd lost contact with you and that she didn't know where you lived. But I never really believed that, not when I was older, anyway.'

He closes his eyes for several seconds.

He loved my mother — still does, I think to myself — and I find myself empathising with him, imagining how he must have suffered when she left him. But it's harder to think about my mother's grief over this child called Louise, who is not me. Until Dermot's death, I had never been aware of any great loss in her life. Surely the death of a child would have left its mark on her? Wouldn't she have held on to photographs of such a child? Wouldn't she have told me about her?

His voice breaks into my thoughts.

'I'm sorry, my dear, but I've told you the truth. I wish with all my heart that your mother

143

were alive and here now. I wish it for many reasons, but most of all so that she could tell you in my presence that our daughter died. But I have something else to show you and I hope it will convince you.'

He hands me a box in which there are several photographs. I recognise my mother and I recognise him. I think I can also see something of my mother and of him in the child she holds on her knee — a little girl with dark blonde curls. I'm on the edge of nausea. I push the photographs away.

'I don't understand it, any of it,' I say, rising to my feet, desperate to get away from this waking nightmare.

'There's one more thing,' he says, and I sink back into the sofa.

This time, he takes something from a sideboard and holds it out in front of him. He doesn't need to tell me what's inside the small white casket.

'Marjorie left Louise's ashes with me. Said she didn't need them to remember her. I must be made of weaker stuff.'

I can't stand any more of this. I have to get out of this house, get back to London and put distance between myself and the grotesque nightmare that my dream has become.

As I leave, David Prescott takes both of my hands in his and squeezes them.

'This has been as upsetting for me as it has been for you,' he says. 'But come and see me again when you've had some time to think about it. We will have to help each other.'

14

It's now several days since my visit to David Prescott and my mind is still in turmoil. I've woken up in a state of confusion every morning, briefly forgetful as I lie for those few minutes in that comfortable space between sleeping and being fully awake. After that, it's downhill, as the marauding ghosts of my mother's past trample through my head and my body. My stomach writhes and knots every time I try to make sense of what David Prescott has told me, which is pretty much all the time. It's as if there are pythons in there, wrestling with each other. I feel sick. The flat is a mess.

I've cancelled my lessons for a week, texting my students to tell them that I have some kind of summer flu and promising to be in touch when I have recovered.

I don't remember much about the journey back to London, beyond getting into the car in Friars Ashby and getting out of it again on Ladbroke Grove. One thing I do recall is hoping that Sandy would be in the flat and then remembering that he was away at his conferences in Vienna and Prague. Maybe it was just as well, because he would have thought I was mad. I'm beginning to wonder about that myself, whether David Prescott really did show me my own death certificate. But I can see the piece of paper clearly in my head, every word etched into my brain. I can see the white casket. I can remember everything he said to me, his voice raised in anger initially and then softening as he talked about what had happened to the child he said was his daughter. *Louise.*

I haven't been back in touch with him since my visit. I want to believe that what he told me was a bag of lies, prepared years ago in case I tracked him down. But even as this scenario takes shape in my mind, I know I have to discount it. It's too fanciful, too far beyond the realms of possibility. And there are the photographs of my mother with him and that child, who, even with the dark blonde hair, looked so much more like her than I ever did.

I know what I have to do, even if the thought of it sends a chill through me. I must check whether the death certificate is genuine. Not now, though. Tomorrow or the next day. What difference will a day or two make? I know I was born on 11 December 1969, in Dublin. I've been able to obtain copies of my birth certificate, with David Prescott named as my father, in the past. I know I exist as Louise Redmond, my mother's daughter. For a moment, I reassure myself that everything can be explained. But then I see the death certificate again in my mind, with all its troubling details — the name, the date of birth and my mother's name. I see the photographs of my mother with the child who isn't me. I hear every one of David Prescott's words ring like gunshots and ricochet around my head until I have to press my hands to my forehead and close my eyes. Sleep is the only refuge and I retreat to the bedroom and, still fully dressed, bury myself in the duvet.

I wake to find Sandy gently shaking me.

'What's the story, hen? You're in a right state, by the looks of things. Come on, you can tell your uncle Sandy,' he says, lying down beside me and drawing me in to him.

So I do, even though I'm afraid he'll be angry with me for not having told him about my scheme to track down my father, for having given a false name and email address to the brewery and for having tricked an old man. Because, as I tell him about everything that's happened, I see how underhand it must all look.

He doesn't give any indication that my behaviour has disappointed him, though. He keeps me folded in his arms as he listens, asks questions, tells me to run over this bit or that bit again.

'How genuine did the death certificate look?'

'It looked genuine. I mean, it didn't look quite like the one I got for my mother, but hers is an Irish one and this is an old English one from the 1970s,' I say, and I hear that my voice sounds calm, normal, that I am making sense, and I feel relieved to be talking about it. 'And, Sandy, the photos . . . '

'Is it possible that your mother had twins, you and another girl, and that this other child died but your name was put on the death certificate by mistake?'

I'm about to say, *Not a chance*, and then I stop myself, because, even if it sounds extraordinary, it does offer a glimmer of hope

147

that there is an explanation.

'I suppose it has to be possible,' I say, but then I shake my head. 'No, it can't be. David Prescott didn't say there was another child.'

'Okay, what about two children, not twins, one he didn't know about because the baby was conceived before your mother went back to Dublin?'

'But what about the date of birth? The eleventh of December, 1969. It's on my birth certificate and it's on the death certificate that David Prescott has,' I say.

And then I find that I can't think any more, can't cope with having to deal with all these outrageous possible explanations. I drop my head into my hands.

Sandy gets up and lifts me off the bed.

'I think you've had enough for now, hen. We can revisit this tomorrow. You need food and I need a drink. But, first, you're in dire need of a shower. Off you go,' he says, steering me into the bathroom.

Oh, the relief of having Sandy look after me! We walk down to one of the Italian restaurants on Kensington Park Road and lose ourselves in the boisterous, noisy atmosphere. I eat the first proper meal I've had in days — and with my husband, whose presence in the flat has been erratic. He has many claims on his attention. Now he's focusing only on me.

I ask him about Vienna and Prague, about *Rosenkavalier*. His face lights up.

'It was terrific. Great production. I called you afterwards, several times. You didn't answer. It went straight to voicemail. I thought you must be out on the razzle with Ursula.'

My earlier suspicions fall away.

Later, at home, I lie awake for a long time, a new torment having taken root in my mind. Perhaps the death certificate and the truth about my father can be explained. Perhaps there really was a sister, or a half-sister, of whom I have no recollection. But what I'll never be able to understand is why my mother kept so much from me, why she lied. Did she really think I was so lacking in curiosity that I might not some day try to find out more about my father and, in doing so, discover her lies?

And if she had kept secret something so fundamental and important as another child, what else had she kept from me?

It strikes me now that I never once saw my mother shed tears, not even when Dermot died. I was the one who wept as his coffin was lowered into the grave, while she stood tall and straight, her black clothes emphasising the pallor of her skin. But there were no tears. It was around then that the need to contact my real father became stronger. I used to talk about it to Sandy. At first, he listened and was sympathetic. After a while, he started becoming irritated whenever I brought up the topic.

'Look, Lou, it's not me you should be talking to. It's your mother.'

'You know she won't talk about it.'

'And you know that I can't help you. Why is it so important to you now?'

'It always was.'

'Was it? We've been married seven years and it's only now that you've started going on about it. Look, hen, it's not great, not having contact with your father, but you're not a child. You're forty — '

'Thirty-nine.'

'Okay, thirty-nine. As I was saying, it's not ideal that you have no contact with him or even a clue where he is, but it's not as if you had a terrible childhood, is it?'

'No, but — '

'Lou, your mother did a pretty good job of bringing you up. And Dermot was as good a father as you could have had. I understand that you want to know your real father, but what are you actually doing about it? Nothing. I can only listen to you. Your mother is the one who can tell you everything, but she won't. So you have to get a grip on this or it'll do your head in,' he said. And then he added, under his breath, 'Not to mention mine.'

* * *

Sheila is silent for what seems like a long time after I give her an account of my trip to Northamptonshire. I've missed two sessions without telling her. I just haven't turned up. I feel I've disappointed her. After all, not only did I lie to Tennyson's in order to find my way to David Prescott, but I also lied to her by letting her think I'd written an honest letter to the brewery. I feel relieved that I can't see her face and register her disapproval.

150

When she finally speaks, however, there's no reprobation. She asks how I feel now about what happened.

'I don't know . . . a little bit panicky. Sandy has put in an online application for a copy of the death certificate because I couldn't face doing it myself. He says it shouldn't be a problem because it's a document of public record. He doesn't even have to explain why he wants it.'

'Have you thought about what will happen when the certificate, assuming there is one, arrives?' she asks.

'All the time. And that's part of the panicky feeling. If the certificate is real, then who am I? I'm afraid I'm never going to find out the truth about anything.'

'Shall we talk a bit about your mother, what she was like when you were very small, what you were like then? What's the first thing you remember?'

I struggle with this question. No single thing leaps out at me. When I think about my child-hood, I see a series of still photographs, so many different images. No one image is dominant. I see myself in a little smocked dress, my hand in my mother's as she takes me about with her. I see her holding her face up to the sun with her eyes closed as we sit on a bench on St Stephen's Green. We're always together, my mother and I. There's rarely anyone else in those early scenes.

My memories become heavily populated by other people only when we move to Drogheda and my mother, though still there, moves back from centre stage.

The only memory that persists over the years is the postbox memory, and yet I can't identify myself as the little girl stretching upwards. But if I'm not that child, who is she? Is she Ailish, the little girl who wrote to Santa Claus in Lapland? Or is she the little girl who died, the other little girl called Louise Redmond?

'It's as if it's all part of a jigsaw that I can't put together because most of the pieces are missing. But I feel I should be able to, if I can just find one piece.'

Sheila asks me whether I think the postbox memory has something to do with wanting to find my real father.

'What do you mean?'

'Is it possible that it isn't a memory at all? That it's part of a story you put together in your mind a long time ago?'

'A story about my father? Something I made up? Something to make him real?'

'Or a way to reach him.'

'And that's me posting a letter to him? I've invented a whole story, but that's the only bit I remember?'

'Maybe it's something we should explore.'

I say nothing. I just stay quiet for a long time and think about what she has said. It sort of makes sense, and I tell her so, eventually, but I have nothing to add, nothing more to offer.

Sheila starts speaking again.

'We've done a lot of work together over the past couple of months,' she says, and, as I hear this, I feel an initial spike of panic, because I'm seized by the conviction that she doesn't want to

152

continue to see me, that she's going to hive me off to someone else.

'But the kind of work we do takes time and I wonder whether we might consider something that could speed things up for you.'

I sit up again, panicking now for sure, waiting for her to elaborate.

'I'm talking about hypnotherapy.'

I don't like the sound of this and I say so.

'It's not something I would recommend as a matter of course, and it certainly has come in for criticism,' she says. 'But I think, in your situation, there may be a strong case for using it. We don't have to do anything straight away, and you have every right to say no. Who knows, you may find a lot of answers as you follow the paper trail. But I want to leave the idea with you. Go home and think about it. Discuss it with Sandy. Take your time. And, in the meantime, we'll carry on here as normal. Is that all right with you?'

I nod. 'If I agree to hypnotherapy, will you do it or will I have to go to someone else?'

'Yes, I'll do it.'

'Okay. I'll think about it,' I say. But, by the time I leave, I've already made a decision. I'm just not sure it's the right one.

15

I have a session with Julia at the studios and, as usual, I'm waiting for her to arrive. I don't mind her being late. It's hot — the kind of London heat that builds up through June and, by July, has driven the air away. I'm wilting. I've had a busy morning and I'm still thinking about the hour I've just spent with an ageing amateur whose rendition of an English folk song, sung in a high, clear, girlish voice, has deeply touched me.

Julia turns up with the usual fanfare — a clatter of kitten heels on the stairs, an apology ringing out even as she turns the door handle.

She looks very pleased with herself. I'm sure I'll hear all about whatever it is later.

We work on technique for a while and, eventually, I move my hand to the pile of songs by Schubert, Fauré and Reynaldo Hahn that sits on the top of the piano.

'Oh, Louise, would it be all right if we tried this? It's really beautiful,' she says, reaching into her music bag and handing me a volume of songs by Puccini.

The song she has chosen is 'Sogno d'Or' — early Puccini, but it already contains some exquisite phrases that will show up again in later works.

We run through it a couple of times, stopping frequently to discuss phrasing. But it's not working. She's not really engaging with it and I wonder why she has picked it.

'Why don't we do it again, all the way through? But this time, take some time to think about what you're trying to get across. Try to imagine you're this young mother, soothing her baby to sleep.'

'Actually, I don't have to use my imagination,' she says. 'I don't have to use my imagination because . . . well, I'm pregnant.'

With her widely spaced eyes and air of complete self-satisfaction, she looks like a cat. I almost expect her to purr.

'Oh,' I say. I hadn't expected this. 'Congratulations.'

I look at her trim little figure, her flat stomach. She doesn't look particularly pregnant, but she's probably the type of woman who won't put on much weight at all.

I don't feel I can ask who the father of her child is. But, as if she can read my thoughts, she tells me who it isn't.

'It's not Ben,' she says, with emphasis. 'It's someone else. Someone I've been with for a while, on and off.'

I'm convinced she's lying about Ben. I feel anger towards both of them. Most of all, I feel a surge of sympathy for Ben's wife, who's about to be cast into that terrible state of marriage breakdown, with all the feelings of despair and worthlessness that I felt. Only it will be worse for her. At least Sandy didn't leave me for someone else. At least, that's what he told me at the time. He and I are fine now. We're close. We share a bed and we have sex. But there's still that big question mark in my mind over what happened to drive him away from me. I can change my behaviour, if I know where I'm at fault. But I still don't know what made Sandy leave or what made him come back, and that's why I can't stop worrying about the future, about the possibility that he may leave again.

'When is the baby due?' I ask Julia, who seems to have abandoned the session in favour of leaning forward onto the piano and having a chat.

'I'm not quite sure yet. I've been far too busy to go to the doctor.'

How extraordinary, I think, that she's telling me all this when she hasn't even confirmed the pregnancy with a doctor. But, then, this is Julia, isn't it? Always upbeat, seemingly frivolous on the outside, but confident about where she's going and what she's doing, and happy to talk about it with anyone in a mood to listen. She has, though, rather taken the wind out of my sails.

'And your, er, partner . . . Is he happy about the baby?' I ask. 'Actually, I had no idea you had one. A partner, I mean.'

'Oh, it's been one of those on-and-off things. We don't seem to be able to live with each other, but we don't seem to be able to stay away from each other, either. He doesn't know yet, but I don't think he'll be surprised. I'm going to tell him today at lunch. Le Caprice — I managed to get a table at the very last minute. We've talked about babies in the past and I know he'll make a

156

wonderful father. Oh, goodness me, is that the time? Would you mind if I shot off now?'

'Of course not. Off you go.'

'See you next week.'

After she leaves, I can hardly think straight. Her announcement has confounded me. It still seems bizarre that she should tell me — someone she hardly knows — about this pregnancy, which is at such an early stage. There's something else bothering me, too, a twinge of something I don't quite understand. And then it all becomes clear. Julia is everything I want to be. She stands for everything I'm not. She's the full package. I'm jealous of her beauty and her vivacity, and I'm jealous of her pregnancy and of the baby that will give meaning to her relationship with her partner, whoever he is.

And then, before I can stop it, another memory bursts through the iron bars I've built against it in my brain, and I see the shocking red of the blood that brought the realisation of Sandy's dream to an end, without him ever knowing it had existed. And I remember the grief I felt for all of us. But, most of all, I remember the relief.

★   ★   ★

All the early signs were there, but I ignored them. I think I must have been hoping that they didn't really amount to anything, that the reason all my bras seemed to be uncomfortable was because the washing machine had shrunk them, and that I was feeling queasy because I was just plain tired. It was only when I realised that I hadn't had a period for a while that it occurred to me I might be pregnant.

'You're looking a bit peaky, hen,' Sandy said one evening. 'You okay?'

I wasn't okay. I was quietly frantic. I hadn't had a period in at least three months and I was still praying it was just one of those blips in my cycle that happened every so often. But I knew.

'I'm fine. A bit tired, that's all. I probably need to catch up on some sleep.'

'You sleep like a log!'

'How would you know, Mr Rip Van Winkle?' I said, laughing. 'You fall asleep as soon as your head touches the pillow.'

I should have told him then, but I argued with myself that there was no point in getting his hopes up until I was sure. I would buy a test kit the following day.

That night, I lay awake into the early hours, veering back and forth between all the scenarios that played out in my head. The pregnancy would be confirmed. Sandy would be the happiest man on the planet and I would bloom into the mother he wanted me to be. I would love our little baby and we would live happily ever after. But, no matter how much I tried, I couldn't imagine this baby as a real person, a girl or a boy, and then the other thoughts would take over, the ones that came out of some part of me that was full of fear for reasons I couldn't explain. Maybe I was terrified that the abortion I had when I was young threatened the pregnancy.

I did the test the following day and it was

positive. I would tell Sandy that night, I told myself. But I didn't. I had planned to, I really had. I was going to cook something out of the ordinary. I was going to open a bottle of some really good wine and I would pour a glass for him but not for me. That would be the first hint. He would lift his brows and say, 'You've forgotten to pour some for yourself,' and I would smile and say nothing. And then his face would flood with delight. But I couldn't get my act together to cook anything fancier than pasta with prawns and chilli and garlic, and when Sandy opened a bottle of wine and began to pour it into my glass, I didn't stop him.

'I think I might go to Ireland for a few days,' I said. 'I haven't got much work lined up for the next couple of weeks.'

'It'll do you good,' Sandy said. 'When are you thinking of going?'

'I might as well go tomorrow, if the prices aren't astronomical.'

'Do you want me to go over at the weekend? I can, if you like?'

'Ah, no . . . I think I just want to hang out with my mother. I haven't seen her at all so far this year. She'll be delighted to have me all to herself. And it'll be lovely to see Dermot.'

My mother was surprised when I called her the following morning and told her I would be on a flight to Dublin that afternoon.

'Is everything all right?' she asked.

'Of course. I just thought it would be nice to see you.'

She told me later she had known I was

pregnant the moment I walked into the arrivals area at the airport, but had waited for me to tell her in my own time. Back in the house with her and Dermot, I reverted to being a child. Over the next few days, I went to bed early and got up late. When I wasn't sleeping, I curled up in a big armchair, reading or watching television. Sometimes I went out by myself, walking all the way into town along the riverbank, or in the other direction, towards the sea. I didn't think about the baby at all. It was as if it didn't exist now that I had come home to my mother; as if, by getting on to an aeroplane, I had left that baby behind in London.

The bleeding began a few days after I arrived. I bought sanitary towels and said nothing to my mother. It was probably my period, after all. But then, a couple of days later, the pains got worse and the bleeding became a torrent. My mother called an ambulance and was about to call Sandy when I stopped her.

'Please . . . please . . . don't,' I begged her.

She gave me a dark look, but she didn't call him. Not then, anyway. When she did phone him, once I was back in the house, she said I was in bed with a stomach bug that was doing the rounds.

'We've all had it, but poor Louise seems to have got the worst of it,' I heard her say. 'I think she's going to have to stay here for a few extra days. No, no, really, don't worry, Sandy, she'll be fine. We'll look after her. There's no need for you to come over.'

When she put the phone down, she sat on the

side of the bed and gave me that look again.

'Are you sure about this? Are you absolutely sure you don't want Sandy to know anything about what has happened?'

I nodded miserably, filled to the brim with guilt and sorrow, but aware, too, of another feeling, a swell of relief that I couldn't suppress.

'I'm sure.'

I told her about the relief I felt at losing the baby and asked her whether it was wrong to think that way.

'No, it's not wrong,' she said. 'If that's what you feel, it's not wrong.'

★ ★ ★

I hand the envelope to Sandy when he returns from the hospital. I've been staring at it since I found it downstairs with the other post.

'Took them long enough,' he says, tearing it open. 'You could have opened it, you know.'

'I know. But I couldn't do it by myself. I needed you to be here.'

He scans it quickly, frowns and holds it out to me.

'I'm sorry, hen. It looks genuine. It's what's registered. But there has to be some explanation somewhere.'

The details are exactly the same as those on the death certificate David Prescott showed me. Louise Redmond, who was born on 11 December 1969, died on 30 April 1973 at Northampton General Hospital. The cause of death was meningitis. The death was registered by Marjorie Redmond.

The sight of the certificate is too much for me and I sit down and weep because I have no other response. It's a dead end — in every sense of the word.

Sandy waits for me to stop crying, stroking my head but saying nothing. When he does speak, it's to tell me that he has come up with a plan.

'Here's what we'll do. We'll go to Ireland for a couple of weeks. We'll go through your mother's stuff and maybe we'll find something. We'll go and see your uncle. We'll go to the old brewery. We're going to sort this out,' he says.

'You can take time off?' I ask, wiping my eyes and blowing my nose. 'When will we go?'

'The sooner, the better. I'll have to give a few days' advance warning and I'll probably end up having to fly back and forth, but how about next week or the week after? I think this counts as urgent, don't you?'

'Yes,' I say. I'm not looking forward to this trip, but it has to be done. And if Sandy is with me, I feel I can handle it, no matter what it throws up. 'And thanks.'

I still haven't agreed formally to the hypnotherapy. It's something left dangling, to be used as a last resort, and I don't feel I'm at that stage. Not yet, anyway. When I mentioned Sheila's suggestion to Sandy, he was less than keen, said he was slightly surprised that she was advocating something like this. But he didn't dismiss it out of hand. I'm still hoping it won't be necessary.

Sheila looks worried when I tell her, as we

enter her therapy room, that I'm going back to Ireland, but her concern visibly lifts when I add that Sandy will be with me. It turns out that she has something to tell me, too. August is holiday month for psychotherapists and it's just a couple of weeks away, which means that, if I go to Ireland next week, this is our last session until September.

'How do you feel about that?' she asks.

'It's fine,' I say.

And it is. I've come to rely on our twice-weekly sessions a great deal more than I ever dreamed I would. I feel safe in that room where I can say what I want, stay silent if I don't want to talk. And when our fifty minutes come to an end, I still feel safe because I know I'll be back in just a couple of days' time. Now, it's going to be a lot longer than a couple of days before I see her again, but it's all right. I know she and I will be back in this room in September.

'Sandy will look after me.'

She smiles and I go to the couch and lie down.

'There's something else,' I say. 'You know Julia? Well, she's pregnant.'

'And how do you feel about that?'

'Peculiar . . . envious.'

'Why do you feel envious?'

'Because it's as if . . . as if she has everything my life needs.'

'Do you mean a child?'

'Yes. No . . . I don't even know! I can't help feeling that, if I'd had kids, things would be different.'

'Do you mean that, if you and Sandy had

children, he wouldn't have left last year?'

'I don't know. I suppose we'd have had a different kind of life.'

'A better life?'

'No . . . just different.'

'We haven't talked much about children, have we?'

'No.'

'Would you like to?'

'Not really, but I probably should, shouldn't I?'

'You don't have to talk about anything you don't feel comfortable with.'

So I lie on the couch saying nothing. Thoughts come into my head and nearly make it on to my tongue. I want to say that I never felt good enough or strong enough to have children, but I can't, even to Sheila, because I'm not even sure that I felt that way.

When I get home, I send texts and emails to all the people I'm scheduled to work with over the next few weeks and cancel the sessions, explaining that I have to go to Ireland on family business. Within minutes, return texts start to come in. Ben sends one of those smiley things — except it's not a smiley because the mouth on the face is turned down — and says he'll miss me. Julia hopes my trip goes well and is looking forward to seeing me again when I return. I feel slightly better disposed towards her, but my envy is still there. It lies low and deep and sharp.

16

Another touchdown in Ireland, but this time Sandy is by my side, holding my hand tightly in his as we leave the aeroplane. We've booked into the modern hotel on the south quay while we work out whether the house is habitable — knowing Joe, it probably is — and we drive straight there to check into our room. Then we head to Angela and Joe for lunch.

They've always been fond of Sandy, and when he accompanied me on some of my visits to see my mother, he sometimes stayed with them, sitting up late into the night with Joe, drinking whiskey and bonding in that strange way men have — not through shared confidences, but through talking about football or rugby.

Joe is eager to take us to the house. The first thing I notice is that the trees and bushes have been cut, so that the house is more visible from the road. The rhododendron, no longer in bloom, is still there, but there's less of it.

We go inside. The little hallway has been demolished and the two pokey rooms on the ground floor have been transformed into one big room. Joe has done a beautiful job with the extension, which lets light flood into the kitchen through enormous sliding floor-to-ceiling glass doors and a huge skylight. The other half of the extension, separated by a small storage area, is a bedroom and en-suite shower and lavatory. It, too, is light and airy, with white wooden Venetian blinds in the window recess. The floorboards, laid over concrete, are beech.

'It's fabulous, Joe, just fabulous! Like something out of *House and Garden*!' I say. 'I love it.'

'You haven't seen everything yet,' Joe says, steering us towards the staircase that had previously been positioned against the wall separating the two rooms, but which has been moved to the far wall. Upstairs, there's now just one big room and bathroom. The ceiling has been taken out to create more height.

'Impressive, Joe,' Sandy says.

'It's turned out well. We've reassembled the beds and put the furniture back, but, if I were you, I'd sling that stuff out as well,' Joe says. He looks at his watch. 'Right. I'd better be off. I have a job out in Termonfeckin. We'll be seeing you down at our place, anyway.'

Joe takes his leave and we take a couple of chairs out to what used to be a dreary old back yard, but is now paved with yellow sandstone slabs.

I'm already thinking about the flowers I'm going to plant in pots and the climbing plants for the wall that surrounds the yard that is now a patio.

'Clematis, maybe,' Sandy suggests.

'What about wisteria?' I say, but then remember that David Prescott's house is hung with wisteria. 'Actually, maybe not.'

Sandy thinks we should do as Joe suggests and chuck out the furniture, replace everything. He looks at his watch. 'It's only four o'clock. We could scoot down to that big furniture place. What do you think?'

An hour and a half later, we've bought a load of sleek, modern furniture that will be delivered tomorrow. When we return to the hotel, we celebrate with a bottle of champagne, delivered to our room, which we drink on the balcony overlooking the river.

We haven't even looked at the boxes. They can wait until tomorrow.

★ ★ ★

We made love last night and again this morning. I could have stayed in that king-sized bed all day with Sandy, just lolling around, ordering food when we needed it, wandering out to the balcony every now and again to watch the endless, fast flow of the river. It felt as if we'd been transported back to those early days when we first got together. But we're here for a reason, so we eventually go to the house.

As we start organising the contents of the boxes we had already sifted through before we went back to London, my phone rings. It's Joe.

'I forgot to tell you — the only thing we found in the attic was a little wooden box with a lock on it. No sign of a key anywhere. You'll find it in the cupboard under the sink, in a plastic bag.'

I go to the kitchen and find the box. It's made of dark wood and is slightly smaller than a shoebox. The lock doesn't look too strong, so I take a knife out of the drawer and twist and lever it until it breaks. I open it nervously and see a photograph of a child — a girl with dark blonde hair. The first thought that comes into my head is that this may be Ailish, who wrote the letter to Santa Claus. But then, in a flash, I recognise her. It's the other Louise, the child that David Prescott told me was his daughter. And lying beneath the photograph is the death certificate. I sag back on to my heels with a strangled sound. Sandy looks up and rushes over.

I can hardly speak. I just hand him the photograph and the certificate, and I see a look of anger pass over his face.

'Duplicitous fucking bitch,' he says. 'She had these all along!'

I used to stand up for my mother whenever Sandy, not unjustifiably, made disparaging remarks about her. But I don't now, although the words deliver a sharp sting. *Duplicitous fucking bitch*. That just about sums her up. I feel a surge of anger towards her. And riding that surge is another feeling — of jealousy. I try to push it away. How can I be jealous of a dead child?

'So Louise Redmond is dead. My mother registered her death and my mother had a copy of her death certificate. And if Louise is dead, who am I? I think I must be losing my mind!'

'Well, if you're losing your mind, I'm losing mine, too. No, neither of us is mad. But whatever your mother got up to is looking dodgier and dodgier. Look, go and sit down. I'm going to plough through this stuff again, just in case we've missed anything.'

But we don't do much ploughing through anything, because the furniture arrives and the old stuff is taken away. We spend the rest of the afternoon moving things around. We dress the beds in the new linen we have bought, hang new white towels in the bathroom. The house is becoming ours now, not just mine.

It's a relief to be able to focus on practical things. I've now seen three copies of a piece of paper recording my death. Any further shock today will be too much.

One of the strangest things about all this is the way my life seems to be splitting in two. As Louise-who-is-not-Louise, I'm a wreck, floundering around on a stormy sea without a compass. I don't know who I am. But when I escape from that no man's land into the new old relationship I'm developing with Sandy, I find I don't quite recognise that identity, either. Maybe it's a version of me I lost a long time ago, but it's a version of me that I'm beginning to like.

I don't say this to Sandy, though. I hold it to myself and think about it often, like a secret that must be kept if the spell is not to be broken.

★   ★   ★

The temptation to tip all the papers on to the floor and scrabble around for just the ones we think may be relevant is huge, but we decide that we could end up missing important things by doing this. The only way to proceed is by systematically going through everything, evaluating every piece of paper, every item. It's boring and backbreaking, and, worst of all, it's slow. But we are moving steadily through it, stopping every

169

now and again for tea or coffee that we take out to the back yard. I still can't call it a patio.

Sandy floats the idea that we take the problem to the police. But I don't want that. At least not unless or until it's absolutely necessary.

★ ★ ★

We've moved out of the hotel and into the house. The days go by and we spend them partly going through the papers, which so far are fairly innocuous, and partly going for long walks. We visit Angela and Joe and Lizzie and Rosie. I see how good Sandy is with the kids. It's *Uncle Sandy* this and *Uncle Sandy* that. They want him to play all sorts of games with them and he's happy to oblige. I love those kids, but I don't have his patience, which seems endless.

One day, it's particularly hot and Sandy is raring to go out to Bettystown. I'm still a little worried about running into Declan, so I suggest we go to Baltray instead, on the other side of the estuary. I haven't been there for years and I'm curious to see whether the old wreck of a trading ship is still there, rising ghoulishly out of the sand.

It's still there, a ghostly hulk, lit by the hazy light of the evening sun, but there seems to be less of it than I remember. The beach is almost deserted. In the distance, the mountains are just visible through the haze.

'I think I fancy a swim,' I say. 'What do you think?'

Sandy isn't so keen. 'The tide is still coming

170

in. Why don't you wait a wee bit longer and then I won't have to run so far to rescue you,' he says.

I slip into my bikini. I may be forty-three, but I'm the fittest I've ever been because I've been going to the gym several times a week with Ursula and, on the other days, swimming at the pool behind Ladbroke Grove.

'Cover yourself up, you brazen hussy,' Sandy says. 'Don't be inciting the menfolk!'

'What menfolk?' I ask, looking around. 'There's only you.'

'Exactly!'

We spread a rug on the sand in front of the dunes and lie down, waiting for the sea to come closer. I use his shoulder as a pillow and we doze peacefully. When I wake up, the waves are just fifty yards away. Sandy is still asleep, his mouth slightly open, and his quiet snores make me think of the sounds a calf might make. I pick my way across the sand and into the waves, shivering as the water curls up around my ankles and, in no time at all, around my waist. I swim out, well beyond my depth.

I look back towards where I know Sandy is, but I can't see him, so I keep the wreck of the ship in my sight and swim parallel to the shoreline, alternating between front crawl and breaststroke. The water is perfect now, warm and glistening, the evening sun casting a golden glow across it. It's so calm that it almost feels like a lake. I turn on to my back and drift for a few moments with my eyes closed.

And then suddenly I feel a pull. I'm no longer drifting. I roll back on to my front and try to remember all the water safety rules that were drummed into me over the years. *Don't fight the current, swim with it until you can move away from it*. But I panic. All I can think of is getting to the shore. So I fix my eyes on the wreck and start to swim towards it, but every stroke seems to take me further away from it. I start to shout.

By the time Sandy reaches me, I'm exhausted, but still pushing against the current. He curls one of his big arms around my neck and shoulders and tells me to lean into him, but to keep using my legs. I have to close my eyes because my face is turned up towards the sun, and even as I start to feel safe because I'm being pulled along by Sandy's muscular swimming, I have no idea where we're going or whether both of us will end up being dragged out to sea.

But we do reach the shore, and we collapse on the edge of the water. Sandy pulls me into his arms and holds me tightly until I stop shaking and my frantic gasps for breath subside.

'Jesus,' he says, when he gets his breath back. 'You're lucky I woke up and heard you. You should have told me you were going in.'

'You were asleep. I didn't want to wake you. I'm sorry. I know I did everything wrong. I shouldn't have fought the current; I should have gone with it. But I just panicked.'

'Just as well I'm a fit hunk, isn't it? Come on, let's get you home.'

We receive some odd looks as we walk back to the car, Sandy barefoot because he hasn't been able to find his shoes, which were probably swept under the waves, and his shirt and jeans sopping wet and stuck to his body.

Back at the house, I shower the sea water out of my hair and skin. Then it's Sandy's turn. He steps out of his wet clothes that are caked in sand, extracting from the pocket of his jeans his wallet, which has miraculously survived, and handing it to me.

'Do me a favour, hen, and see if you can rescue any of the money in there.'

I take the wallet to the kitchen and pull out the sodden wad of sterling and euro notes, separating them and spreading them out across the table to dry. They're crumpled and wringing wet, but they can be ironed. The credit cards I wipe dry in a tea towel.

Then I take out the other bits of paper in a third section of the wallet and start to separate them. They've suffered more damage than the banknotes. Taxi receipts from Vienna and Prague, his ticket for the Staatsoper, credit card receipts. I notice that one of the receipts is for a restaurant, but the date has been obliterated by the water and the salt. We've been there, but not recently, maybe not even in the past year. Someone else has mentioned the same restaurant during the past few weeks. I rack my brain, but I can't remember who it was.

When Sandy emerges from the shower, I wave the receipt at him.

'So which of your women were you entertaining?' I joke.

He takes the receipt, looks as it and tears it up.

'A very unimportant one,' he says, pinching my nose.

A few hours later, Sandy's mobile rings. He looks at it and frowns.

'Bugger. It's the hospital.'

It's very much a one-sided conversation, his only non-monosyllabic contribution being 'Is it absolutely necessary?' When I hear this, I know he is being asked to return to London.

'I'm sorry, hen,' he says. 'Bit of a bummer. I've got to go back to a meeting about a patient. They've called it for tomorrow afternoon. I'll go over in the morning and, if I'm lucky, I'll be able to get back tomorrow evening. To be honest, I'm amazed we've managed more than a week here without me being called back.'

I'm disappointed, but I knew it was likely to happen, especially when he had taken time off at such short notice. If he's away for just a day, I can't complain.

17

Sandy has already left when I wake up. I have a vague memory of him kissing me on the nose. He has opened the curtains, so that the sunlight is streaming in. It's so strong that I have to squint into it while I decide whether to doze for a while longer or get up. I get up. I want to get back to the papers.

I have a quick shower and then make coffee and toast, which I eat on the floor in the sitting room, papers strewn all around me.

I find my First Communion and Confirmation certificates. Although my mother had no interest in religion, she was happy enough that I shouldn't stand out as being different. So, like the other little seven-year-old girls in my class, I wore a long white dress with a lace veil and a little pearly tiara, and went to the altar with my hands joined as if in prayer, to receive the body and blood of Jesus for the first time.

I root around among the stuff scattered across the floor and I find an old black-and-white photograph showing a group of little girls dressed like miniature brides and beaming at the camera. We had spent months preparing for that day, rehearsing for the first time we would go to confession, stand inside the dark box and wait for the priest to slide back the grille and hear us own up to all the terrible sins we'd committed in our seven-year lifetimes.

I smile now, remembering how I'd agonised over whether something was a sin and, if so, whether it was a mortal or venial sin. How small those worries were. But, back then, they were worries that dominated my life.

I made my First Communion in the church to which my primary school was attached. It wasn't far from where we lived in Drumcondra and I've always assumed that I was also baptised there. But I can't assume anything any more. A baptism certificate isn't a legal document, but if I can find mine, it will have on it the names of the church and the priest who baptised me. If he's still alive, he may be able to help me with even the smallest bit of information. I scrabble among the papers, but can't find it.

Richard, though, may be able to tell me what I need to know. I dial his number and I'm pleased to hear the lift in his voice when he hears me speak.

'Ah, Louise, you're back in the country. Are you going to come and see me?'

'I am,' I say. 'But I'm going to be knee deep in paper for the next few days, and I was wondering whether you might be able to fill in a couple of blanks for me in the meantime.'

'I can certainly try.'

'Was I baptised? I think I must have been because I went to a convent school. But I haven't found a baptism certificate yet.'

'Yes, you were. In fact — ' he breaks off and clears his throat — 'I stood for you.'

'You're my godfather?'

'Yes. I'm sorry . . . I haven't been a very good one.'

176

'Oh, it's all right. Maybe my mother told me, but I don't remember. I don't think I ever even asked who my godparents were. Did I have a second one?'

'Yes, but I can't remember her name. I think she may have been an old school friend of Marjorie's.'

'And the church? Was it in Drumcondra?'

'Why would it have been there?' is his response. 'No, it was here in Dalkey. We were all there.'

'All?'

'Well, Marjorie, myself and my wife, the other godparent and, of course, our parents.'

This is something I hadn't been expecting. My mother's parents, who had rejected their daughter for having a baby out of wedlock, attended my baptism, which took place in their local church in Dalkey. It doesn't make sense and I say so.

'They were strict, but they weren't cruel,' Richard says. 'Look, I wanted to tell you this when you came here earlier this year, but you seemed so agitated that I didn't want to upset you further. I don't know what Marjorie told you, but if she told you that our parents threw her out of the house — '

'She didn't exactly say that, but that's the impression I've always had.'

'It wasn't as simple as that.' He sighs. 'They hit the roof, of course, when she came home and announced she was pregnant. But they never cast her out. She stayed here, in the family home, until she had you. And she could have continued to live here, but she insisted on moving into a flat

177

when you were a few months old.'

'Drumcondra,' I say. 'That's where we lived.'

'It wasn't, then. The flat she moved into from this house was in Rathmines. She was there for a year or more. It was a nice little flat. My parents paid the rent and went to visit her occasionally, and she brought you here, too, sometimes. And then, all of a sudden and for no obvious reason, she moved out of the flat. We only found out when the landlord contacted us. She hadn't left a forwarding address. It was hard on my parents. They weren't the most demonstrative people, but they did love her and they were terribly hurt by it.'

I listen, bewildered. I might have doubted Richard had he told me all this during my first visit, but a lot has changed since then. My mother, I now know, was a consummate liar. She lied about everything. What I can't even begin to understand is why.

Richard is speaking again.

'We didn't hear from her for years and my parents were too proud even to try to contact her. I probably should have made more of an effort but . . . well, Sadie, my wife, and I were having a few problems. Anyway, Marjorie had been settled in Drogheda for a very long time when she got in touch with me, and by then our parents were both dead.'

I had thought of my uncle as having had a charmed life, inheriting the family home in a beautiful area. Now I'm learning that impressions are not to be relied upon. Certainly not mine.

I briefly consider mentioning the death certificate and the 'other' Louise before I ring off, but decide that this is not something for the telephone. I'll take the document I found among my mother's papers with me when I visit him, maybe later in the week. And I'll make sure I also take the letter to Santa Claus in Lapland from the little girl called Ailish.

But I need to ask Richard whether he had been aware of my mother's time in Northamptonshire.

'I think I know why she cut everyone off,' I say. 'Did you know that she moved to England at one point?'

'England? No. No, I had no idea. When was this?'

'When I was very small. Or when someone was very small.'

'What?'

'It's a long story, Richard,' I say, weary now of the conversation and unable to face the thought of recounting the details of my visit to David Prescott. 'And it's not one for the phone. I'll come up later in the week. I'm sorry, but it's all getting a bit complicated and a bit much.'

There's a silence that lasts several seconds.

'Would you like me to obtain a copy of your baptism certificate?' Richard asks eventually. 'I can have it for you when you come.'

There's no need for a baptism certificate now. I've learned more from this telephone conversation than anything a record of my church baptism will show. But I might as well have it.

One more document to add to the strange collection.

'If you don't mind,' I say.

* * *

Sandy phones at six o'clock to say the issue surrounding the patient he and his colleagues have been discussing is much more complicated than he had thought it would be. He sounds agitated.

'I'm really sorry, hen, but I'm going to be here at least through tomorrow morning. Will you be all right?'

'I'll have to be, won't I,' I say, and I immediately regret my snappy tone. 'Sorry, I don't mean to sound like a witch. It's all this bloody paper. I feel as if I'm drowning in it. And I discovered something else today.'

I tell him about my conversation with Richard and he whistles.

'Bloody Nora! So she was the one who rejected them, not the other way round. Look, why don't you leave everything until I get back. If anything dodgy is going to turn up, I want to be there.'

'You'd better hurry back, then.'

* * *

I've invited myself round to Angela's for the evening, partly because I want company and partly because I want to fill her in on all the latest developments. Joe, despite having worked

180

all day, is only too happy to take over the cooking, leaving Angela and me to sit in the garden, making inroads into a bottle of wine.

Maybe it's the result of her training as a nurse, but Angela has always taken everything in her stride and barely reacts to what I tell her.

'I had no idea whatsoever that she'd lived in England. She never mentioned it. I wonder if my father knew. And this death-certificate business . . . Do you think it's real?'

'Yes. Well, in that one does exist in the name of Louise Redmond, who was born on the same day I was born and whose death was registered by a Marjorie Redmond. But it just can't be right — except, how many Marjorie Redmonds are there who have daughters called Louise Redmond, born on the same day in 1969?'

'You know, Louise, I really don't think this is something you can sort out on your own. It's gone well beyond that stage. My advice is to go to the police when you get back to London,' she says.

'But what will they do? They'll probably just say that there's obviously been a bureaucratic mix-up somewhere along the line. And then why would they bother to get involved when the death certificate was issued in England, but the birth certificate in Ireland? And there's still masses of stuff I have to go through. Maybe everything will become clearer when I've looked at all of that.'

'Pity she never kept a diary,' Angela says drily. 'We'd all be the wiser.'

I'm not so sure about that. I find myself

thinking that, even if my mother had kept a diary, it would almost certainly turn out to be a work of fiction.

18

Bombshells have become par for the course over these past few months, but the one that lands this morning has nothing to do with my mother and the turmoil she has left for me to sort out. And the strange thing is that, when it explodes all around me, I'm not even that surprised. It's as if things have somehow come together and are finally starting to make some kind of sense.

My day starts with my mobile ringing, waking me up. It's the opening of Mahler's eighth symphony — my ringtone for Sandy — and it's big and loud. I love when it bursts into life with the massed choirs singing *Veni, Creator Spiritus*, although not at seven o'clock in the morning.

'Hello?' I say, turning the greeting into a question with an upward flick in intonation, hoping he's not calling to tell me that there's a new delay and he won't be coming back today. We have only a few days left in the house, in the huge bed dressed in white linen. On Sunday, we fly back to London.

'Lou, are you all right?' he asks, and I assume he's checking to find out whether anything untoward or upsetting has turned up among my mother's things.

'Why wouldn't I be?' I say. 'Slightly hung over. I went to Angela's last night, so you can imagine. But otherwise not a bother on me. Are you all right? You sound a bit . . . anxious.'

'No, no, I'm fine. I just felt bad about leaving you for a whole night when we have so much to do and with everything else that's been happening. But I'm coming back today. I have a flight around three, so I'll see you between six and seven.'

'Wonderful.'

I'm about to end the call when I hear him start to speak again.

'Lou . . . '

'Yes?'

'I do love you.'

'I should hope so,' I say, using the response he used to make when it was me telling him I loved him. When I put the phone down, I'm smiling. It's already turning into a good day. I feel I can handle anything it throws up. I haul myself out of the bed, shower and dress, and walk down to White Nights, where I order a big cup of coffee and a croissant.

It's eight o'clock and the air is still cool, but it's going to be another hot day and this is the perfect start to it. People are crossing the little pedestrian bridge in both directions, going to work, going about their business, and I can hear the distant hum of the heavy stream of traffic that bypasses the town centre. The river looks clean and bright in the early sunshine. I wonder where the swans are. Perhaps they're still asleep.

I'm so relaxed that I almost don't hear my phone ring. If it's Sandy telling me he's not coming after all, I'll murder him, I think to myself as I scramble inside my bag for the phone. It's not Sandy, though. The number that

184

flashes up is a London landline that I don't know.

'Hello,' I say.

'Louise?'

It's a female voice and I don't immediately recognise it because I'm hearing it out of context, but within seconds I realise it's Julia.

'Julia, hello. I'm still in Ireland.'

'Yes, I know,' she says, and even as I wonder why she's calling me, I have a feeling that she's not going to tell me anything I want to hear. Her speaking voice seems to have dropped a tone and there's no hint of that honeyed sound that is so seductive.

So I wait for her to tell me the reason for her call. But, all the time, I'm telling myself I know exactly why, because now it's all making sense. And I'm half relieved because I know now why Sandy left me that first time. I don't have to wonder any more. But the other half of me is devastated as I listen to Julia say how she hates herself for having to tell me this, but she has no other option because Sandy is the father of the baby she's going to have, and that he loves her but is torn between leaving me — because he feels guilty about doing something like that when I'm in such a parlous emotional state — and moving in with her and the baby.

She's still talking non-stop when I put the phone on the table, and I leave it there, leave her talking to the wind. I don't want to hear any more. I don't need to.

Eventually, I put the phone back in my bag without checking whether Julia is still on the line. She must have cut it at some point because, after a while, it starts ringing again. I look at it, but I don't answer. It's Sandy.

I look at the river, see how fast it's flowing. I could lower myself into the waters that are dark below the glistening surface and let myself be taken out to the sea. But the thought is a fleeting one. It wasn't so long ago that I had to learn how to survive without Sandy. I can do it again.

He keeps trying to call me through the morning, but I just let the phone ring. I could answer, talk to him and hear what he has to say. I have questions that are torturing me. How did he meet her? Was it through the choir? It must have been. And why did he choose her? Was it because she could have a child? Did he compare her with me and find me less lovable, less beautiful?

And I think back to this morning when he called me so early and told me he loved me. I thought he simply wanted to make sure I was all right. But now I know he was checking to see whether Julia had already called. Maybe he thought he was safe and could get back in time for some damage limitation. But the damage has been done. I think that maybe I could have coped if he'd told me about the initial betrayal. After all, he came back to me. But I can't deal with this new one.

A text comes through:

Louise, please let me tell you the truth. I did have an affair with her, but it's over. It has been over for a long time. I love you.

I text him back:

> No more lies. Don't come back. I don't want to
> see you.

I go back to the house. I take Sandy's things out of the wardrobe and put them into one of the black plastic bin bags. They're destined for the charity shop. I haven't gone through them. If there's further evidence of his betrayal, I can't bear the thought of finding it.

Sitting in the kitchen and drinking mug after mug of strong tea, I torment myself with images of Sandy and Julia together, planning a future with their baby. I think about his trips away from London. He went to conferences all over Europe. Vienna. Prague. Berlin. Rome. Was she with him on those trips? Or had he invented some of them and gone to stay with her for days at a time, knowing I wouldn't check up on him? I sob until my ribs are too sore to cope with any more weeping and I wipe away the mixture of tears and snot running down my face. I've had enough and now I want to know everything, but I want the truth. If I talk to Sandy, I'll get only lies.

I search through my phone and find a number for his friend, Geoff, whose flat he stayed in when we were separated and who also sings in the choir. I once thought of Geoff as my friend, too.

'Hello, Geoff, it's Louise Redmond. Do you have a minute?'

He's uncomfortable talking to me and at first

denies all knowledge of Sandy's affair. But I persist, telling him about Julia's telephone call earlier this morning.

'Geoff, this woman sought me out, came to me for lessons. And all the time she was screwing my husband and probably laughing at me behind my back. Now she says Sandy is the father of her baby and is planning to leave me, once and for all. I need the truth. Did he meet her through the choir?'

'I'm afraid so. She joined about a year ago. Look, I'm not trying to make excuses for him — '

'It sounds like that's exactly what you're about to do!'

'She set her sights on him. He didn't really stand a chance. She was very determined.'

'Oh, for God's sake, Geoff, don't give me that rubbish. She clearly didn't have to try too hard.'

'She could have had any of us, Louise, myself included.'

For a moment, I'm sidetracked. I switch my hatred of Julia to envy. How extraordinary to have such power over men. But my anger takes over again.

'Do you know what really pisses me off, Geoff? He left me and he never told me why. He let me think there was something wrong with our marriage, because he said there was no one else. And, all the time, he was with her, and everyone knew about it. Everyone except me.'

'Louise, I have to say I'm a bit surprised about this latest development — the, er, pregnancy — because I thought he had ended the whole

188

thing. He hasn't been to choir for a while, either. He took a break because he wanted to fix things with you. Have you heard Sandy's side of things?'

'Why would I want to hear his side of things? What would be the point? I know what he's done. I've had too many lies. From everyone.'

Angela comes round. She's sympathetic, but says I need to speak to Sandy before I start to think about cutting ties with him.

'I should have known it couldn't last,' I say.

'Well, it lasted long enough,' she says. And then, softening her tone, she adds, 'You've invested a lot in your marriage. Do you really want to let it end because of an affair?'

'Angela, am I really hearing this from you? It's more than an affair! She's pregnant. He's been carrying on all the time I was convinced we could make a go of things. Would you forgive Joe if he had an affair? If he'd had an affair and said it was over, but was lying?'

'I don't think I'd want to know if he'd had an affair,' she says. 'But now that you know for sure that Sandy's had one, I think you should talk to him.'

'I can't.'

'Do you want me to talk to him?'

'No! Don't, Angela. Please.'

Geoff said Sandy hadn't stood a chance against Julia. But maybe I was the one who had never really stood a chance, not against a woman like Julia, who could give him a child.

Sandy, busy at the hospital, busy with choir rehearsals and concerts, hadn't made an issue of having children. I had been ambivalent and I had been afraid. I had seen us as a perfect couple. And now I curse myself for having been so stupid, so sure that we could survive as a couple without a family. I couldn't have been more wrong.

19

I immerse myself in what I have to do at the house, anything to keep the torment of imagining Sandy with Julia at bay. There are more photographs, reams of them. I've seen most of them before. My mother's wedding to Dermot: she in a light blue dress with her hair up and carrying a small bouquet of white flowers; he in a dark suit and smiling happily at the camera; Angela and I standing beside them in our matching blue bridesmaids' frocks.

I pick up a small black-and-white print that I had long ago forgotten. I'm dressed for my first day at school, holding a little case. Seeing it takes me back to that morning, the first time I can remember being separated from my mother. She had prepared me for it, but at the last minute I rebelled.

I cried, big crocodile tears that made no impression. Then, as my mother took my hand firmly and led me to the door, I pulled and screamed. 'No! No! NO!' She wasn't having any of it.

'Come on, Louise, you're going to love school,' she said. 'There'll be lots of other little girls, just like you. There's nothing to be afraid of.'

But there was. The nun waiting for us stood like a black statue at the entrance to the school and, as we climbed the granite steps, I kept my eyes on the huge crucifix that dangled from the belt around her waist, unwilling to look up at the pale, pasty face that had glared at us as we approached.

'Good morning, Sister. I'm sorry we're a little bit late,' I heard my mother say, and I could tell that she was making a special effort to be polite, because her voice was all sweet and sticky, as if she had spooned lots of jam into her mouth and the words were coming out covered in it.

'Good morning, Mrs Redmond,' the nun said, and even now I fancy I hear a sneering emphasis on the *Mrs*. But I'm probably imagining that.

'And you are Louise?' she said to me. I said nothing, kept my eyes fixed on that crucifix and the big rosary beads that dangled beside it.

'Look up at me, child,' she said, and I did, because, although her voice was low, there was a sharpness to it that forced me to raise my head.

'You can leave her with us now, Mrs Redmond, and come back to collect her at half past two,' the nun said, dismissing my mother, who bent down to kiss me before retreating down the steps, promising, as she moved away, that she'd come back in just a few hours to take me home.

I wanted to break into a run after her, but I was too frightened. Instead, I followed her with my eyes until tears blurred my vision and I could no longer see her. The nun told me to walk beside her.

She hadn't introduced herself, but she was the head nun, Mother Bernadette.

Pre-school education wasn't generally available in Ireland in those days. There was no gentle introduction to the world of learning. We started primary school around four or five in what was called Low Babies, learning to read, write, do arithmetic — basic stuff that continued the following year, in High Babies. These names may have given the impression that the system recognised how young we were, but some of the nuns were tough.

I was too timid to be anything but well behaved. And I was already able to read and write before starting school; my mother had spent hours teaching me to recognise letters and words, and had guided my hand as it pulled pencil across paper to form them.

'What's your name?' asked the girl I was put sitting beside on that first day. She was dressed like me, in the school uniform — a little navy dress with a white collar and mother-of-pearl buttons down the bodice. Her hair was dark red and as straight as mine was full of kinks.

'Louise. What's yours?' I managed to say before Sister Philomena, who was in charge of our class, spotted that we were talking to each other and walked down to us.

'Empty vessels make the most noise,' the nun rapped. Her cheeks were bursting against the tight white coif she wore under her veil. 'Now, no talking.' And she turned and walked back up to the front of the class, her heavy black habit making a swishing sound as she moved. As it turned out, Philomena's bark was worse than her bite; she could look and sound fierce, but underneath it all she was soft. But I didn't know that yet and I was cowed into silence. The other girl was made of sterner stuff. 'My name's Ursula,' she whispered. 'We can be friends if you want.'

I smile as I think back to how my first real friendship started. How could two girls so different in personality — one forward and bold, the other on the timid side — form such a strong bond so early in life? She became the sister I had longed for and I suppose that, for her, I was relief from a family of boys in which she stuck out as the only girl. When my mother told me we were moving to Drogheda, I cried for days, because the one thought in my head was that I would never see Ursula again. But my mother helped us to keep in touch, so we remained firm friends. And when I moved to London, Ursula did, too, to study journalism.

As I recall that first day at school, it occurs to me that perhaps Ailish was one of the children in my class. I can't remember, but maybe Ursula can. I dial her number in London.

'Ursula, I want to ask you something. Remember school, St Celestine's?'

'Will I ever forget it? What about it?'

'Do you remember whether there was a girl called Ailish in our class?'

'Hmmm. No, I don't think so. There was an Aileen, though.'

'Aileen McCormack!' I say, and for a moment I think I've misread the name scrawled on the letter as Ailish rather than Aileen. But when I check it, I see that I haven't made a mistake.

'Why do you ask? You haven't bumped into her, have you?'

'No,' I say, fishing around in my head for an answer. 'I was just thinking about those days.'

'Are you managing to have some fun? Is Sandy still there?'

'No,' I say. 'He had to go back.'

Although she's my closest friend, I can't bear to talk any more about what Sandy has done, and I'm afraid that, if we continue to talk, I'll blurt it all out.

'Listen, Ursula, I'm sorry, but I can see the delivery man coming to the door with stuff for the house. I have to go,' I say. 'I'll give you a buzz later, or maybe tomorrow.'

* * *

One of the cardboard boxes contains a stack of my old drawings and paintings, all done before the piano became my big interest. I'm touched that my mother held on to them. Some of them are surprisingly good, even imaginative. I can't remember having painted most of them, but I can easily work out who the people in them are meant to be. The grown-up lady in the high heels and dress that flows out from the waist, and who appears in several paintings, is clearly my mother. The two little girls holding hands are Ursula and me. They must be, because one of them has red hair and the other is dark. Sometimes there are boys with the two girls and I work out that they must be two of Ursula's four brothers.

195

I look at each drawing and painting in the stack, enjoying this diversion from the main task, until I come to the still life: a bunch of grapes in a bowl. Another reminder of the past, but this one stirs up a different kind of feeling.

Mother Bernadette didn't teach. Perhaps her duties as head of the school were too all-consuming. Perhaps she just didn't like children all that much.

Our main contact with her was on Wednesday afternoons when, for half an hour, just after the lunch break, we had a period called Instructions, which was taken by Mother Bernadette and brought the whole school together. This could cover any topic, and not necessarily one that had anything to do with religion or education.

Sometimes she inspected our uniforms, checking that our white collars were clean, that no buttons were missing and that the hems of our dresses were a good inch below the knee. Any child found to be wearing clothes not sanctioned by the school was given a written reprimand to take home to her parents. My mother made sure I was always correctly kitted out.

When I fell foul of Mother Bernadette, it had nothing to do with dress or even behaviour, because I was a fairly docile child. But I was also an artistic one, mad about music, art and ballet. I loved drawing ballet dancers and spent hours sketching dancers in different poses — arabesques, jetés, pas de deux. It was the pas de deux that turned out to be my downfall.

One Wednesday, shortly before Instructions, I

196

was sitting at my desk, absorbed in sketching a pair of dancers, male and female. I had given the ballerina a short tutu. My male dancer was wearing what classical male dancers tended to wear — tights and a codpiece. I had no idea quite what a codpiece was, but I drew it without thinking about it, copying from a picture on a greetings card, because I drew what I saw.

Unfortunately for me, Mother Bernadette came into our classroom to start us moving towards the assembly hall and, failing to catch my attention, walked down to my desk to see what I was doing. Her look was one of disgust. But she said nothing, just turned her back on me and left the classroom, a black crow gliding silently, malevolent and predatory.

We all moved into the assembly hall, where Instructions took place. I was shaken by what had happened, uncertain of what I had done that was so wrong and had so clearly disgusted the nun.

'Miserable oul' wagon,' Ursula whispered. 'Don't mind her.'

I wasn't comforted. I knew Mother Bernadette had something in mind for me and, whatever it was, I was dreading it.

We sat in the hall, waiting for Mother Bernadette to arrive. When she made her entrance, we all stood up and, when given the signal by her, sat down again.

At this point, two of the younger nuns scuttled in, one carrying a small table, the other a large tray.

'Louise Redmond, come up here,' Mother

Bernadette called out.

I walked up slowly towards her, dropping my head in shame and fear. I was to be made an example of, but I still didn't know how she was going to do it.

The younger nuns took several things from the tray and laid them on the table: a bowl of black grapes, a small jar filled with water, a sketchpad and a box of watercolour paints.

'Now, Louise, do you know why I have brought you up here?' Mother Bernadette asked. Her question was addressed to me, but her eyes were fixed on the assembled school.

'No, Mother,' I mumbled.

'Oh, come now, surely you remember what you were doing?'

'I was drawing, Mother.'

'You were drawing. Yes, indeed, you were. But *what* were you drawing?'

I started to tell her that I was drawing ballet dancers, but she stopped me, holding up her hand.

'I don't think the school needs to hear about the sinful shapes you were drawing,' she said. 'And now, Louise, you clearly have some talent for art, so I am going to show you how you can exercise this talent without offending God.'

She proceeded to paint the bowl of grapes, slowly and painstakingly, ignoring the big clock on the wall and stretching the Instructions period long beyond the half hour. I stood beside her, mortified.

I can't have been more than eight or nine years old at the time. Even then, I would have

198

preferred six strokes of the cane on my hand. The pain would have burned for a while and then it would have gone away. I didn't tell my mother about it, though, because she would have marched straight in and shouted at Mother Bernadette, and I was afraid of the consequences for myself if she did.

I look at the watercolour in front of me now, tempted to tear it into tiny pieces and throw the shreds into the bin. I hesitate, though, because, despite its provenance, it's a good painting. That's one reason to keep it. But there's another. If I hold on to the painting, I'll be taking charge of it. I can decide not to let it disturb me, but see it instead as just a relic of the time in which I grew up.

I'll take it to the framer later. And then maybe I'll call Ursula and we'll both laugh and wonder how we managed to grow into relatively normal adults.

20

The next time I see Declan is by design.

I'm still in bits over Sandy, devastated by his second betrayal. It has only been a week since he went back to London. I'm not yet used to being without him again. I don't want to go to bed at night because that's when I'm weakest, when there's only me in the vast bed and the emptiness of my future without Sandy stretches into the early hours. And when I wake in the morning, the desolation is the first thing I'm aware of as my body comes to life. I don't want to be miserable. I don't want to be the tragic figure I'm letting myself become. I can't even think about going back to London. It would be too much of an effort, so I just drift from one day to another.

I've been walking most evenings on the strand at Bettystown, hoping I'll see Declan. I don't have a plan for him and me. I just want to walk beside someone, someone like him, throw sticks for his dog to chase, and then sit beside him in a pub with a glass of Guinness and a packet of Tayto crisps. But when I finally see him on the strand, walking towards me, I quickly become aware of how attractive I find him. And when he stops in front of me, I tell him I'm glad to see him.

We walk for a while, up and down the strand, and eventually we go for a drink. He asks me how things are with Sandy. I grimace and shake my head. I don't want to talk about it.

'What about Áine? How is she?' I ask.

'She's in Italy. We have a house there, in Liguria. I've just come back, but Áine is staying until the end of the summer.'

'Are the boys with her?'

He nods.

'So you're home alone?'

'I suppose so,' he says, giving me a nervous look. 'Apart from Bran.'

Something brazen has got into me, something that reminds me of the night of my birthday, when I picked that guy up in the wine bar and took him home. But this is different, surely? This is Declan. We were lovers once. We can be again. We don't have to make a meal of it, fall in love or anything like that. So, emboldened, I lean forward and suggest that he come back with me and I'll cook something. 'You're not in a rush. We can talk for as long as we like. And if you don't want to drive, you can stay over.'

'What are you saying? That we should sleep together, have an affair?'

'Well . . . '

'With no strings attached?'

I nod. 'Why not?'

He looks disconcerted, anxious. He shifts in his seat.

'I don't know, Louise,' he says, shaking his head. 'I was in love with you once. I don't know if I could risk that again. And, anyway, I'm married. I'm not the affair type.'

'Oh, it's all right,' I say. 'It was just a mad idea.

I think I probably wanted to turn back the clock on everything in my life. And you were a good thing in my life.'

He looks at his watch and says he'd better think about getting back to Bran, who will almost certainly be destroying the inside of the car. He's jittery now, eager to be out of the snug and away from me. In my head, I can hear the nuns saying how important it is not only to avoid sin, but also to avoid *occasions of sin*. If this counts as an occasion of sin, it certainly hasn't led us to anything very dangerous or serious. Impure thoughts have been entertained, certainly by me, but no mortal sins have been committed.

We leave our drinks unfinished and walk to the little car park. There's an awkward exchange of small talk, followed by an equally awkward, embarrassed embrace. But the awkwardness and embarrassment are his. I feel exhilarated by our encounter, by the sense that anything is possible, even revisiting the past and not being hurt by it.

I turn on the engine and I'm driving away when I hear him calling out to me. I look into the rear-view mirror and see him running after the car. I can keep driving, go back to the house. Or I can stop the car and wait for him to approach, knowing that this latter option may not be good for either of us.

I stop the car and roll down the window fully. He leans in and kisses me. No awkwardness this time.

'Wait for me. I'll get my car and follow you,' he says.

★ ★ ★

The affair, if it can be called that, with Declan
dulls the pain of Sandy's betrayal, makes me feel
alive, desired. When he turns up, it's always with
Bran in tow. I don't mind if he brings the entire
dog community of Skerries, as long as he turns
up. His intensity bothers me, though. And he's
full of questions. Am I likely to get back with
Sandy? It doesn't look that way, I tell him. Would
I ever think of living in Ireland again? I don't
know, but I doubt it, I say. I've been away too
long.

Sometimes, I join him in Bettystown to walk
on the beach in the evening, when the families
have gone home and there are just a few people
ambling along the hard sand by the water's edge.
But mostly we stay at the house, putting Bran in
the yard so that we can go to my bedroom
without having to watch the dog look at us
reproachfully as we close the door to keep him
out. The sex is easy and comfortable, just as sex
with Sandy was easy and comfortable. But it's
not the same. It doesn't leave me with that
feeling of everything in the world having been
made right. And hours later, long after Declan
has gone home, the ache of Sandy, of having lost
him, gnaws at my stomach as I get into bed and
turn off the light.

Declan has offered to help me with the sorting
out of my mother's papers. I've thanked him, but
told him I can manage. I haven't told him
anything about the mess I'm in, and I see no
point in doing so. And if I tell him that my

mother had a child called Louise Redmond with the same date of birth as mine, and who died when she was three, and that I have no idea who I am, he will surely put on his psychiatrist's cap, wonder about my state of mind and step back from our affair. He's too cautious a man to do otherwise. And who could blame him?

21

I'm having one last check through the pile of papers that I've designated as rubbish before I throw them into the recycling box. I've seen the big brown Manila envelope before. It contains about a dozen greeting cards and envelopes, all the same, with a bland landscape on the front and the inside left blank. She must have had a stock of them for use when a thank-you note was called for, although they don't strike me as her style. When she bought Christmas cards, she ignored the robins and reindeer and snow scenes, and went straight for medieval and renaissance paintings of Madonna and child, because, despite her lack of religiosity, she saw Christmas as a religious festival that had at the very least inspired great art.

I aim the Manila envelope at the recycling box, but, as it sails through the air, the cards start to fall out.

'Bugger,' I mutter, annoyed at having to get up from the floor, where I've managed to find a relatively comfortable position, to pick them up.

I'm gathering up the cards and envelopes when I notice that one of the envelopes has an address scrawled on it in block capitals. I recognise them as my mother's block capitals because of the squiggly *D* in *Dublin*.

MRS MARY O'CONNOR

10 WALTER SQUARE
CRUMLIN
DUBLIN

I stay calm. I've developed a technique to try to hold panic at bay when I think about the Crumlin episode. I press my tongue against the roof of my mouth, just above my teeth, clench my fists and tense every muscle and sinew in my body. It works most of the time, and it does now. I look at the envelope again, but there's nothing inside it, nothing else written on it. Perhaps she has written on one of the cards. But, when I check, I find that each one is blank, pristine.

Sandy had wanted me to stay away from Walter Square. But Sandy's advice doesn't count for anything now, so I walk down to the railway station. I have no particular plan sketched out in my mind beyond getting myself to Crumlin, to number ten, Walter Square. I have no idea what I will do when I get there.

On the train, I stare out of the window, but take nothing in. I have no idea how many or which stations we have passed. Why was my mother writing to someone who lived in the square? Was it someone she worked with? There are too many questions piling up in my head, crowding my brain. I try to make myself stop thinking about them, but I can't, and I become more and more confused.

When I reach the square, I avoid looking at the green postbox, but I know exactly where it is. It's almost too hot and sultry to be out of doors. There are a few children playing in the garden in the middle of the square, under the watchful gaze of their parents, and one or two people are sunbathing. But otherwise it's quiet, except for the summer buzz of insects and the chirruping of birds.

I ring the doorbell at number ten and wait for what seems a very long time before I hear footsteps coming towards the door. The woman who appears in the doorway is young, probably in her late twenties, with long blonde hair and a honey-gold bloom to her skin that can only have come from a sunbed.

'Hello,' I say. 'Is Mrs O'Connor in?'

'Mrs O'Connor?' she asks in one of those strange modern Dublin accents that didn't exist in my day. 'I'm sorry, there's no Mrs O'Connor here,' she says.

'Oh,' is the only response I can come up with. I hadn't really expected to find Mary O'Connor, but I'm bitterly disappointed that I've come all the way back here only to hit a dead end. 'I'm sorry to have bothered you.'

But as I turn away to walk back down the little pathway to the gate, the young woman calls after me.

'Are you all right? You look a bit knackered. Why don't you come in and have a cup of tea?'

She takes me inside and I have a strange feeling as I walk through the door that I should know this house, but there's nothing I can put my finger on. As in most of the older inner-city houses bought by the young and upwardly mobile, walls have been knocked through to create one big room, which in turn leads through to an extension that opens on to a garden at the back. Floors that would once have been covered by old dark-patterned carpet or linoleum are now covered by expensive-looking wood.

'I hope I'm not disturbing you too much,' I say.

'Oh, you're not disturbing me at all,' she says, pointing towards a rectangular exercise mat and the paused video on an enormous television screen. 'I was just finishing my Pilates exercises when you rang the doorbell.'

The tea is lapsang souchong and we drink it without milk; another far cry from the Lyons or Barry's tea with full-cream milk that would have been drunk in these houses in the old days.

'My boyfriend and I have lived here for a couple of years. We know a few of the neighbours, but they're mostly like us. I mean, they haven't been in the square that long either. I don't think there's anyone called O'Connor. Do you know how long ago she might have lived here?'

I shake my head. 'I don't know very much about her at all,' I say, and I find myself telling her a little bit of my story, about my mother having died and my need to find anyone who can help me trace my father. I don't tell her more than that. I don't mention the death certificate.

'My mother once worked at the brewery and, when I saw the envelope addressed to someone in this square, I thought there might just be a tiny chance the woman was still here and might be able to tell me something,' I say.

She gives me a long look. I can tell that she

wants to help me. It's written all over her face. For all the signs of upward mobility and pampered lifestyle, she's just a nice girl, and a nice girl with a lot of time on her hands.

'Look, I'll ask around and see if anyone knows anything. Do you want to give me your phone number? My boyfriend's an estate agent. I'll ask him. He might be able to do a bit of digging.'

'That's very kind of you.' I pull out a piece of paper from my bag and write down my mobile phone number and my email address.

'My name's Joannie, by the way. And here's my phone number and email.'

I had forgotten how kind strangers can be.

$$\star \quad \star \quad \star$$

Richard shows no surprise when I arrive, unannounced, at his door. He's too much the gentleman for that.

'Am I disturbing you? I'm sorry to turn up out of the blue. It's just that I was in Dublin and I felt I wanted to see you. If it's not convenient, I can come back another time.'

'No need whatsoever to apologise, Louise. You're welcome here whenever you want. I hope you'll remember that. Now, what can I offer you?'

'I think I need a drink,' I say. 'I mean, a proper drink.'

'A gin and tonic?'

'That was my mother's drink. Yes, a gin and tonic would be perfect.'

We sit outside. It's the middle of August, still

summer, but the sun has lost much of its earlier heat and intensity. Already, in the late afternoon, there are hints of an autumn chill.

Richard makes small talk, about the garden, the books he's reading and his grandson's decision not to go to university straight away, but to go travelling for a while.

'Did you go off like that, Louise? Travelling?' he asks.

'No, the gap year wasn't really a thing in my day,' I say. 'Not in my circle, anyway. I went straight off to music college, in London.'

'Ah, you didn't study here in Dublin? I had taken it for granted that you did. We have a perfectly good academy in Westland Row, you know.'

'Oh, I do know. And other places, too. But Mamma encouraged me to go to London. She thought I'd have a better chance of a career there, better connections.'

'And has your career worked out well?'

'It has certainly been different from what I'd imagined. I started off as a singer, but it didn't work out for all sorts of reasons. To be honest, I knew a long time ago that I was never going to be a Marilyn Horne or a Janet Baker. I think I even knew it all along. But Mamma convinced me that I was going to have a big career. Anyway, I developed serious vocal problems, lost my voice and had to find it again. So now I teach singing. But it's not a substitute — I love it.'

'So you don't sing at all now?'

'No. Apart from when I want to demonstrate something to a student.'

210

'And do you miss it?'

'Not in the slightest. When I think back now, it's pretty clear to me that I never really enjoyed it as much as I thought I would. I loved learning the stuff, and I really enjoyed the rehearsals. But the rest of it was very stressful. Going to auditions and not being offered roles. Getting a gig and then going down with a heavy cold. And whenever I did get a gig, it was always a bit of an anticlimax. I don't think I had the right temperament, anyway. I prefer to take a back seat, be the support rather than the main act.'

'Very unlike Marjorie,' Richard says, smiling. 'She rarely took a back seat.'

I've been struggling to find a way of telling him about the death certificate, but now he has provided an opening in the conversation by mentioning my mother.

'There are things I have to tell you, Richard,' I say. 'About Mamma and about me. Things I don't understand.'

He sits back and listens as I tell him about how I tracked down David Prescott, about my shock and distress at being presented with the death certificate, about the photographs of my mother holding the small blonde child.

His frown deepens as I relay each detail. He remains calm, but when he speaks there's a slight tremor in his voice. I know he's shocked. How could he not be?

'I don't know what to make of all this, where it leaves you. That Marjorie had a copy of this death certificate is . . . well, disturbing, to say the least. I was very worried when you rang off the other day. You said, 'when I was very small', and then you said, 'when someone was very small'. Now I understand what you meant.'

He reminds me that I told him during that call that my mother had lived in England for a while.

'What have you discovered about the time she spent there?' he asks.

'Well, David Prescott was transferred back to Northampton and she eventually joined him. He lived with his wife in a village outside the town and my mother lived in a house he found for her in Northampton itself. I suppose it explains why she left Rathmines, but it doesn't explain an awful lot else. Anyway, according to David Prescott, the child died and my mother came back to Dublin.'

'And that's it? That's all you know?'

'It's a lot more than I knew the last time I saw you.'

'Sorry. Yes, it's quite a development. I don't know what to say. There are only two possible explanations I can come up with. One is that David Prescott is a fantasist and has invented this other child . . . '

'No, he's not a fantasist. The death certificate is real and that child, whoever she was, was real. Sandy wrote off for a copy of the death certificate and we also found one in the house. It was in a box that had been hidden away in the attic, and there was a photograph of that child with it. I haven't got them with me because I wasn't planning to come out here, but I'll bring them the next time I come up.'

'Maybe I can help. I'll try to see what I can

find upstairs. There are still a lot of things, old things, stored up in the attic here. But it may take rather a long time. You can imagine how big the space is.'

'That would be great. I'd much rather sort all this out without having to go to the police or whichever authorities would be relevant.'

'Oh, is that what you're thinking of doing? I would have thought it a little premature to be involving the Gardaí at this stage.'

'It's what Angela thinks I should do. But I'm inclined to agree with you. There are still loads of papers in the house, all jumbled up. For someone so neat and elegant, she left things in an awful mess.'

Richard laughs. 'Oh, yes, that was very typical of her. When she lived here, her room veered between calm and chaos, but she never walked out of the house without looking absolutely perfect.'

He looks at his watch and insists I stay for supper and spend the night in Dalkey. 'We can get to know each other a bit more,' he says. 'But I think we have time for a walk before we think about food. It will do us both good.'

As we walk companionably down to the harbour, I find myself telling him more than I had intended. I tell him about Sandy, about his leaving me and coming back, and about his second betrayal.

He doesn't say anything, just listens. And then, after a long silence, he tells me he has never been entirely sure whether infidelity matters a great deal, if at all, in the longer term.

'We all betray each other, in so many ways,' he says. 'It's just a question of degree. And as time passes, we begin to wonder why we have wasted so much of it on something that will inevitably lose its importance. That's the way I see it, at least.'

'Are you suggesting that what Sandy has done won't matter to me at some point? It wasn't just a one-off thing. When he first left, last year, he told me we both needed a break from each other, but all the time he was having an affair. And he was still having the affair when he came back. And now she's pregnant, and she was the one who told me — he didn't have the guts. Maybe he thought he could have the two of us.'

'But you don't know what he thought because you wouldn't listen to him when he tried to talk to you. You don't even know that the baby is real.'

'Oh, it's real, all right. Why wouldn't it be? You wouldn't make something like that up. And I didn't need to hear what he had to say. I didn't want to hear more lies. Anyway, whose side are you on? You haven't even met Sandy, but you seem to be taking his part.'

'I'm not trying to make excuses for him, Louise. But are you really ready to walk away from your marriage? How will you feel about it in, say, ten years' time? Will you regret not giving it another chance? And if you do take Sandy back, isn't it possible that ten years, even five years down the line, the pain of this will just be a memory?'

As I think about this, Richard starts speaking again.

'I'm going to tell you something, something that will shock you.'

We're still walking, but now Richard slows down the pace, though he avoids looking at me.

'Peter isn't my biological son. Sadie and I never . . . never managed to consummate our marriage. My problem, not hers. And then one day she mentioned that she was pregnant, and I said that was good news, and eventually Peter was born.'

I stare at him.

'That's it? She told you she was going to have a baby that you knew couldn't be yours and you just said it was fine? There was no discussion?'

'None whatsoever. It wasn't necessary. I hadn't been able to give my wife what she wanted and needed. I felt a great deal of pain, naturally. But I also felt a kind of relief, if you can understand that.'

'Did you not think of talking to someone, to a doctor, about your — ?'

'About my impotence? Here, in Dublin, in the 1960s? No. It wasn't a subject I was able to discuss with anyone. Even with Sadie.'

'Yet you're talking to me about it.'

'Oh, I'm an old man now. It doesn't matter any more. It stopped being important a long time ago. What's important is that I have a son.'

'Do you know who Peter's biological father is?'

'Does it matter? In every respect, I became Peter's father. He knows the truth, or at least most of it. He knows who his biological father is, as do I. But, in every other sense, I'm his father and he's my son. We accept each other. We love each other. I loved his mother — not in the way she would have wanted, I admit — and she found a way of compensating for that, a way that hurt me very much. But good came out of what she did.'

'Did she keep her affair going?'

'Yes, but so discreetly that, if I hadn't wanted to know whether or not it was continuing, I could have ignored it.'

'But you wanted to know.'

'Yes. And the knowledge was a torment. But it was also a comfort, because I knew that, as long as she continued that affair, she would stay with me.'

He stops walking and stands to face me before speaking again.

'I'm telling you this because you have a long history with your husband. He has certainly betrayed you. But we are all flawed, Louise, and I hope that whatever decision you eventually make about your marriage will be in your best interests. The decisions I made proved to be the right ones for me. And for my wife and son.'

We continue our walk in silence, and I wonder what it has cost him to tell me about the tragedy of his own marriage, his inability to perform a fundamental act of intimacy that would have cemented his relationship with his wife. Yet, at the same time, I'm aware of a tiny thought forming in my mind, a question as to whether his marriage really was the tragedy I see it as. He

216

had a wife who had been unfaithful to him, but out of that betrayal came the son he would probably not otherwise have had.

And then I think of my own marriage, try to think of Sandy's betrayal as something that he and I can deal with together. Would I really be capable, some time in the future, of looking back and seeing all this as a barely significant blip in our marriage? And what about this baby? If I were to take Sandy back, how could I deny him contact with his child? But if I slam the door finally on what has been mostly a great marriage, will I regret it some day?

Thinking about this is too much for me and I force myself to stop. I look at Richard, who's walking quietly beside me, his eyes fixed on the road ahead. I slip my arm through his.

'Thank you,' I say. 'I'll think about everything you said. But not now. It's still too raw. It still hurts more than I can bear.'

22

Despite having intended to maintain a certain amount of distance, I can't help being curious about Declan's life. He lives in a big old house with outbuildings, one of which his wife, Áine, has turned into a studio where she paints.

'Is she good?' I ask. We are lying in bed after a particularly energetic and satisfying bout of sex.

'Not bad,' he says. 'Actually, she's more than not bad. She's very good. One of the local galleries has sold a few paintings of hers.'

'What kind of stuff does she paint?'

'Landscapes, seascapes. Portraits of the boys.'

'And of you?'

'I'm not the best sitter. She tried once, but got exasperated with me.'

He sounds proud of his wife. I tell him so and ask why his marriage isn't working.

'I never said it wasn't working,' he says. 'As marriages go, it's a good one. We complement each other. If we were a business, we'd probably get some kind of award.'

'So I got the wrong end of the stick. You're not dealing with marriage fatigue or failure. You just want a bit of excitement, is that it?'

'No, Louise,' he tells me, looking steadily into my eyes. 'You've got the wrong end of the stick there, as well. It's not excitement I'm after. I could have gone after excitement before, but I didn't. I didn't marry Áine for excitement. I married her because I found her attractive — in her personality and in her looks — and because we got on well. I knew we'd have a good marriage, and that has turned out to be the case. I love my wife. I've never been unfaithful to her before. So, as they say in America, go figure.'

His speech makes me uncomfortable. I've wanted to see his marriage as something steady and boring, something he fell into because it was comfortable and easy. It's clear that this isn't the case. He loves his wife, but I'm the girl who let him down. And, despite being a psychiatrist, he hasn't worked out that he wants me *because* I'm the girl who let him down, the girl he needs to come back to him so that everything can be sewn up nicely.

I'm trying to find a way of telling him this, but he's not ready to stop talking.

'Yourself and myself, we didn't see each other for years and now we see each other every day. I tell lies to my family when they call from Italy. I tell them I'm doing this, that and the other to explain why I'm not always at home when they call or why I have my mobile switched off. All I can think of is you and being with you, having sex with you. But what are you thinking? Oh, sure, I know you're enjoying what we get up to, and I know that it probably helps you cope with your marriage breakdown. But is there anything beyond that? I doubt it. And here's something else that bothers me: I never did understand why everything changed so drastically between us, all those years ago. Did I do or say something to upset you? What did I do that was bad enough to make you drop me without explaining why?'

This is the moment I should tell him that he and I conceived a baby together and that, encouraged or persuaded — I'm not sure what the difference is, in this case — by my mother, I got rid of it, had it scraped out of me in a clinic in London, and chose to tell him nothing about it.

But I don't say anything, because I don't want to revisit that particular time in my past. I don't want to feel again the emotional pain that lingered for a long time and that I eventually found a way of shutting out. And I don't want to hurt him. But I do want to be at least partly honest with him.

'I'm sorry, Declan,' I say. 'I can't remember what happened. It was too long ago. And I don't know what to tell you about what I'm thinking. I don't know if there's the remotest chance of Sandy and me getting back together. Sometimes that's what I want, and sometimes I'm so angry that I don't think I could ever forgive him. When I'm with you, I feel good about myself. Yes, I love the sex. It's brilliant. And I wouldn't be doing it if I didn't feel something for you. The trouble is that I just don't know what I feel or how much.'

He turns away from me to look at his watch, which he's left on the table beside the bed, gets up without a word and goes to the shower. I start to follow him, but he closes the door and I hear the lock turn. When he comes out again, wet and wrapped in a towel, all traces of me washed away, I'm overwhelmed by a sadness that surprises me and that I can't disguise. I start crying. He throws the towel aside and pulls me to him and we fall back on to the bed. I'm holding on to him without having had to explain myself, keeping him in thrall to my questionable charms. It's a small victory for me, but it doesn't feel like one. It feels more like a trick.

⋆ ⋆ ⋆

'Hi, there! It's Joannie.'

The voice is jaunty, bright, and for a couple of moments I'm confused, unsure of whether the person on the other end of the line is trying to sell me something or whether I should know her and am having a brief memory lapse. The affair with Declan has softened my previous sense of urgency and I've done little work on the papers. But then I remember the young woman who was so kind to me when I went back to Walter Square in search of Mary O'Connor.

'Joannie, how are you?'

'Grand, thanks,' she says. 'I have a bit of news for you. My boyfriend did a bit of checking up on this Mary O'Connor. There's no Mary O'Connor registered on anything to do with the house, but the name on the deeds was Thomas O'Connor. He seems to have bought it in 1975, but he must have been living there before — renting it, like — because that was the address for him before it all went through.'

'Yes. He would have been working at Tennyson's and paying rent on the house. Tennyson's built the square. Everyone who lived there in those days would have been renting. I

221

suppose the brewery would have sold off all the houses eventually, when it closed down in Dublin.'

'There's a bit more. The house was transferred in 1984 to a Liam O'Connor. That would have been this Thomas O'Connor's son, I suppose.'

'Is that who you and your boyfriend bought it from?' I ask.

'No. There were a few people in between. Liam O'Connor sold the house in 1998. But here's the interesting thing: it was the auctioneer my boyfriend works for that handled the sale, and it looks like Liam O'Connor had already moved when he put the house on the market, so there's an address for him down in Kerry. Have you a pen handy?'

'No, give me a second. I'll go and get one,' I say. It's a white lie. I always have a pencil handy, ready to mark a score or, when I answer the phone, ready to write a lesson or session into my diary. But I need to step away from this conversation for a few moments and try to understand why my heart is beating so fast, and slow it down. When I pick up the phone again, my voice is as jaunty as Joannie's.

'Fire away,' I say, and she reads out an address near Kenmare that sounds as if it might be a farm or a smallholding.

'No phone number?'

'No, sorry. And he may not be at that address any more,' Joannie says. 'Even so, you might still be able to track him down.'

'Joannie, you've been incredibly helpful. I'm really grateful,' I tell her.

'Ah, sure, it was no big deal,' she says, downplaying the extent to which she has gone out of her way to help me.

It is a big deal, though. I have no idea who Liam O'Connor is, who Thomas and Mary O'Connor were, and it may be that they have nothing to do with my mother. But I won't know that until I find them.

I call directory enquiries and ask for a number for Liam O'Connor at the address Joannie has given me.

'That number is ex-directory,' the operator says.

I want to scream in frustration.

23

I feel as if I've been here forever. It's still August, but there's a sense that the summer is over. I haven't been able to face going back to London. I have no idea whether Sandy is in the flat or whether he has moved in with Julia. I've sent texts and left messages telling people I've had to stay on in Ireland for a while because of family stuff. I sit outside White Nights with my coffee, quiet amid the bustle around me, unable and unwilling to think beyond the present. The river is flowing as fast as ever, people are going about their business, moving back and forth across the little bridge. Occasionally, I see someone I recognise, but even when I catch his or her eye, there's no discernible flicker of acknowledgement. Have I changed that much? I could call out to them, approach them and say, *Hello, do you remember me?* But I don't.

Part of my reluctance stems from an admission that, despite having lived for years in this town, I failed to put down real roots here, created no lasting foundation for strong friendships capable of standing the test of time. It would be easy to blame my mother for having been so interfering, but I could just as easily blame something in myself, an inability to stand up to her — until Sandy appeared on the scene.

What would be the point, anyway, in trying to resurrect one of these old friendships, if that is what they can be called, that I know I won't keep up? If you leave something, you can't go back to it. And yet I have, in a way, gone back to Declan, haven't I?

I feel a bit like Oisín, one of those mythological heroes in the stories my mother used to read to me. He fell in love with a fairy princess called Niamh and went to live with her in Tír na nÓg, the land of the ever-young. After three hundred years, he was starting to miss Ireland and wanted to go back for a visit, so Niamh gave him a white horse for his journey and warned him that, if he dismounted and set foot on the soil, he'd never return to her. But his girth broke and he fell to the ground and immediately became a withered old man and died. I feel as if I'm still on the horse, but only just.

Leaving Ireland wasn't my idea. Drogheda was a great town. It had its own personality, despite being so close to Dublin. People were lively and kind, and I was happy there. At some point, I would have had to leave it to go to university or music college, but, even then, Dublin rather than London would have been in my sights. I was doing well with my piano studies, which surprised my mother. Most children I knew hated practising their scales. Not me. I loved the regularity of it, the certainties of where the notes had to go, the way I could spread my fingers and know where they were going to fall. Learning the piano had been my idea and it was Dermot who had initially encouraged me. It was Dermot, too, who paid for my singing lessons, driving me up to Dublin regularly to see a well-known teacher.

My mother, having smiled indulgently at me from the sidelines, only began to show serious interest in the possibility that I might have a career when invitations to sing solos at local concerts started to come in. And when it finally came to making a decision about whether to go to university to study history or to go to music college, and I was adamant that I wanted to be a singer, my mother stunned me when she told me I should think about auditioning for the top London colleges.

Now, thinking about how I always ended up doing what my mother wanted, I feel a surge of bitterness that becomes physical, a rush of sourness from my stomach into my mouth. But, just as quickly, an image comes into my mind of my mother in the hospital, at first agitated and frequently gasping for the oxygen mask, then eventually frail and silent as the increasing doses of morphine take effect.

It's too painful to think about her final days, so I make myself look at the paper, order more coffee and think about anything but her suffering. I turn to the exercise book where I've been making notes about everything that has happened.

Louise Redmond 1 (me), born 11 December 1969.
Louise Redmond 2, born 11 December 1969, died 30 April 1973.
Death certificate for Louise 2. Real.
Father of Louise 2 is David Prescott, ex-Tennyson's, my mother's lover.

David Prescott saw Louise 2 die of meningitis in hospital in Northampton.
Marjorie Redmond, my mother, registered the death of Louise 2.
Marjorie Redmond was the mother of Louise 2.
Marjorie Redmond had a copy of the death certificate of Louise 2
Marjorie Redmond had a photograph of Louise 2.
David Prescott says he is not my father.
Who is my father? Is he still alive?
Who am I?

And then I write down the details of my recurring memory, of the little hand stretching upwards, and of the episode in Crumlin when the memory seemed to merge with reality as I found myself standing in front of the green postbox in Walter Square.

My writing is fast, but it's behind the speed of my thoughts, which are racing ahead to the other things that don't appear to be directly connected: the letter to Santa Claus that I found in my mother's trunk; the envelope addressed to Mary O'Connor at 10 Walter Square. I'm just starting to write these down when, my head bent over the exercise book, I become aware of someone standing in front of me. I look up.

'Jesus, Ursula, what are you doing here?'

'What do you think? I was worried about you. You haven't been answering your phone. So I rang Sandy.'

'Ah.'

'Ah, indeed. Look, I want to know what's going on. Sandy didn't give too much away, said

227

I should hear it from you first. So, are you going to tell me?'

'I'll tell you later. But you were right all along. He was a lying bastard and I was an idiot. But it's not just the Sandy thing. There's a lot more going on, and I'm sorry I haven't told you. Here, sit down and have a look at this.'

I push my exercise book towards her. 'That's about the gist of it,' I say.

She eventually looks up from my notes, shaking her head in bewilderment.

'Okay, I don't understand this at all, but it looks pretty messy. You'd better give me the full story,' she says.

I'm getting fed up of retelling the story. Sometimes, I do it quietly to myself, feeding in the facts one by one, trying to make sense of them by creating links between them. It's always the same, though. It never makes sense. But I go through it all again for Ursula, who exhales loudly as I finish the story and sit back.

'Oh, I forgot one thing, but it may not be connected,' I say, telling her about the ancient letter from Ailish to Santa Claus.

'The explanation has to be that your mother had twins. It's the only one. And the Ailish thing kind of supports that.'

'Not according to David Prescott,' I say. 'Well, it's not that he said there were no twins involved. It's just that he mentioned only one child. I think he would have mentioned a second.'

'Unless he's lying. Unless he's got a reason for wanting to keep you, the other daughter, out of his life.'

228

'But why?' I ask, bewildered. 'And then there's the fact that both of us were called Louise. Why would my mother have called us both Louise?'

She waves my question away. I love the way Ursula is so certain about everything, right up to the moment when she can't be certain any more. She grabs hold of things, pursues them until they either work or don't, but she exhausts them before abandoning them and moving on to the next theory.

'I don't know. But we're only going to find out by talking to David Prescott. He's the key to all this now. From everything you've told me, I'm absolutely convinced about that.'

I look out across the river, feeling as insubstantial as the glimmers of sunlight that land on the water momentarily, only to vanish just as quickly. I'm convinced of nothing, anchored to nothing. But I'm grateful to Ursula for her faithfulness, her insistence on helping me find answers, and if she thinks David Prescott can provide them, I'm ready to try to believe her.

'So,' she says, 'I think we should go and see David Prescott, and sooner rather than later. My flight back to London is the day after tomorrow. Why don't you come with me?'

'I can't. I have to go down to Kerry.'

I tell her about my visit to the house in Walter Square and the information Joannie has given me.

'I rang directory enquiries for a phone number, but they wouldn't give it to me.

Ex-directory. I think I'm going to go down there, though.'

'But that's madness, Lou! You can't go off haring down the country on spec. And, anyway, that O'Connor chap is probably nothing to do with anything. For all you know, your mother was doing some Lady Bountiful thing when she worked at that brewery, sending pretty cards to the appreciative locals on behalf of the company. No, Lou, the answers to all this are closer to home. David Prescott is our man. He knows more than he's told you. It's a matter of asking the right questions.'

'I'm not even sure I know the right questions,' I say.

'No, but I do,' she says. 'Ring him up and ask when he can see us. But do it later. I'm starving. And I need a drink.'

As we stand up to leave the café, my mobile rings. Declan. I let it ring, but I don't answer. Ursula gives me a sidelong look that I ignore. She doesn't need to know that I'm seeing him again after all these years. It's not that she'd disapprove. She'd probably be delighted and say, *Go for it, girl*. But, if I tell her about it, I'll be giving the affair an importance it doesn't have. It's an interlude, no more than that.

We repair to the old Franciscan church, which has become an art gallery with a restaurant. When I was living here in the eighties, the church was still thriving. Drogheda was a town of churches and tall spires. Most of them are still there and attendance remains relatively high. But times have changed and religious vocations are

230

down. You rarely see a nun.

Ursula, as if reading my thoughts, starts giggling.

'What's the collective noun for nuns?' she asks.

'A coven?' I say, and I immediately feel a bit mean. There were some wonderful nuns in both my primary and secondary schools, clever and hardworking women who did their best to educate their pupils, but it was often the ones like Mother Bernadette who stayed in our memories.

'Not bad, but no. Try again.'

'I give in.'

'A superfluity! But they're not so superfluous now, are they?'

'Do you remember that old witch, Bernadette?' I ask.

'Will I ever forget her? I remember that time she made you stand beside her, in front of the whole school, while she painted the grapes.'

'Believe it or not, I found that painting of the grapes the other day. I took it to be framed. We could go and collect it later.'

'I can't believe you're paying good money to put it in a frame,' she says, a look of incredulity spreading across her face. 'I'd have chucked it into the bin. Bad memories. But you always were a weirdo.'

'I'm turning bad memories into good ones. It's a psychotherapeutic exercise I've set myself,' I say. 'And it's not a bad painting. You'll see.'

'You're turning into an eejit. Now, are you going to tell me the whole Sandy story?' she says.

I love Ursula. She's my best friend in the whole world. We survived being parted when my mother and I moved away from Dublin, and we've both ended up in London. But Ursula doesn't have a high opinion of men and I know that, once we get down into a serious discussion, there's a danger she will launch into a rant about their deceitful ways. That will make me feel worse than I feel already. Still, she deserves to know what has happened.

'Okay, so . . . you were right about the first time he left. It *was* for a woman. When he came back, he was still carrying on with her. And now she's pregnant. End of story,' I say.

She gapes at me in astonishment. 'Christ on crutches,' she says, and she's about to continue speaking, but I take both of her hands and pull them towards me.

'I can't face talking about it, Ursula. Not right now. It's too public and, if I start crying, it'll be embarrassing for both of us. Anyway, I'm going to need another couple of glasses of wine before I'm able to tell you the whole story.'

It's less a statement than a plea. Ursula looks as though she's about to say something, perhaps tell me that I need to talk about it here and now, but then she relents and gives a short sigh.

'Okay, let's eat and then we can go and get that painting.'

24

Back at the house, Ursula wants me to call David Prescott and arrange for her and me to visit him. But I can't quite bring myself to inflict Ursula on him. She would be too direct. He would find her rude. I do, though, take her point that it would probably be worth seeing him again. So I tell her I need to think about what to say to him, and then I make sure we focus on Mother Bernadette's dark watercolour of the grapes, now safely contained within its new frame of bleached oak.

'It's going into your room,' I say to Ursula. As much as I like the look of it in the new frame, I don't want the painting in my room, or in the sitting room.

Ursula is in the downstairs bedroom, taking from her bag the few toiletries and T-shirts she has brought with her.

'You've travelled light,' I say.

'Yeah, well, I wasn't planning on staying too long,' she says, coming forward to take the painting from me so that I can drive a nail into the wall. 'You're keeping the house, then?'

'I think so. What do you think of it?'

'The bee's knees and the cat's pyjamas. If you could transpose this place to London, you'd be in clover.'

'It was so dreary before, wasn't it? I don't know what possessed her to move here. She must have known it could be turned into something like this, but she obviously had no intention of doing anything to it.'

'I can hardly remember what it was like.'

'Have a look at these,' I say, handing her my phone with a series of before-and-after photographs.

Ursula swipes through them.

'Yeah, it really was, if you don't mind my saying so, a bit of a dump. And Marjorie had such good taste. It's as if she suddenly decided to become an old woman when Dermot died. I wonder . . .'

She breaks off and starts walking towards the bathroom with her toiletries, but I stop her. 'What do you wonder?'

'Guilty conscience.'

'What?'

'Well, I just wonder whether she was punishing herself for something by moving into a grotty old house.'

I raise my eyebrows.

'Maybe she'd . . . I don't know . . . had an affair at some point when she was married to Dermot, or something, and then, after he died, she felt guilty about it, so, consciously or subconsciously, she needed to punish herself.'

'Ursula, that's nuts! It's off the wall. My mother sold the other house because she wanted Angela to have some money after Dermot died. Maybe this place was the only thing available for the money she had to spend. She didn't have an affair. I would have known. Everyone would have known. You can't keep anything secret in this town.'

'Is it as off the wall as you finding out that Marjorie had that death certificate all along? Or that she had two kids, both called Louise. She managed to keep those things secret, didn't she? Yeah, I'm beginning to like this guilt-and-self-punishment theory.'

'But she and Dermot were devoted to each other. She was truly happy with him!'

'If you say so. But things happen . . . just saying. Anway, I'm having another thought — about how there came to be two kids.'

'Okay. I'm listening.'

'Your mother had twins. They came as a shock and she realised it would be difficult, even impossible, to cope with two babies. She was a single mother, after all. So her parents persuaded her not to tell David Prescott that there were two babies and they arranged for one of them to be fostered out to someone.'

She stops. 'Are you with me?'

I roll my eyes.

'So off my mother went to England with David Prescott, entirely happy to leave one of her two babies behind with a foster family? And then when one baby died she returned to Ireland to claim back the second? No, Ursula.'

'You have to admit, though, that it's not entirely impossible.'

'But, Ursula, if that's what happened your theory that David Prescott is a crucial part of the jigsaw falls apart, doesn't it? Because, if he was told that only one child had been born and still believes that, he's hardly going to be able to tell me anything, is he?'

'Ah, but he might have had his suspicions. Really, Lou, I don't get the feeling you asked him too many questions when you went to see him. It's understandable. You had a terrible shock. But I still think he can tell us — you — an awful lot more than he did during your visit. He's still your best chance of unravelling this mess.'

Her second-child theory makes no sense whatsoever. Richard, my uncle, would have been aware of another baby. And my own childhood memories pour cold water all over it. If I had been left with foster parents, I would remember them, even in a small way. But I have no memories of anyone else in my early life. There was only ever my mother.

★ ★ ★

I'm still not entirely convinced, but Ursula has persuaded me that we must visit David Prescott before doing anything else. So I take my mobile out to the yard and press his number. My nerves are jumping around as I wait for him to answer. This will be our first contact since I went to see him, way back in June, over two months ago. He told me as I was leaving that I should visit him again. He probably meant it at the time, but he may be less than pleased to hear from me now.

As I wait for him to pick up, I agonise over how I should address him. Mr Prescott? David? Neither seems appropriate. He resolves my problem by saying, 'David Prescott,' when he answers.

'Oh, hello, it's Marjorie's daughter,' I say. I don't say *Louise* because I don't want to cause him even a fraction of the anguish he felt that day when I told him I had the same name as his dead child.

'Louise,' he says softly, and I feel my throat catch as I realise the enormous gift he has just given me by using my name.

It's then that I decide for certain that I can't take Ursula to see him. She'll push and prod, question and doubt, and I won't subject him to that. But I will go to see him, not just because I want to hear what else he can tell me, but also because I want to see him. Even if he's not my father, he is the man my mother once loved.

'Louise?' his voice interrupts my thoughts.

'I'm sorry; I got a bit lost for a couple of seconds. I was thinking I might come and see you. It's just that I have so many things I need to know about my mother and you're the only one who can help me. Would you mind?'

A small silence. Hesitation. And then his voice comes back, firm and steady, and he tells me he would very much like it if I came to visit him. We agree that I will drive up to Friars Ashby on Saturday.

When I go back inside, Ursula pours me a glass of wine.

'So? Do we have a date?'

'Yes. Well, not exactly. He's up for a visit, but I said I'd call him about it once I was back in London.'

'Well done,' she says. 'We're in business.'

I don't dare tell her now that I have no

intention of taking her with me to Northampton-shire.

My plan is to fly back to London with Ursula the day after tomorrow, drive up to David Prescott the following day and, as soon after that as possible, return to Ireland. There are, after all, the various papers to be sorted out. And there's the trip to Kerry, which I'm determined to make because of the link between my mother and Liam O'Connor's family, even if it may have been a tenuous one. And maybe talking to Liam O'Connor will help me find the connection — if there's a concrete one — between what happened that day in Walter Square and my recurring memory of the green postbox.

But Ursula is probably right about the importance of seeing David Prescott again soon. There are still questions I can ask.

'I'd better tell Angela I'm going back to London. Let's phone for a taxi. I don't think I should drive after the wine.'

Sitting in Angela's garden, we drink a bottle of white wine and Joe quizzes Ursula on the state of her love life. She drives me mad sometimes, but she's been a constant in my life since that first day at primary school and, as I listen to her talk about her latest conquest, I feel a rush of affection towards her.

She's my age, but still looks and dresses as she did in the eighties, mostly in black — leather jackets, jeans and T-shirts — never a dress, but occasionally a black leather skirt. Sometimes she throws in the odd flourish of grey or khaki. She still has her hair cut in a razored bob, still lines her eyes with the blackest kohl. Age certainly hasn't withered her so far. Men are drawn to her tall, slim body encased tightly in black, like a spider, and she pulls them in, just as a spider might. I've seen the performance so many times that I no longer marvel at it. I just feel slightly sorry for the men. She takes up with one, stays with him for a while — it could be a few months, it could be a few years — and then moves on.

Her latest conquest is young, about thirty. I've known other women involved with younger men who worry about the age gap and the inevitability of their lovers dropping them. But not Ursula. The only thing she's bothered about is that her toy boy is starting to talk about the long term. 'I'm going to have to start letting him down gently,' she says.

We all laugh, but I feel a rush of pity for the young man who's about to have his hopes crushed.

25

I manage to get a seat on the same flight as Ursula, and, as we part company at Paddington, I promise I'll call her as soon as I've spoken to David Prescott on the telephone to arrange the visit. I send Declan a text. *Sorry,* I write, *have had to return to London for a few days. Will text when coming back.* No response.

Now that I'm back in London, the only thing I can think of is Sandy and whether, in refusing to talk to him, I'm cutting myself off from something that can be put right. During the short Tube ride to Ladbroke Grove, my mind and body veer between the pain of his betrayal — a physical pain that stabs at my stomach — and the desperate need to see him and to be convinced that we can get beyond this. I stand nervously by the doors, ready to spring out when the train stops, torn this way and that.

When I walk into my building, I see the first indication of his absence in the empty post basket. There's nothing lying around, either for him or for me, which probably means he's been here to pick up his post and start moving his things out, bit by bit. I feel sick to my stomach.

Inside the flat, I go straight to our bedroom, terrified that, when I open the doors on his side of the wardrobe, there will be nothing of him left. So, when I fling open the doors and see that most of his clothes are still there, I sit back on the bed and start crying with a feeling of relief that overwhelms me. I think about what Angela has said, what Richard has said. Right now, I want him back. I dial his number, but it goes straight to his voicemail. It's all right, I tell myself. He's with a patient. Or he's on a train.

The kitchen is relatively tidy, but I see the pile of envelopes and bills, some opened, some not. The milk in the fridge is fresh and there's some cheese and a few tomatoes. Relief hits me again. He hasn't left. Not yet, anyway.

I run down to Portobello and stock up on food. But when I've put it into the fridge and cupboards, when I finally sit down with a mug of tea, all the doubts and the hurt come back, and I tell myself I'm stupid even to be thinking of trying to revive this marriage. All through the rest of the afternoon, I swing between hope and despair, drinking mug after mug of tea. I rehearse how I'm going to talk to him. When he lets himself in this evening, he'll be surprised to find me waiting for him. I won't crack. I'll be firm. I'll hand him a glass of wine and tell him I'm willing to listen to what he has to say. No crying. He can tell me his story and then I'll ask him the questions I've prepared. Why should I take him back after he betrayed me twice? Why did he tell me the first time that there was nobody else involved, when there clearly was? And if he wants to come back to me, where does this leave Julia and the baby?

But I don't get to ask him any of these questions because he doesn't turn up. And eventually, after a long, nervous wait, I sit down by myself and eat the blue-cheese risotto I've made, his favourite comfort food, and drink the entire bottle of wine. How stupid I was to think I could make everything all right again, just because I wanted to, because Richard and Angela had made me believe I had the power to do it. How stupid. How pathetic.

★ ★ ★

The following morning, I get up at seven and set out early for Northamptonshire. I have a headache from last night's wine. My mobile rings as I'm sitting in traffic in north London. Ursula. I don't want to have to lie to her and I don't want her to think I'm avoiding her, so I let the call go to voicemail and then I switch the phone off completely.

The wisteria that hung around the house in the spring is no longer in bloom. The peonies, too, have had their day. But the garden is a colourful riot of late-summer flowers. David Prescott opens the door as I walk up the path to the house. Unexpectedly, he opens his arms to me, a gesture I find so touching that I have to pretend there's something in my eye.

'Welcome back, Louise.'

Again, he's used my name, for which I'm silently grateful.

I've brought my birth certificate, the baptism certificate obtained by Richard, my marriage certificate. I've brought some of my music diplomas. I show them all to David and he scrutinises them.

'What can I say? Clearly, they're all genuine. Whatever 'genuine' means.'

'I have some other things to show you,' I say, this time putting my mother's copy of the death certificate and the photograph in front of him. 'I found these in my mother's house. They were in a wooden box in the attic. I want you to know that I believe what you told me. This is the proof. But there are so many more things I don't understand, things I've discovered since I came to see you. I thought there might be a chance . . . that you might be able to help me make sense of some of them.'

'I can try,' he says.

So I tell him about the envelope addressed to Mary O'Connor at 10 Walter Square and the information Joannie gave me about the house having been bought by a Thomas O'Connor, who was probably Mary's husband, and transferred to a Liam O'Connor, who was probably their son, who eventually sold it and moved to the south-west of the country, to Kenmare in County Kerry.

'There was indeed a Thomas O'Connor who worked at the brewery. I'm afraid I can't remember which house he lived in, but we're probably talking about the same man. He had a wife and two small boys. They were about four and five years of age, I think, though they may have been younger. I don't recall his wife or whether Marjorie was in contact with her. She certainly never mentioned it.'

'Could you find out a bit more about them from Tennyson's? I don't think I would have a hope of getting anywhere, but you might be able to.'

'I can certainly try,' he says. 'But, my dear, do you really need to find these people? The most likely thing is that Marjorie got to know this Mary O'Connor during her time at Tennyson's and was simply sending her a card to keep in touch.'

'You're probably right. But I still have to do it. I have to find out who I am and what happened, and that means I have to check out everything that doesn't make sense. Okay, I know an envelope addressed to someone called Mary O'Connor doesn't necessarily mean I've come across another mystery, but the address was Walter Square, and something horrible happened to me there, a while back.'

I tell him about the strange merging of reality and memory when I found myself in front of the green postbox in the square, the sheer terror that had made me flee from the place.

'How upsetting for you,' is all he says. Although he has acknowledged that my mother has left a huge mess behind her, maybe he thinks I'm a little crazy after all.

I revive the conversation by mentioning that my closest friend had wanted to accompany me to see him.

'But you came alone.'

'Ursula can be a bit, well, demanding. She's a journalist. She works for a tabloid. I won't tell you which one — you'd be appalled. She doesn't take any prisoners, just shoots. She came up with a load of theories about you and my mother and so on. I love her to bits, but I was afraid she might upset you.'

He smiles. 'I suspect I might have been able to cope.'

'Actually, you'd like her, I think. She's up front about everything. She doesn't dissemble. Doesn't lie.' As I say this, I remember with shame that I used a lie to make contact with him. 'David, I'm so sorry for deceiving you before . . . '

He raises his hand, signalling me to stop.

'Please don't apologise. You did what you felt you had to do. And now, aren't you going to tell me about your friend's theories?'

'I have to warn you . . . they're a bit crazy.'

'I have a strong constitution,' he says.

So I talk him through Ursula's theory — that Marjorie gave birth to twins, but told him she'd had only one child and allowed her parents to find a foster family for the other twin. He listens, but I can tell from his expression that he's finding it difficult to keep track.

'And when — when she went back to Dublin she contacted the foster family and took the child — me — back. That's what Ursula is suggesting.'

'What an imagination your friend has,' he says as I finish speaking.

'All right, I know it seems far-fetched, and probably is, but it has to be at least possible,' I offer.

'Of course, it has to be possible. Anything is possible — except in this case. Marjorie was not expecting twins. If she had been, she would have told me. I would have known. We were always honest with each other.'

Honest with each other. I've heard that one before, but I keep my mouth shut.

'I've been doing some thinking of my own,' David continues. 'Isn't the likeliest and simplest explanation that Marjorie adopted you when she returned to Ireland after our daughter died? Hasn't that occurred to you?'

'No, that's impossible,' I counter. 'There would be records. And my birth certificate says clearly — look, you can see it — it says that Louise Redmond was born on the eleventh of December, 1969. And your name is there, too. Birth certificates don't lie.'

'Oh, my dear, anything can be changed or falsified. The question that we don't seem to be able to get to the bottom of is *why*.'

My visit to David Prescott has thrown no new light on anything and I find myself regretting my decision not to bring Ursula with me. There's little point in staying, but, just as I reach out for my bag, he starts talking about my mother, telling me that, contrary to anything I might believe, she had not longed for a baby, but had taken every precaution against having one, as had he.

'We were both horrified when Marjorie discovered she was going to have a child. For reasons that will be obvious to you. An 'illegitimate' child — what a ridiculous, cruel term — was branded for life. An unmarried mother was gossiped about, looked down upon. Those were not good times, and anyone holding them up as an idyllic era needs his head examined.'

'I know,' I say, remembering the way the nuns looked at my mother during those first weeks when she delivered me into their care every morning.

'But I'm veering slightly off course.' He stops and looks about him. 'Do you mind if I have a cigarette? I stopped smoking many years ago, but I keep a small supply for use in times of need.'

'Like now?'

'Like now,' he says, going out of the room and returning with a cigarette, already lit.

'When I first met Marjorie, she was vivacious, flighty — even fast, you might say. All the things you might expect in a young and beautiful woman from a fairly privileged background. I must admit that those things were part of what I found so compelling about her, along with her intelligence, of course. But having Louise, our daughter, transformed her into something even more beautiful. She was so kind and compassionate, devoted to her child. Louise was the centre of her world and I had to take a back seat. Not that I minded. I adored my daughter.'

I recognise this picture he's painting of my mother and, like a child entranced by a fairy tale someone is reading to her, I want to hear more.

'So what happened when . . . when your daughter was born?'

'For the first few months, Marjorie stayed at her parents' house. She had given up working, of course. When she was ready to leave, we found her a flat in Rathmines. I saw them every day.'

I ask him where his wife featured in all this, whether she had had any inkling of what was going on.

'She may have known, or suspected, but she never said anything to indicate that she did. I didn't flaunt Marjorie in front of her. I didn't leave clues lying around. When Louise died, I lived two different existences for a long time. With my wife I tried to behave normally. When I was alone, I grieved. I kept the casket and the death certificate locked in a suitcase. Celia would never have pried. I think I told you when you came before that my wife and I couldn't have children together. If she did find out about Marjorie and Louise, I would imagine she reconciled herself to their existence because of that, and because I stayed with her. But,' and he leans forward and says earnestly, 'I want you to know that I loved my wife. It's true that I would have left her for Marjorie, but, as you know, it was Marjorie who left me.'

Even now, decades after he last saw my mother, it's clear that he hasn't stopped thinking about her. The look on his face and the shine that lights up his eyes when he says her name tell me that.

'But didn't you try to persuade her not to leave?' I ask.

'I did. Of course, I did. But it was pointless. And it made me suspect that, had we not had a child, our relationship might not have lasted as long as it did. Louise became the cement between Marjorie and me. When she died, everything fell apart because Marjorie saw no

248

point in continuing.'

We've been talking for a long time and David's face looks tired and strained. As if reading my thoughts, he says, 'It's one thing to think about these things. It's another to talk about them. I'm afraid I need to be by myself for a while. Would you mind? You can stay here and I'll just go and sit in the garden and have a cigarette.'

'No, don't worry. It's fine. I should be getting back to London.'

As I pick up my bag, I remember the silver cigarette holder.

'I almost forgot. I brought something for you. Something of my mother's,' I say, taking it out of my bag. 'I thought you might like to have it.'

His eyes brighten in recognition. He holds it, stroking it with his thumb.

'I gave it to her. A birthday present,' he says. 'If only I had known then that smoking would kill her. But, thank you, Louise. I shall treasure it.'

He takes my hands in his and wishes me a safe journey, looking so tired and sad that I'm reluctant to leave him. It reminds me of those times I couldn't wait to get back to London, yet was filled with guilt about leaving my mother, so my heart would ache until I was in the air.

I wipe away a tear as I drive away.

26

I've forgotten about the August bank holiday. Notting Hill is already revving up for Carnival when I get back home, late in the afternoon. Shops are boarding up their windows and the empty residents' parking bays tell me that the exodus of those who can get away has begun. The sunlight is pouring into the kitchen, blasting its way through the dense foliage of the trees outside. It's hot and it's going to get hotter and stickier. I don't want to be here for the two days of relentless heat, noise and crowds, so I start thinking about whether I should go straight back to Ireland or ask Ursula if I can go and stay with her. I call Ursula.

'Can I come to your place for a couple of days? It's Carnival weekend.'

'Of course you can. And you can tell me how you got on with David Prescott.'

'Ah. Look, I'm sorry, I thought it was better to go on my own because — '

'Don't tell me now. Save it for later. When are you coming?'

'In the next hour or so. You sure it's okay? I'm not putting you out?'

'It's okay and you're not.'

Just as I finish talking to Ursula, the landline rings. I pick it up, expecting it to be one of those marketing calls because most people who want to get hold of me use my mobile. But it's Angela.

'I've been trying to get hold of you all day,' she says.

'Oh, sorry, Angela, I've been out. I had to switch off my phone and then I forgot to turn it back on. Is everything all right?'

'Yes, everything's fine. But I have someone here who wants to talk to you.'

After a few seconds of silence, I hear another voice.

'Louise.' It's Sandy. He sounds awkward, unsure of himself. Tired. 'I flew over last night. You weren't at the house, so I went to the hotel. I thought you might be at Angela's. We've been calling you. We were . . . I've been worried.'

I almost feel like laughing. When I was waiting in a state of high anxiety for him to come back to the flat last night, he was on an aeroplane to Ireland.

'I need to see you, Louise. I need to tell you what's real and what's not and put things right. I don't want to lose you. I love you.'

This is what I've wanted, prayed for. He's on the phone and he wants me back. It's not too late. I could tell him I'm taking the next flight to Dublin because I need to see him too and can't bear the thought of losing him, no matter what he has done. But I can't go that far. Something stops me. My wounds have stopped bleeding, but they could burst open again at any moment.

'I don't know what to say, Sandy,' I hear myself saying.

'Just say . . . Just say that you'll meet me and listen to what I have to say. Please.'

'Okay. But I'm not promising anything.'

'I'll try to get on the next flight back to Heathrow.'

'No, don't.' Am I really saying this? Does my voice really sound so cold? 'I'm going to stay at Ursula's for a couple of days to get away from Carnival. I can see you on Tuesday, if you like.'

'I love you, Louise,' he says again.

I have no answer to that, so I just say goodbye.

'I'll see you on Tues — ' I hear him say as I end the call.

I throw a few things into a small case, make sure the windows are closed and walk to the car. The air is heavier now. By midday tomorrow, the area will be heaving, the sound systems throwing out heavy-duty noise at decibel levels that make you think you're going to have a heart attack, even if you're on the other side of the street. 'You're turning into a grumpy old bat,' I scold myself, remembering for a moment the times when I was a committed Carnival-goer, dancing in the streets, high on a mix of reggae and sunshine.

I wonder whether Sandy will stay at Angela's for the weekend or come back to London, to the flat. I wonder whether I have made the right decision in putting off seeing him until next week. But it's all too much to think about. I get into the car, turn the radio on to a pop-music station and head to Ursula's.

She doesn't say it outright, but I can tell Ursula is annoyed that I went to see David Prescott without her.

'Sorry, Urse. I know we agreed that you would come with me, but then I thought it might be a bit much for David if two of us turned up.'

'So what did he have to say? Did you ask him the right questions?'

'They weren't the right questions, but I did ask them. I asked him if it was possible that my mother had given birth to twins but that she only told him about one of them and had the other one fostered. And I mentioned your suggestion that when his child died, my mother turned around, went back to Ireland and told the foster family I'd been left with that she wanted me back.'

'What did he say?'

'Oh, Ursula, you're such a gobshite sometimes. Can't you hear now how ridiculous the whole idea was? Of course he said no. *No, no and no.*'

'Well, it was worth a try,' she says, indefatigable as ever. 'So, what's next?'

'I'll probably go back over in the next month or so and see if I can get hold of this Liam O'Connor. I'm not overly optimistic about what I'll get from that, but at least I'll be doing something. After that, I don't know what the next move is going to be. It's not really something I can go to the police with, is it?'

'What about a private detective?'

My first reaction is to laugh. People like me don't hire private detectives. But then I see that this might not be a bad idea.

'Do you know any?'

'No, but I could help you find one.'

'Look, there's something else I have to tell you.' I launch into an account of the phone

253

conversation with Sandy.

'Sounds like you're going to be more forgiving than I would be, but if that's what you want . . .'

'I don't know what I want any more, Ursula. And there's one more thing. Remember Declan?'

She nods.

I lower my eyes. 'I've been seeing him.'

'Jesus, you're a dark horse! And what does 'seeing' mean, exactly?'

'Do I have to explain?'

'Power to your elbow. So is this why you're not running straight back into Sandy's arms?'

'I don't think so, but it's a good question, I suppose.'

'And have you told Declan about . . . ?'

'No. I couldn't. It would . . . He wouldn't just hate me for it. It would wreck him. I know it would.'

'Listen, Lou, ordinarily I wouldn't say a bloke has a right to know whether the girl he's been screwing is pregnant or not, or whether she has an abortion or not, unless she chooses to tell him,' she says. 'But this is different. It's not just about a baby and an abortion; it's tied in with everything that has happened to you. I think you have to tell him. But not for his sake. For yours.'

* * *

On Tuesday afternoon, I'm back home. There's no sign of Sandy having returned to the flat. He calls me around five o'clock and asks whether it would be all right for him to come around at seven.

254

'I thought we might go out to dinner, talk then,' he says. 'I've booked a table at that French place in St John's Wood, the one with the garden. But I can cancel it if you'd rather not go out.'

'No, it's fine. See you at seven.'

When he turns up, he doesn't let himself into the flat, but rings the bell, and when I open the door, we exchange awkward half-smiles. I'm torn between a desperate urge to throw my arms around him and a nervousness that makes me stand back from him. I keep my distance. He doesn't make any attempt to embrace me, either. Neither of us is taking it for granted that we'll get beyond this.

'Angela and Joe were on good form,' he says by way of conversation, turning the engine on and pulling out into the traffic.

'When did you get back?'

'A couple of hours ago. It's okay, I can stay at Geoff's or I can stay at a hotel. I'm not assuming anything.'

The restaurant is full, inside and out. Sandy has booked a table in the garden, the most romantic place we could be, because it's filled with the scent of jasmine and lit by flickering candles. But there's nothing romantic about the situation we are in and, for a moment, I feel vexed that he has chosen this place. Is this all he thinks he needs to do to win me back?

Throughout our marriage, I've always allowed him to set the framework for any serious discussion, deferring to what I had always seen as his superior emotional and psychological awareness and sensitivity. Apart from the night he told me he was leaving for a while because he needed space, his approach has usually been to ease us into any potentially difficult conversation, to wait until the prospect of an angry eruption has passed. Now, I'm sure, he would like us to ease gently into the things we have to talk about, after we've chosen the food, after we've had that first glass of wine. But I'm not deferring to him now. He has fucked up big time. He has lost any right to determine the rules of engagement.

'So,' I begin, as the waiter disappears with our drinks order, 'what have you got to say?'

'I'm sorry I caused you such pain,' he says slowly, looking down at his hands. 'I want to make it up to you. I want to stay married to you.'

'You might want to look at me when you say stuff like this, Sandy. You're not convincing me.'

'I'm ashamed of what I did, Louise.'

'What about Julia? And the baby?'

'I don't love Julia. I never did. I was seduced by her. I love you. And there's no baby.'

'What? She had an abortion?'

'There never was a baby.'

I stare at him, looking for the lie. His face is a map of shifting expressions that I'm unable to read.

'You mean you're going to tell me she made it up? That you didn't continue the affair with her after we got back together? Oh, Sandy, please, no lies.'

'I'm not lying. I did stop seeing her. I stopped going to choir. There was just one night when I agreed to see her because she'd been badgering me, and . . . well, I ended up getting pissed. It was just that one time. It meant nothing. Then she told me she was pregnant and I knew it wasn't impossible.'

'And that's your excuse? You got pissed and she took advantage of you. What did she have that you found so irresistible? Do you remember that night you walked out on me, last year, when you told me we needed a break from each other? Why couldn't you have been honest with me? You told me there was no one else involved. You let me think there was something wrong with our marriage.'

'But there was.'

'Something wrong?'

'Can't you remember?'

I shake my head. 'No. But now that we're talking about it, you'd better tell me.'

'Look, I did lie about Julia. But she was just a part of the whole thing. You and I weren't getting on. I feel bad saying this, because I understand so much more now, after everything that's happened since your mother died, but all you seemed to think or care about for so long was finding your real father, even though you were doing nothing about it. And it was as if nothing else mattered. I felt as if . . . well, as if I didn't matter, either. I felt that I just wasn't enough for you. I'm not excusing what I did — I'm really not doing that — and I know how pathetic and ridiculous I may sound right now, but we'd stopped being the way we used to be. Julia . . . Julia just happened to be there.'

I want to dismiss what he's saying, tell him that he's right and that it does sound like a pathetic excuse. But, even as he's still speaking, I try to cast my mind back and, with every little push, I remember the spats we had. They were always the same. I would mention my father and my latest idea for finding him or for tricking my mother into telling me where he lived. It got to the point where Sandy would refuse to discuss it and pick up a paper or turn on the television. And then I stopped talking about it. I stopped talking about a lot of things. Maybe our marriage had become so difficult that Sandy had needed to get away from it. But why had he taken up with someone else? Why Julia?

'Did you know she was coming to me for lessons?'

'Not at the time. I had no idea. That was . . . '

'A bit sick? Yes, it was. The whole thing was a bit sick. But I want to know more about the baby. You said there never was one. Did she make it up?'

'I really don't know. I think she convinced herself she was pregnant.'

'And if it hadn't been a false alarm? Would you have left me for her? Again?'

He doesn't answer straight away.

'If there had been a baby . . . ' He leaves the sentence unfinished.

I wait, my heart beating time in milliseconds. And, when he speaks again, it's not what I want to hear.

'I honestly don't know.'

27

I've been apprehensive about my first session with Sheila after the break, having to tell her that everything has been a sham, nothing but lies. All the lies my mother told. Sandy's lies. I had been so confident as I walked away from our final session before I left for Ireland. Now I'm in a worse position than I was when I started my therapy.

'I'm afraid I've gone backwards, not forwards,' I say. And, as I lie down on the couch, the floodgates open. Almost without stopping for breath, I tell her about the shock of Julia's phone call and Sandy's treachery. I don't tell her about Declan. He's not significant. He's not really part of the story. And, anyway, if I do tell her about him, we will end up going back all those years to the abortion. I'm fed up of talking about the distant past. I want to move forward.

'You've had quite an eventful few weeks,' Sheila says when I stop talking. She shows no sign of surprise, but seems to take it all in her stride. I can sense that she's waiting for me to start talking again, but I say nothing. I'm emotionally exhausted after the rush of information I've given her.

'Would you like to talk a bit more about what happened with Sandy and Julia?' she asks eventually.

'What's there to talk about? It's all out in the

open now and he's promised to be a good boy. But only because there's no baby, after all.'

'Do you think Sandy became involved with Julia because he wanted a younger woman who could give him a child?'

'I don't know. I'm fed up thinking about it and trying to understand it. But I think he became involved with her because she's beautiful and she flattered him. She flattered me, too. That's how she seduces people. I think he's convinced himself that he wants to make our marriage work now. But I think he would have left me for her, for good, if there really had been a baby.'

'How does that make you feel?'

'Not great. Inadequate. It's as if . . . well, I get to hold on to Sandy only because Julia wasn't pregnant, after all. It doesn't exactly bolster my confidence, does it?'

'Don't you think there are other reasons Sandy wants to stay with you?'

She has a point. There must be other reasons. I close my eyes and think back over the years, conjure up a pageant of scenes from our life together that make sense of what she was saying. It seems simple: we love each other, so that should be enough to start us off on the right track again. Yet his betrayal still tears through me like a sharp knife, and the only thing I can pin it on is my failure to give him a child, even though he has brought up my obsession with my real father as something that had introduced tension in our marriage long before his affair with Julia. But I can't bear to think too much about all this. It's easier to put the blame for everything squarely on Sandy.

I sit up and turn around to face her.

'You knew of Sandy professionally. Aren't you shocked by all this, by the way he's behaved?'

She gives her head a small shake. 'Louise, it doesn't matter what people do for a living. We're all human. We all act out what's going on inside us. Even someone like Sandy.'

★   ★   ★

My first day back at the studios was filled with back-to-back sessions and, though I was exhausted at the end of it, I was exhilarated to be doing normal things again. There was a sealed envelope waiting for me when I arrived. Inside was a note from Julia with just two words written on it: *I'm sorry.* Ben came for a lesson and asked shyly about Julia's whereabouts. I told him she had decided to go to someone else. He looked disappointed, but said nothing more.

I've seen Sandy several times. It's as if we're dating, getting to know each other again, except that he's the one who wants to talk about the future, while I'm stuck wrestling with the past. We are careful in our dealings with each other. Sometimes, when I feel his hand on my back as he guides me to a restaurant table, an electric current runs through me and, for a second or two, I'm ready to capitulate. But the thought of Julia is still too raw.

We talk about her. It's a tiny bit of comfort to learn that he didn't move in with her when he left me last year, but really had stayed at Geoff's flat. 'She was an interlude, that's all. I was bewitched for a while. She was never meant to be long term.' That's what he says, over and over again.

'There's something I don't understand,' I say one day, remembering the session when Julia told me she was pregnant and I had assumed then that the baby was Ben's. 'When did Julia tell you she was pregnant?'

He lowers his eyes. 'It was that time when I told you it was the hospital calling. I'm sorry.'

'But . . . now I'm confused,' I say. 'She didn't tell you until then? I thought you had lunch with her at Le Caprice.'

'That was . . . I'm sorry; that wasn't long after the night . . . you know . . . the night I got pissed and . . . ' He trails off and coughs. 'She asked me to meet her for lunch, just as friends. So I went, because I thought that was the right thing to do. But she wanted us to continue and started going on about how she might even be pregnant.'

She wanted us to continue. The *us* stings. I let out a moan and Sandy grabs my hands and squeezes them so tight it hurts.

'I told her not to be ridiculous,' he says. 'And it was ridiculous. It was only a few days after . . . and I'd been drunk, but I'd used a condom. I'm not that stupid.'

'Yet you ran to her when she called you in Ireland. You believed her then.'

'I didn't know what to think. She said the condom must have been faulty. All I knew when she phoned was that I had to go and talk to her and find out what was happening. I think she

262

already knew she wasn't pregnant when she called you.'

★ ★ ★

We talk about our childless marriage and whether it might have been very different had we been honest with each other about what we'd wanted and what we'd feared.

When we first got together, I was curious about his first wife and how I compared with her, but over time I stopped thinking about her. Everything was about Sandy and me. Now, though, I want to know and understand more. Had childlessness been a choice for her, or for both of them? Or was it simply that they hadn't got round to having children? And had Sandy discovered at the age of fifty-one that the prospect of becoming a father had exposed a desire he never imagined he would feel?

'I don't remember Elizabeth and I ever talking about kids. I suppose we might have had a couple, if we'd stayed together, but we were young and completely focused on our careers,' he says. 'I didn't really think consciously about kids until I met you.'

'Not consciously enough that you ever actually talked about kids in a serious way with me,' I say. 'So why Julia? Did you sit down and talk about kids with her? I won't be cross if you tell me the truth. I just want to know what it was about her that made her so irresistible.'

He throws his hands up in a helpless gesture. 'She was . . . lively and good fun. Most of the men fancied her like mad and I suppose I was flattered that she was interested in me.'

'You're a complete fuckwit.'

'I know.'

There's something else I want to know. Why he came back to me that first time.

'I missed you. And . . . you needed me.'

I persist with another question, over and over again. 'If we'd had a child, children, do you think you would have had an affair with Julia?'

His answer is always the same. 'I don't know.'

But we talk in short bursts, because neither of us is capable of sustaining such openness for long, so we talk about other things. He tells me he has been offered a job in Dublin.

'Are you going to take it?'

'I don't know. It depends on you.'

'When did this Dublin offer come?' I ask.

'A few months ago. When we were still apart. Well, it wasn't really an offer, then, just an approach. To check whether I might be interested.'

'And were you?'

'At the time, not very. But that was . . . '

I finish his sentence for him: ' . . . when you were still with Julia.'

'Look, I wasn't with her all the time. I was just seeing her occasionally. It wasn't what you'd call a relationship. But that wasn't the reason. I didn't see any point in leaving London and it was all very much up in the air. Now they've come up with an offer and I've said I'll think about it.'

'Why? Is it because of the job itself or because

you think it's what I would like?'

'The job's a senior one. It wouldn't be much different from what I'm doing now. But it might be good for both of us. We'd be starting again.'

It's not an unattractive idea. We could sell or rent out the London flat and buy something in Dalkey or Killiney, or in Howth, on the other side of Dublin Bay. We'd be close to the city and close to the sea and the mountains. I could teach there, too. It would take a bit of effort to establish myself, but maybe that would be a good thing, to have time to get used to such big changes.

I never thought I'd return to Ireland and now the possibility that I might, that both of us might move there, frightens me as much as it excites me.

But what if we can't repair our marriage and we drift apart, though? At least in London I would have most of the life I've built up over the years. I would have Ursula. Being alone in Dublin would be hard. As part of a couple, I might be able to form new friendships, but as a woman in her forties and on her own — that's something I don't want to think about. And I'm not in the mood for final decisions now, for giving a definite yes or no to anything.

'I'm sorry. I can't think about that now,' I tell him. 'I can't think about anything right now. It's too soon.'

There's already an autumn chill in the night air and, when I open the windows, a resinous smell insinuates its way into the flat from the trees in the communal gardens at the back. It

265

was around this time last year that Sandy walked out. I could take him back and try to write off the year that has passed. But I'm not ready to forgive him and I'm not sure I ever will be, because every time I think about a future with him, I also think of him with Julia, imagine their bodies in a tangle of physical desire, and my stomach feels as if shards of glass are flying around inside it. I don't know whether I will ever be able to trust him again.

28

I see Sheila every Tuesday and Friday morning at nine o'clock. We talk, me lying back on the couch, saying whatever comes into my head, although 'whatever' still doesn't include Declan. Sheila listens and occasionally interjects with a comment or question, quietly helping me to explore my mind and my feelings.

How do we really remember things? I want to know. How much of what we tell about our childhood is real and not just a set of tableaux, like a series of film stills, borrowed from the memories of others? I am learning just how unreliable our memories are.

I pour all this out to Sheila, and I wonder what she makes of it. I don't know if the sessions are helping me, but I like her calmness. I like knowing that, when one session ends, I'll see her in just a few days, and I like the fact that I'm doing something to discover what has been happening to me and why.

We talk about the postbox memory and whether it has become more vivid. It hasn't, because I haven't allowed it to. Every time it starts to come, I'm afraid it will merge with my breakdown — I call it that because I don't know what else to call it — in Walter Square and bring back those feelings of terror.

'So you deliberately suppress it. How do you do that?' Sheila asks.

'I just fight it. I force myself to think about something else. Do you think that's not a good idea?'

'I don't think it's necessarily a *bad* idea, but that memory is trying to come out and you've probably been suppressing it unconsciously for years.'

'You're going to suggest hypnosis again, aren't you?'

'Only if, and when, you feel ready,' she says.

So much of me wants to reject anything that will push me deeper into that strange memory, potentially opening up something that will make me wish I'd never embarked on this psycho-therapeutic journey. But I want to end the craziness of the past few months and get to the bottom of this huge box of horrors that my mother's death has opened. And it's autumn now, the time of year I've always seen as a time of new beginnings, after the long summer.

'I'm ready,' I say. 'When can we do it?'

★　★　★

I'm to undergo hypnosis today. I'm apprehensive, nervous, anxious. No, I'm much more than those things. I'm utterly terrified. I trust Sheila, but, as I walk up the path towards the white-stuccoed house, I think that my trust in her is not unlike that of a child in its mother. And, as I know only too well, mothers are not infallible. Nor can they always be trusted to do the right thing.

The temptation to turn away is strong, but my

need to dig deep for the truth about my recurring memory and the connection with that postbox in Walter Square is even stronger, and I climb the steps and press the doorbell. As I wait for Sheila to open the door, I look around me at the trees in bloom, at the houses on the other side of the leafy street, at everything, taking it all in so that I'll know, when I leave, that nothing has changed, except perhaps me.

Sheila smiles as she opens the door and we walk silently to the room she uses for psychotherapy sessions. We never converse on this part of our journey. We save that for the room at the back of the house. I've come to know that small room intimately, its walls painted a light warm grey, the blue Persian rug that covers much of the floor. There are no paintings on the walls, but there's a window that frames a tree directly outside and, as the sunlight penetrates the dense foliage, there's a kaleidoscopic effect that I find quite calming, almost meditative. I wonder how it will change in winter, when the branches are bare.

I lie down on the couch and start chattering about anything and everything — the time it took to drive here, how difficult it is to find shoes that are both stylish and comfortable, how agitated I've been in the humid weather.

And then, gradually, I settle down and hardly notice that Sheila is talking more than she normally does, telling me how it's possible to relax by thinking oneself into a beautiful garden.

I think about a garden I visited once in Ireland, the garden at Kilruddery in County

Wicklow, in the shadow of the Little Sugar Loaf. I had been to a concert in the Orangery and, during the interval, the rain stopped and a rainbow stretched across the sky and everything was bathed in an extraordinary watery light, tinted by the lapis and purple shades of the mountain. Richard's garden comes into my mind, too, with its feel of the Mediterranean and the views that made me think of the Bay of Naples and the French Riviera.

She asks me to imagine walking down steps into a garden where I will feel quiet and peaceful, to think about the flowers and plants in it. So I think about sitting on a wooden bench, surrounded by roses in shades of white and pink, and by oleander of the deepest red, intoxicated by the scent of jasmine. In this garden, spring and summer blend into one.

And then, when I've become comfortable and dreamy in this imagined sunken garden, Sheila takes me to another place, the garden in the middle of Walter Square. What is it like? Are there flowers in it? Trees? Yes, there are some trees. But there are no flowers because it's winter. Are there people in the garden? Children? No, no one; it's quiet and empty.

Perhaps it's time to walk for a little while outside the garden, Sheila suggests. How many gates are there? Four, I say. Metal gates, with railings. So I choose a gate and walk through it. It's becoming dark now and I shiver, because it's getting colder. I'm walking now around the square, past the houses with their curtains closed and their lights on. I'm running, running, and now I see the postbox, the green postbox, only now I stop skipping because there's someone there, someone I can't see. I want to run away, but I can't. Terrified, I start to scream.

Sheila puts her arms around me, the first time she has ever done so.

'It's all right, Louise, you're safe,' she tells me.

But I don't feel safe. I've walked towards a dangerous place in my mind and have gained nothing.

29

David Prescott calls with some information he has been able to glean from Jill Tomlinson about the O'Connors, who lived at 10 Walter Square.

'You told me that, according to this young woman who now lives there, the house was sold to Thomas O'Connor in 1975, didn't you?'

'Yes,' I say. 'Joannie told me she presumed the brewery sold it to him then because that's when his name appeared on the deeds.'

'Well, this is where it becomes interesting, because the brewery didn't sell the house to Thomas O'Connor. It gave it to him, which is very generous, even for a company like Tennyson's. All the other houses were gradually sold, over the years, to the workers who lived in them, at prices well below market value. Except this one.'

'Was Jill able to find out why?'

'No. There's no background documentation other than the record showing that ownership of the house was transferred to Thomas O'Connor.'

'What do you make of it?'

'I'm mystified, as is Jill. When I transferred from Dublin, I had no contact with the business there. It was a separate entity. And when Marjorie left me, I forced myself to forget about Ireland, have nothing to do with it. I doubt whether there's anyone still alive who might be able to explain it. But as to the question of whether any of this has anything to do with Marjorie — '

'It *does* have something to do with her. That address and the name O'Connor were on the envelope I found in the house,' I cut in.

'That may just be a coincidence. Marjorie may have got to know them during the time she worked at the brewery and was still in touch with them. As for the house . . . Perhaps Tennyson's felt that the O'Connor family needed help, for whatever reason, and gave it to them. But it does seem unusual. And the lack of documentation makes me think that the decision to give the house to the O'Connors must have been made at the highest level, perhaps by the Tennyson family.'

'Are you telling me there's no point in pursuing the connection with the O'Connors?'

'No, not at all. But I don't think you should raise your hopes that these people — assuming you track them down and they're willing to talk to you — will be able to provide you with all or even any of the answers. You want to know who your father was. You may never know the truth about that. But, at the moment, it's much more important for you, and for me, to find out why you have on your birth certificate the name and date of birth of my daughter. And that's something I don't think you're going to be able to do by just getting in touch with people here and there who may or may not be able to provide you with little pieces of information that you hope will solve the mystery. It may be time to consider involving the authorities, both in

Ireland and in England, to bring in professional help.'

'Ursula, for what it's worth, thinks we should hire a private detective.'

'In this instance, I think your friend Ursula may be right.'

I can't think of any reason not to hire a private investigator at this stage. But I'm still reluctant to take that step. And I want to talk to Liam O'Connor before I commit to anything else. So I suggest that we leave it just a little while longer, giving me time to go to Ireland, before we embark on the private-detective route.

'That's fine,' David says. 'Just don't leave it too long, though. I won't be around forever.'

'I'll go to Ireland in the next couple of weeks,' I tell him, adding, 'You're welcome to come with me, of course.'

'No, my dear, it would be lovely to go back to Dublin, visit old haunts, see Richard again after all these years. But I'm too old now to travel. All the airport hassle is too much for me, these days. And, to be quite honest, I think I might find it rather too unsettling. I'm sure the place has changed for the better, in many ways, but I prefer to remember it as it was when I lived there.'

'I can understand that. Sometimes, when I go back, I'm bewildered by all the things that have changed and keep changing. If you did go back to Dublin, you'd be shocked. You wouldn't recognise a lot of it. The landmarks are still there — the GPO, Trinity, Christ Church and so on — but they've knocked down and redeveloped an awful lot. Even during my time.'

'There's something I've been wanting to ask you,' he says. He pauses for a few moments and I wonder what's coming.

'Was Marjorie happy? I've often wondered, over the years . . . '

How should I answer? I can tell him I always felt there was some regret in her life, and maybe that will satisfy him, but it won't be true. Even now, when I look back and scrutinise the near past and the distant past, I have no memory of her having displayed any mood or emotion that suggested the smallest bit of unhappiness. I tell him the truth, or at least the truth as I know it.

'I think so. She had a nice life with Dermot. You might say he was a rung or two below her family, on the social scale. He was a draughtsman who started his own construction company. But by the time she met him, I don't think that mattered to her. I think maybe she'd reached the point where she didn't want to cope all by herself any more. I think she wanted someone for herself and a father for me. But he wasn't a consolation prize — he was a good-looking man and he was clever and musical. They got on brilliantly.'

'And was he a good father to you?'

'Oh, yes — though more like a favourite uncle. He always stood up for me when my mother was cross with me.'

I can almost hear a smile in his voice. 'Ah, yes, Marjorie cross could be very formidable. I presume Dermot had a very relaxed approach to life?'

275

'He did.' I laugh. How well David knew my mother! 'Actually, now that I think about it, he was rather like you in a way that I can't quite explain. He gave out a sense of calmness and reliability, I suppose.'

'I'm not entirely sure I can be described as calm and reliable, but if that's a compliment, I accept it.'

'You are calm. And I think you're reliable,' I tell him. 'And . . . ' I pause for a moment before I am able to continue. 'I really do wish you were my father.'

I hadn't planned to say that, but now that I've come out with it, I am half-expecting him to say that he, too, wishes he was my father. So when he simply says, 'Thank you, Louise,' and ends the conversation, I'm conscious of something like disappointment.

And there's something else bothering me, something he did say, but I can't, for the life of me, remember what it was. All I remember is that, whatever it was, it struck me as vaguely puzzling in that fleeting moment I heard him say it.

30

It's October already, but we're having an Indian summer. I'm sitting on the left side of the plane and, as we descend over Dublin Bay, I can see all the way through the clear evening sunlight to the Wicklow Mountains. I think enviously of Richard and his garden with its glorious views, imagining him pottering about among his plants. I should call him and arrange to go to Dalkey. I'll call him from Drogheda.

My first task, though, will be to find Liam O'Connor. I could drive down to Kenmare on spec, but if he no longer lives at the address I have for him, it would be a long way to go for nothing. And if he is still living there and sees a complete stranger on his doorstep, he may not welcome the intrusion. I have an idea. Maybe Joannie can help me. I call her when we land.

'Joannie, I've just arrived at the airport. I need a huge favour from you.' I explain that there's a phone number for Liam O'Connor, but it's ex-directory. Maybe she could ask her boyfriend to call directory enquiries, explain that he's the estate agent who sold the house in Crumlin years ago and needs to contact the seller because something valuable has been found in the house. 'I know it sounds ridiculous, but it's all I could come up with.'

'Yeah, it does sound ridiculous all right.' She laughs. 'Leave it with me. I'll see what I can do.'

An hour later, I'm in Drogheda, turning the key in the front door. The house, *my house*, is bright and warm, so different from what it was when my mother lived here. And yet, despite all the work we've done, all the changes we've made, I have a sense that she still inhabits it in some ineffable way. Her clothes are gone and the old dark wardrobes and chests of drawers have been replaced by light, modern equivalents. But when I close my eyes for a moment, I see her walking through the house, examining everything we've done and pronouncing it to her liking.

I call Angela, who's expecting me to join her and Joe for dinner, and tell her I need half an hour to get my act together. Just as I end the call, the phone rings again. It's Joannie. She sounds pleased with herself.

'I have a number for you,' she says.

'I'm stunned. How did you manage that?'

'I have my ways. Let's just say I can be very persuasive when I want to be.'

We both laugh.

I stare at Liam O'Connor's number. I have no idea what I'm going to say to him. If I tell him too much, he may think I'm a complete nutter. If I tell him too little, he may be suspicious of me, anyway.

A woman answers the telephone. She's probably his wife.

'Hello?' is all she says, but from that single word, the way she elongates the second syllable and curls it up into a question mark, I can tell that her accent is pure Kerry.

'Hello. I wonder if I can speak to Liam O'Connor,' I say, trying to sound calm and confident.

'And who are you?' she asks, the sing-song lilt changing in a flash to something cooler and darker, overladen with suspicion. It takes me by surprise. I wasn't expecting to have to get beyond such a fierce gatekeeper.

'You won't know me,' I begin, searching in my head for the words that will convince her to let me speak to Liam O'Connor.

'Are you from the papers?' she cuts in, her voice now as sharp as a razor blade, even as it moves up and down chromatically through several tones.

'No, no, I'm not from a paper or anything like that,' I tell her quickly. 'I'm a teacher, a music teacher. I'm from London.'

'You don't sound like you're from London.'

'What I mean is, I live in London. I've lived there for years. But I'm from Drogheda. And Dublin, originally,' I say, adding, for no particular reason, 'Drumcondra.'

'And what is it you want with Liam?'

At this point, I realise that I have no hope of maintaining any control over this conversation or of getting to speak to Liam O'Connor, so disconcerting has been the intensity with which she has thrown questions at me.

'To be honest,' I say, faltering, all of the intended confidence replaced by weariness, 'I'm not sure. It's to do with his mother and my mother.'

I'm half-expecting her to put the phone down,

but, to my surprise, her voice falls back into the softer lilt and she tells me to 'Hang on for a minute.'

Several minutes go by and I start to wonder whether she has cut the line. But eventually I hear the sound of low voices coming nearer, the sound of movement through whichever room the phone is in. There's a clattering sound as someone picks up the receiver, and then a voice.

'This is Liam O'Connor.'

The voice is deep and low, the accent unmistakably Dublin. But it's the rougher sound of the inner city, rather than the well-modulated tones of the wealthier southern suburbs.

'Thanks for taking my call,' I say.

I'm buying time, still searching for the explanation that will persuade him to see me. But I'm sure now that he's the son of Mary O'Connor, because the woman didn't correct me.

'How did you get this number?'

'I . . . I got it from directory enquiries.'

'We're not in the directory. They shouldn't have given it to you.'

'They must have made a mistake. I'm sorry.'

Silence. I'm expecting him to put the phone down, but he starts speaking again.

'So what is it you want?'

He is much more polite than his wife, but he makes me nervous.

'My name is Louise Redmond and I live in London, but I was brought up in Drogheda. Well, Drogheda and Dublin,' I say, groaning inwardly as I listen to my inane repetition. How stupid and irrelevant this must sound. What does it matter where I'm from? I need to find a way of telling him why I want to see him.

He waits, says nothing.

'I . . . I'm sorry, but it's really difficult to explain on the phone. I'd like to come and see you.'

'I'm not going to see you unless you tell me why. You told my wife it was something to do with your mother and my mother. Who's your mother?'

'Her name was Marjorie Redmond.'

'That name means nothing to me. My mother is dead now, and she never mentioned a Marjorie Redmond. So why do you want to come down here?'

'Look, your wife asked me if I was a reporter. I swear to you I'm not. The reason I need to see you is because I found your mother's name and address in my mother's house. My mother died a few months ago and I never heard her mention your mother's name, so I don't know what the connection was between them, but there must have been one. My mother left things in a bit of a mess and I'm trying to sort them out. All I'm asking is that you see me for even just fifteen minutes. Please.'

'What age are you?' he asks.

'Forty-three,' I answer, before I have time to think that his question is an odd one.

'Where are you now? In London?'

'No, I'm in Drogheda. I came over this evening.'

Silence.

Then he asks, 'When were you thinking of coming down?'

'Could I come tomorrow?'

'No, I'm busy tomorrow. The day after will be okay. Have you the address?'

'Yes.'

'We'll see you then, so.'

The strange conversations with Liam O'Connor and his wife play over and over in my head as I drive to Angela's. Why would the wife have thought that I might be *from the papers*? Why would a newspaper be interested in them? I stop the car and tap *Liam O'Connor, Kenmare, Kerry, Dublin, Crumlin* into a Google search box in several different combinations, but come up with a confusion of results, none of which offers any clue as to why Liam O'Connor would be worthy of newspaper gossip.

Angela and Joe have never heard of Liam O'Connor, but Angela is broadly supportive of my plan to go to see him.

'It's good that you're doing things, checking them out. But don't be upset if you drive all the way down to Kenmare — and it's a very long drive — and come back with nothing very much at all.'

'Oh, don't worry. I'm prepared for the trip to be a waste of time, but I have to do it. It's something I have to tick off.'

Joe makes the point that I've already established in the telephone conversation with Liam that my mother's name rings no bells. 'So I don't understand what more you can get out of him by driving all the way to the wilds of Kerry,' he says.

'I don't know, either. But I'm going to ask about Tennyson's and about his family. Maybe he met my mother but didn't know her name. There are loads of questions I can ask.'

'Well,' Joe says, opening a second bottle of wine, 'as herself says, don't be disappointed if it all comes to nothing.'

31

The following evening, I drive out to Bettystown, half-hoping to see Declan on the beach with Bran. But there's no sign of him among the few lone walkers exercising their dogs.

It's probably just as well. He has been in my mind a lot. I've failed him twice. But, while I'm undecided as to whether I should tell him about the abortion, I still feel a need to see him, at least to make some kind of reparation for the way I cast him off all those years ago and for my more recent treatment of him. I was never in love with him, not before and not now. I used him as a human comfort blanket to deal with the break-down of my marriage. It is as simple as that.

What I should really do at this juncture is leave Declan alone, but I convince myself that he and I can still be friends. I send him a text telling him I'm back in Ireland and that it would be lovely to meet for a drink. He doesn't respond and I tell myself that his obvious unwillingness to see me is probably for the best.

I walk briskly into the wind, the sound of the sea in my ears and the taste of it in my mouth. My thoughts feel free, unanchored, and the images they conjure up float and bump into each other. My mother and David Prescott. My mother and Dermot. The old flat in Drumcon-dra. The letter from Ailish to Santa Claus. Sandy. Sandy and Julia. Liam O'Connor. Richard. The little hand reaching up to the green postbox is there, too, but it moves quickly in and out of my mind as I stride along the strand, still disturbing, but diluted by the other images that are flying through my head.

Back at the house, I take out a road map and start to work out my journey to Kenmare. It will be a long drive. The route-planning website gives a driving time of more than four and a half hours, but I decide it will be safer to allow six hours, even more. I will set off at eight, tomorrow morning.

I'm so absorbed in my route planning that I almost miss the sound of the door being tapped on lightly. Assuming that the caller is one of the neighbours, I open it without checking the spyhole. It's Declan.

'Oh. This is a surprise.'

'Is it? You sent me a text saying you were here.'

'And you didn't reply. So it's a surprise.'

'Can I come in?'

'Of course. I'm sorry; I don't mean to be rude. It's just that you haven't been in touch, you haven't responded to any texts. But I'm glad you're here. I went to Bettystown earlier. I looked out for you.'

'I did actually set out for Bettystown. Bran is in the car. But I decided to come straight here.'

'I'm glad you did,' I say, without thinking. And then, because I don't want to give Declan the wrong idea, to lead him on, I add quickly, 'You can advise me on my route to Kenmare.'

'You're going to Kerry? When? What for?'

'Tomorrow morning. I'm going to visit some . . . some old friends of my mother.'

'How long will you be down there?'

'I'm not sure. A day, maybe two.'

'A long way to go in the car for just a day or two.'

'Well, I may stay longer. I'll see. Look, are you hungry? I did a shop this morning. I have pasta, cheese, eggs, bacon. We could do a carbonara. And I have lettuce and tomatoes for a salad. Or we could go out.'

'Let's stay here,' he says. 'Look, I'm not . . . I'm not assuming anything. I just wanted to see you. That's all.'

I turn away, not wanting to let him see how pleased I am by what he has said, and start pulling things from the fridge and the cupboard.

'Here,' I say, handing him a big saucepan. 'Get the water on for the pasta. I'll get going with the other stuff. And why don't you bring Bran in? He'll keep us on the straight and narrow.'

When we sit down to eat, he quizzes me about what I've been doing in London, how often I'm likely to come back to the house.

'I don't know, but often enough, I hope. A few times a year, I suppose. Maybe a lot, during the summer. I still have a lot of things to sort out in my head, but I'm sure of one thing. I'm a Londoner now, Declan. I'm not coming back here.'

'And Sandy?'

I'm still attracted to Declan. It wouldn't take much to tell him that Sandy and I are finished, which wouldn't be entirely untrue because I still can't get beyond the affair with Julia. There's still a wide gap between Sandy and me that may never close. What would be wrong with having the occasional comfort of Declan? I could make it work. I could reach my hand out to him now and tell the lie that's already forming on my tongue, the lie that will send us scooting upstairs to my bed tonight and other nights.

But I stop myself. No more lies.

So I look at him and tell him the truth.

'We're not back together, but we're working on it.'

He's angry and disappointed, asks me why I gave him misleading signals. I have no excuse.

'Declan, I'm sorry. I don't know whether things will work out with Sandy — they probably won't — but I have to give it a chance. It's not great between him and me, if that helps. I did miss you. I'm attracted to you. It's easy and lovely to be with you, but there's no point, is there?'

He glares at me and then he shrugs.

'No, you're right. There isn't much point,' he says. 'Still, it was great while it lasted, wasn't it?'

I smile. 'It was.'

I think about Ursula's advice, that I should tell him about the abortion. It may not bother him at all. After all, he has two boys. And I think about the promise I have just made to myself. *No more lies.* But I see that he's trying to be nonchalant, while his eyes show that he's hurt and upset, and I know that this is one truth I'm never going to tell him.

★　★　★

I sleep badly. The night is hot and sticky. There's not a breath of air moving the leaves in the trees

287

outside. Everything is dark and still, and I lie awake, desperate for sleep, yet unable to calm my mind. The ghosts of thoughts and images dart through my head, but disappear just when I think I'm getting an inkling of what they are. I drift off, wake, drift off again.

And then, in the middle of all the chaos in my mind, I remember with utter clarity what has been needling me since I spoke to David Prescott a few days ago.

He said it would be good to *see Richard again after all these years.* I'm sure of this. Yet Richard, I remember with equal certainty, told me he had never met my mother's boss and couldn't recall his name. He said the name David Prescott means nothing to him. Our minds can play tricks over the years. Maybe Richard had simply forgotten. Maybe David had assumed he had met Richard, but hadn't. But I remind myself that, when it comes to anything to do with my mother, there are no simple explanations for anything.

My plan was to get up early and be on the road by eight for the long drive to Kerry, but the disparity between what I am being told by my mother's brother, on the one hand, and by her former lover, on the other, is like a parasite burrowing into my brain. I can't call either of them too early in the morning, so I hang around the house nervously, drinking coffee and jumping up and down to straighten picture frames or pick up balls of dust poking out from under chairs.

Shortly after nine, I call David, apologising for phoning so early in the day and hoping I haven't got him out of bed. But he has been up and about for a couple of hours.

I get straight to the point.

'I just want to check something with you. The other day, you said something that made me think you'd met my uncle before. Did you ever meet him?'

'Yes. Many times. We got along very well, actually. When he came to visit Marjorie, we would sometimes slip off to the cricket together.'

'He visited her in England?'

'Several times. But you sound surprised. It wasn't that difficult to move between Ireland and England, you know,' he says.

'And did he know about your daughter dying? I'm sorry, I have to ask you.'

'I don't know. I had no contact with him after Marjorie left. He didn't contact me, either. I have no idea what she told him. Why are you asking all these questions?'

'I had the impression from Richard that you and he had never met, but maybe it was just me misunderstanding what he was saying.'

I change the subject quickly and tell him I'm about to go down to Kerry to see Liam O'Connor, thank him when he wishes me a safe drive and put down the phone.

I'm puzzled. Richard said clearly that he had never met my mother's boss and that he couldn't remember his name. Yet David has just confirmed that they knew each other quite well. Richard told me he hadn't known about the time my mother had spent in England, yet he made several trips to see her.

I tap his number into my phone.

'Ah, Louise, are you back? I've found some more photographs for you. I think you'll find them very — '

'Richard, you told me you couldn't remember the name of my mother's boss. You said you'd never met him. But you did know him! And you told me you didn't know my mother lived in England for a while. But you went to see her there a few times. And you even went to cricket matches with David. What's going on? Why did you lie about those things? Is lying a Redmond disease?'

'I-I-I'm sorry,' he falters. 'It was your mother . . . She didn't want you to have any contact with David. I argued with her, but she insisted. She made me promise.'

'But, Richard, she's dead! What harm would it have done to help me find David Prescott?'

He says nothing, but I can tell from his breathing that he's uncomfortable and agitated.

'And the death certificate. Did you know about that?'

'No! I knew nothing about that. Louise, please believe me. Yes, I lied to you about having met David, and I accept that it was probably wrong to do so. As you say, Marjorie is dead and that promise was one I shouldn't have kept. But the death certificate — I knew nothing about it. I would never have kept anything like that from you. Marjorie contacted me to say she had ended the relationship with David and was coming back to Dublin. She said she needed time on her own, but she asked me to help her out financially.'

'And you did?'

'Yes, we opened a bank account for her and I paid money into it every month.'

'Enough to pay rent?'

'More than enough to pay rent. She was my sister. She needed help.'

'But you didn't see her?'

'Of course, I saw her. Every now and again we met for lunch at the Shelbourne.'

'And where was I?'

'You were at school. I did ask if I could see you, but Marjorie wasn't keen.'

'And what about David? Didn't you try to contact him?'

'No. No, of course not, because — '

'Because she asked you not to?' I can't help the sarcasm. 'Look, tell me just one more thing. Did you know I wasn't David Prescott's daughter?'

'No!' he says, and with such conviction that I have to believe him. 'As far as I knew, he was your father and you were his daughter.'

He sounds convincing. And how can I challenge what he says about my mother having extracted a promise from him not to put me in touch with David, especially when I know how persuasive she could be.

'I feel very sorry about having helped Marjorie to deceive you. Why don't you come up now and we can talk about it all?'

'No, I'm sorry, I can't today. Or tomorrow. I'm going down to Kerry. I'll call you when I get back. Bye.'

'Kerry?' I hear him ask as I end the call.

32

The house, a long stone cottage, is a few miles outside Kenmare, standing by itself against a mountainy backdrop. As I get out of the car, the front door is already opening and a tall man of about forty-eight or fifty comes out and walks towards me. I take in his dark curly hair, run through with grey, his eyes that are a startling blue, and I wonder why I have a feeling that I know him. An even stranger thing is that I almost feel he knows me, too, because the look he gives me is a deep one.

He takes me inside the house, where a soft-faced woman of about the same age is waiting. This is the woman who answered the telephone.

'This is my wife, Imelda,' he says. 'You must be tired after the drive.'

The sun is still warm and he suggests that we sit in the garden at the back of the house. Imelda brings a pot of tea and slices of home-made fruit cake on a tray, and leaves us. The mountains rise up in the distance, blue and dark at the same time.

It's one of the most beautiful places I have ever been, but I can tell by looking at Liam O'Connor that he hasn't had an easy life. There's a quiet roughness about him and his education has probably been of the most basic kind, but there's a strong intelligence behind his eyes.

He pours tea, offers me a piece of cake and waits for me to speak.

'I didn't want to say too much on the phone,' I say, 'because, to be honest, I'm still not sure I understand any of it.'

So I repeat what I've already told him, that I was born in Dublin, grew up partly there, partly in Drogheda, and that my mother, Marjorie Redmond, has recently died. He listens, says nothing. Waits.

'She was once a secretary at Tennyson's,' I continue, and now I notice that his eyes narrow slightly at the mention of the brewery.

'In Dublin?'

'Yes. The thing is . . . I wanted to get in touch with people who lived in Walter Square in the 1960s and 1970s. You and your family — you were there then, weren't you?' I ask.

He shoots me a look filled with anger and hostility.

'You know we were there!' he says, getting to his feet. 'So you lied on the phone about not being a journalist. Raking the bottom of the barrel for a story, I suppose. Well, if you don't mind, I won't be talking to you, so you've come all this way for nothing.'

'No! No, I'm not a journalist. I'm a musician. And I'm not trying to get a story. I don't know anything about you. I just want to know who I am!'

This appears to throw him and he sits down again.

'What's this all about, then? Why are you here?'

'It's just that I've been going through my mother's things and I found a piece of paper with your family's address on it — 10 Walter Square. There are a few things I'm trying to sort out. My mother . . . left a bit of a mess behind and I was hoping I might be able to clear at least part of it up by talking to you. I don't know anything about your family. I know your name and address only because some people helped me find out who had lived at number ten.'

He's still listening to me, but I can tell he's not convinced that I've come all the way to Kerry just to satisfy a desire to know who lived at the address I found in my mother's house. So I tell him the whole story, about my attempt to find out who my father was, about tracking down David Prescott and being shown the death certificate with my name and date of birth on it.

And as he listens, I see that his face changes, becomes tighter, and that the frown that has appeared on his forehead grows deeper. He's staring at me in a way that I find frightening.

After a long silence, he looks towards the mountain and, when he returns his gaze to me, his expression has changed, has become less hard, though his eyes are still that piercing blue, the blue of the mountains and the sea.

'You told me you were forty-three. What date were you born?' he asks.

I'm slightly puzzled by his interest in my age and date of birth.

'The eleventh of December, 1969.'

He seems to think about this for a few seconds, nodding as if making calculations in his head.

'It's true we were there. At number ten. All of us,' he says, speaking so quietly that I have to lean forward to hear him. Again, I catch a glimpse of that sad quality he has about him.

'What do you know about us, about the house we lived in?' he asks, and something in his question leaves me with a feeling of disquiet.

'Nothing,' I say.

'The worst thing happened there. I try not to think about it too often, but I'll never get it out of my mind. And it's even worse for my sister.'

He gets up and says he'll be back in a minute. The evening is soft and beautiful and there's only the gentlest of breezes, but I have a feeling that whatever he's going to tell me will blow me apart.

When he returns, he's carrying a crumpled old plastic bag from which he takes several newspapers, yellowed and ancient. He hands one of them, the *Evening Herald*, to me and points to a news item on the front page. The headline is big and bold, shocking. I begin to read, but after just a few words I have to stop. My head explodes with pain and my stomach heaves so strongly that I can't stop its contents from shooting out of me. And then I hear myself crying out. 'No, no, it can't be! It's impossible! No . . . '

★　★　★

I'm shivering, despite the warmth of the evening sun. Imelda rushes out with towels and a bathrobe, and wraps me in them until I stop shaking. Then she takes me to the bathroom, where she gently removes all my clothes and puts me sitting in the tub. And I sit there, naked and weeping, as she runs the shower hose over me, washing me with soap and a sponge until I'm clean again.

When I'm dry, Imelda takes me to a bedroom, gets me to lie down on the little single bed and pulls the covers up around me.

'I'm going to leave you to rest for a little while,' she whispers. 'Just close your eyes and try to sleep.'

But there's no prospect of sleep. I close my eyes and a terrible scene opens in my mind, like a film being acted in front of me. I see Walter Square and a little girl, underdressed for the cold night in just a skirt and jumper, running along the pavement towards the green postbox, her shadow dancing behind her, thrown about by the street lights. I hear her little shoes making the lightest tap-tapping sounds. And now I see and hear other things, too — the Christmas lights glowing brightly in some of the windows, the bare branches of the trees, the ghosts the little girl's breath makes in the cold air, the sound of her voice as she warbles away to herself. I hear bells ringing, the Angelus bells. It must be six o'clock.

And I see the postbox, the oblong mouth placed too high for such a little girl, so that she has to stand on tiptoe, has to strain and stretch to get her little arm high enough to reach it.

But she never does, Mamma, because you were there, ready to snatch her away.

Did she cry, Mamma, that little girl, when you took her? Did she call for her mother, the one who would die not knowing what had happened to her daughter, whether she was alive or dead?

Did she call for her sister, her twin sister, who had to grow up with part of her missing?

How did you comfort her, Mamma? Did you even try?

And how did you choose that little girl, Mamma? Maybe you just happened to be there on that night and acted on impulse, on the spur of the moment. You were always very impulsive.

Or was it all part of a plan? Did you see that other mother with her little twin girls in their matching navy-blue coats and envy her, ask yourself why she should have two when you had none? Did you think that other mother — *my mother* — wouldn't miss one of those little girls?

Oh, Mamma, how could you have done such a thing?

★   ★   ★

'Five, four, three . . . '

Mammy is counting the seconds to switching off the light and me and Nora are stifling giggles and pulling up the blankets so that they nearly cover our heads.

'No more talk from the pair of you. If you're still awake when your daddy comes in, there'll be wigs on the green.'

297

'Night, night, Mammy,' we say together in a pretend whisper. She closes the door and we wait.

'Nora,' I say when I think Mammy has been gone long enough and isn't standing outside the door. She does that sometimes.

No answer.

'Nora?'

Still no answer.

'Stop pretending to be asleep,' I say. But she's not pretending. She's asleep, and even when I shake and tickle her, she doesn't wake up, just makes funny little noises and turns around in the bed, away from me, and curls up tighter.

It's not much fun being awake without Nora, so I try to fall asleep too. I think about the Sandman and how he's going to come and sprinkle sand in my eyes. I don't want sand in my eyes, because then, when I wake in the morning, my eyes will be sore.

'Well, now,' Daddy says, every time I worry about the Sandman, 'you'd better be asleep when he does his rounds and then he won't come anywhere near you.'

But even thinking about the Sandman doesn't make me fall asleep. I'm far too excited. It will be Christmas soon. The day before yesterday, I heard Mammy say it was the Feast of the Immaculate Conception already and the country people were up in Dublin doing their shopping and it would be no time now until Christmas. But when I asked her to help me write to Santy, she said Christmas was still ages away and that she'd help me do it another time. So I asked

Liam to help me write it. I made all the words myself, but he showed me how to do it. I put the letter in the envelope and he helped me write on that too. And then I licked it closed and Liam took a stamp out of one of the drawers in the dresser and I licked that too and stuck it on the envelope. I put the letter under my side of the mattress.

Now I'm afraid Santy won't get my letter in time, so I reach under the mattress and pull it out. I have it in my hands now. I know what it says by heart. Audrey comes into my head and I wonder how she is. We left her in the hospital with the other dolls. I don't think she's coming back in time for Christmas. I heard the nurse tell Mammy that they were very busy and they'd do their best, but it might be the New Year before they were able to fix her. That sounds like a long way away.

I sit up in the bed and climb across Nora. She moves a bit and turns around, but doesn't wake up. I find my clothes and put them on over my nightdress, and then I sneak out of the room. I can hear Mammy and the boys talking in the front room, and the television is on as well. I tiptoe to the back door and open it as quietly as I can. Dingle, the cat, stands up and gives me a cross look, so I put my finger to my lips and whisper, 'Sssssh.' He lies down again and goes to sleep.

It's cold outside and I wish I'd put my coat on as well. So, instead of walking, I run and skip, and I warm up quickly. There's no one in the street. Patsy Houlihan said they had their

Christmas tree up already and, when I pass her house, I see it through a chink in the curtains, all lit up and covered in decorations. Mammy says it's too early to put the tree up, that it will spoil the excitement of Christmas if we do.

I'm nearly at the postbox now. I hear a sound and then another, like footsteps, but not really, not like normal footsteps. And I hear someone breathing. I look around, but there's no one there.

I'm at the postbox now, but the slot is too high for me to reach. I stand on tiptoe and stretch and stretch. I'm nearly there. I hold my letter to Santy with the tips of my fingers to push it into the slot. And then something happens. There's a lady, a tall lady in a dark green coat, and she's smiling and holding my hand and telling me I have to go with her because my mammy told her to find me.

'But I have to post my letter to Santy first,' I say.

She takes the letter from me, but she doesn't put it in the postbox. She says we can post it another time. She keeps holding my hand tightly and we hurry through the square. But then I see that we're not going back to my house and that's when I start to cry.

'It's all right, Louise, don't cry,' the lady keeps saying. Why is she calling me Louise? And I keep crying because I want my mammy and my daddy and Nora and Liam and Tommy, and she says I'll see them soon, but first I have to go with her. It takes a long time to go where she wants us to go and I keep having to stop because I'm so tired.

And I'm cold, too, and I start crying again, so she takes off her coat and wraps it around me and picks me up, and then I start feeling sleepy and my eyes feel sore, and I wonder whether the Sandman is a lady, after all.

33

Sleep does come eventually, perhaps because my mind and body are worn out with the trauma of it all, and when I wake, I know I've been asleep for hours because the room is pitch black. I turn on the little bedside light and pull on the dressing gown Imelda has left for me at the bottom of the bed. I want to pee, but I don't know what time it is. The O'Connors may be in bed asleep. So I open the door quietly and pad barefoot in search of a bathroom.

But then I hear low, quiet voices and I follow the sound in the dark. Liam and Imelda are sitting in the kitchen, facing each other across the table. She's holding his hands in hers. They both look up as I enter and I almost feel I should apologise for breaking into their privacy. But then Liam stands up and holds his arms out to me and I fall into them. It's the saddest homecoming imaginable.

We sit up, talking through the night, Imelda getting up at intervals to make tea, and Liam tells me how my mother — how can I call her anything else? — destroyed their family.

I can't bear to look at the newspaper reports again, but I force myself to scan them, and read about the disappearance of a little girl on a cold winter night, not long before Christmas. The eleventh of December, 1973. The child's mother, Mary O'Connor, had put her twin daughters,

Ailish and Nora, to bed. Their older brothers, Thomas and Liam, were doing their homework. It was their father, Thomas, coming in from his shift at the brewery, who discovered that Ailish wasn't in the room she shared with Nora, and raised the alarm. But by then someone had spirited the little girl away.

'What happened to them, your — our — parents?'

'They never got over it. My mother died just a few years ago. She was living down here with us. Went to her grave with her heart still broken. He died a few years after you were taken. Cancer. You were his favourite of all of us.'

'They thought I was dead.'

He nods. 'She kept hoping, my mother. My father wanted to move back down here, where they were from, get away from Crumlin. But she wouldn't move. Stayed there for years. She wanted to be there in case you came back somehow,' he says. 'And it turns out that she had good reason to hope.'

He leaves the room and comes back with a bundle of envelopes held together with a red ribbon. He unties the ribbon and spreads out the envelopes on the table. They're all stamped and addressed in block capitals to Mrs Mary O'Connor, 10 Walter Square, Crumlin. He takes one and hands me the card that's inside it. I recognise it at once. It's the same as the blank cards I found among my mother's things. But it's not blank. Written in block capitals are the words *DO NOT WORRY ABOUT AILISH. SHE IS WELL AND HAPPY.*

My mother's squiggly *D*. On the envelope. On the card.

'They're all the same,' Liam says, as I take another of the envelopes. 'The first one came a few months after she — you — disappeared. After that, one arrived every year, around the anniversary of you being taken, the eleventh of December. They came for years. Then they stopped. There are fifteen of them. You can count them.'

'But didn't you tell the Gardaí about them? Surely they would have done something?'

'We did. But they said the cards were probably from a crank. Anyway, when all was said and done, we were only a working-class family with no grand connections. We had no standing, no position.'

When I look at the envelopes, I see that they were all posted from different towns, the length and breadth of Ireland. And now those trips my mother took me on, those birthday visits to Cork, to Galway, to Belfast — to all the postmarks on the envelopes — come back to me. This was what they were all about; nothing to do with my mother just wanting to spend time with me. What was in her mind? Did she really think that she could comfort a woman whose child she had taken?

'When is my real birthday? When was I born?' I ask Liam.

'The seventh of October, 1969.'

So I'm two months older than I thought I was.

I go to my holdall and retrieve the little envelope, battered and crumpled, and hand it to

Liam. He scans the envelope and pulls out the letter, and when he looks up from it, his face is white and filled with anguish.

'I helped you to write that letter to Santy. I'd forgotten all about it . . . Is that how you were taken? You ran out to post it? Oh, Jesus. We could never understand it. We thought someone had come in the back door and taken you from the room. We asked Nora over and over again if she'd seen anyone come in.'

'You were in the front room. You and Thomas and Mammy. I went out the back door. I'm starting to remember bits. I remember that night.' I nod towards the letter. 'I found it in my m — Marjorie's house, after she died. There was something about it that bothered me, but I didn't know what it was.'

How has it been possible to bury all memories of a life that was turned into something else in the flash of a single moment? Was I so frightened at being taken by a stranger that, out of some basic need to ensure my survival, I made myself forget my sister and brothers, my parents?

Over the next few days, Liam and Imelda tell me about the family I should have grown up with. Nora, my twin sister, lives in America. Thomas, the oldest of the four of us, is dead.

'What happened to him?'

'Life got a bit too much for him. He walked into the sea.'

I open my mouth to say something, but I have no words, either to express my sorrow or to ask Liam to tell me more.

'He was never right, after you were taken. I

think he blamed himself in some way. Being the oldest and all. He took to the drink in a big way.'

'Was he married?'

Liam smiles sadly. 'He was. He was married to a lovely woman. Moya. We'll bring her over from Tralee so you can meet her.'

'Kids?'

'Three. Twin boys, backpacking in Australia, and the girl is working in Dublin.'

'When you asked me about being from the papers . . . was it because of Thomas?'

He nods.

'That all happened last year. It wasn't that Thomas was well known, but Moya is, because she's involved in local politics. So we started getting calls from journalists and we knew it was only a matter of time before they'd be writing stories about the family struck by tragedy a second time. It was horrible.'

'But did they write anything? I did actually google your name, after you mentioned the papers, but couldn't find anything, even about what happened when I was taken.'

'No, they didn't in the end. Moya put a stop to it. She talked to the editors and told them the whole family history, and they agreed not to run anything. Astonishing, really, when you think about it. When you rang, I was afraid you might be one of those cut-throat types, out for a big story and damn the consequences. There was a lot in the papers after you were taken, and you'd probably find it all in a newspaper library. But I don't think there's much on the internet. Because it happened back in the seventies, and because there was no body found, the story just fizzled out.'

Liam brings out reams of photographs and I pore over them. I look more like my father, Thomas, than my mother, Mary. He is the big dark one; she, a tiny little woman with wavy fair hair. Nora's hair is red, the deepest auburn. Mine is a dark cloud that threatens to obscure my face. We look different. I'm the taller, the sturdier-looking, the more boisterous-looking of the two. But when I examine the photos closely, I see we have the same eyes, the same quizzical expression on our faces. I see that we're always standing next to each other or looking towards each other.

'The pair of you were so close,' Liam is saying. 'You did everything together. But you were such a bold little thing, no fear at all. You'd stand up to anything.'

I don't recognise the child he is talking about. Perhaps I'd learned on that night all those years ago, when I sneaked out of the house to post my letter to Lapland, that fear was a good thing to have, after all.

My brother is a quiet, cautious man, not given to impulsiveness. He hasn't told my sister that the miracle they'd given up hoping for has happened, that I'm alive and have come back. He needs to know who and what he is dealing with before he makes that phone call to America.

He tells me more about Nora.

'She's a singer,' Liam says. 'It's funny that the two of you ended up doing music for a living.'

He looks proud as he hands me a CD with the

name Nora O'Connor emblazoned on it. The cover, an arty black-and-white portrait, is of a fine-boned woman with long, wavy, lived-in-looking hair, who looks nothing like me.

'She's not famous or anything, but she has a good following. Sings in folk clubs all over America, but mainly in New York.'

'Can we hear it?'

He puts the CD into the player and I listen, transfixed by the sound of my sister's voice as she sings a mix of Irish traditional songs and songs she has written herself. But there's one song that smashes into my heart and my memory. I don't immediately recognise it because Nora has slowed it down so that it's not faithful to the dancing beat of the original composition by James Molloy. It's more beautiful, because the slowing down has heightened the sense of yearning in the words. But there's something else about it that rings in my head. I close my eyes and, somewhere in the distance, behind Nora, there's another voice singing the same words in a high tenor voice.

Oh, the days of the Kerry dancing,
Oh, the ring of the piper's tune . . .
Oh, to think of it, oh, to dream of it, fills my heart
with tears . . .

'Are you all right?' Liam is asking.

'Yes, it's just . . . that song. I know it. I've always known it. But I think . . . I think I remember it in a different way . . . from before.'

'My father used to sing it. He always wanted

308

to come back down here. Never did, of course, while he was alive. It's why Nora has it on the album.'

Later, I lie awake in bed, the song playing over and over in my head, my eyes filled with tears that renew themselves every time I wipe them away. I am weeping for all of them, for the father who dreamed of returning to his home county, the mother who never stopped hoping that her stolen child would be returned to her, for Liam and Nora, and for Thomas, my brother who died before I could get to know him.

And then I think of the woman I still call my mother, whose grief for her own dead child on what would have been her birthday overwhelmed her and pushed her into an appalling act, and I weep for her too.

34

Angela, normally so composed, cries when I tell her about everything.

'I had an awful feeling it might be something bad,' she says when she's finally able to speak. 'But I'd never have imagined this.'

Sandy wants to jump on a plane and fly straight over, but I don't want him here. Not yet, anyway. I'm learning to love my new family and there's no place for anyone else, not even him.

'I need time with them, just me and them,' I tell him. 'I'm sorry, but . . . '

'It's okay, I understand,' he says. But I can hear that he's hurt by my having excluded him, by my telling him that I don't need his support.

I'm still finding it difficult to think of myself as Ailish, as anyone other than Louise, daughter of Marjorie Redmond. Even Liam, who's having to adjust to the reality that the sister he thought he would never see again has reappeared, stumbles so much over which name to call me that most of the time he doesn't use either.

'Come, I want to show you something,' Liam says, and he opens a door to a small room.

'My mother kept all your clothes and toys. Just in case,' he says. 'I thought about getting rid of it all when she died. But I couldn't just throw it out, even though . . . '

'Even though you thought I was dead.'

He nods. 'We kept all the newspapers, too,' he says, pointing to a yellowing stack.

I look at the small piles of clothes, skirts and jumpers, folded neatly, several tiny pairs of shoes, a navy-blue wool coat with a Peter Pan collar. I brush away tears as I touch them. There are drawings, too, done in bright crayons, of cats and dogs, houses, trees, people. And there are sheets of paper with words scrawled on them — a child's attempts at writing.

'Was I already at school?' I ask.

'You were too young to go to school, but Thomas and I used to help you and Nora with the reading and the writing.'

I've almost become used to the internal turbulence that each new discovery, each new revelation brings, but the shock of seeing the doll is visceral. She stands out among the other smaller toys, lying on top of one of the little piles of clothes, her jointed arms stretching upwards. I reach out and touch the pink dress, the dark brown nylon hair, the shiny plastic face. I put my fingers on her lash-framed blue eyes, eyes that once opened and closed but don't move any more because of the glue that holds them in place.

I break down and Liam gathers me in to him, holding me tightly until I stop sobbing.

'Her name is Audrey,' I say. 'After Audrey Hepburn.'

'That's right.'

'We took her to the Dolls' Hospital.'

'Yes.'

'I remember going to the Dolls' Hospital. I

remember handing her over to a man and a woman who were dressed up as a doctor and nurse. But I don't remember going back to collect her.'

'You were taken while the doll was in there,' he says. 'The people who ran it brought the doll back to us after they heard about what happened.'

I've remembered that doll and the visit to the Dolls' Hospital all my life, but my memory was skewed. I thought she was part of my life with Marjorie. I thought Marjorie had taken me to the Dolls' Hospital.

Oh, Mamma, did you have to steal my memories as well?

★ ★ ★

I wait with Imelda in the garden, fraught with anticipation and anxiety, as Liam makes the call. How will Nora take the news she never thought she would hear? Will she resent me for having so easily forgotten her?

Imelda is reassuring. She reminds me of Angela, except that Angela is sturdy, while she's small and thin. But they both have the same strength, the same calm air about them.

Nora has been living in New York for the best part of twenty-five years, Liam has told me, and I calculate that her move away from Ireland must have coincided roughly with mine to London. She hasn't married, but has lived with a succession of men, none of whom she has brought to Ireland.

Liam eventually comes out and nods to me. I follow him inside and he tells me to sit in front of the computer. I hadn't expected this. I'd expected to talk to my sister on a telephone. Now I'm going to see her.

My apprehension is so great that I avoid looking at the screen as I sit down in front of it. But then I bring my eyes level with it and I find myself looking at my sister. Neither of us speaks. We stare at each other and then we both start crying and laughing at the same time. My sister. My twin.

We don't look very alike at all. Her hair is long and wild, and it glints auburn and chestnut in the early morning sunlight streaming in through the window of her kitchen. She's delicate and translucent, beautiful. I drink in every feature, desperate for some stirring of recognition, but there's none.

'I can't believe it,' she says, over and over. 'How did you find us? Liam told me a little bit, but not very much.'

So I tell her about the memory I retained over the years, the one that refused to be buried, and how it led me eventually to the truth about what had happened.

'Do you remember everything now?' she asks.

'Not everything, but it's starting to come back. I remember you asleep and I remember leaving the house and trying to post the letter . . . but not much else.'

I stop. I can't tell her what I remember about the fear I felt when the woman I've thought of all my life as my mother took me away from everything that made me feel safe. And I'm afraid of what else I may remember. Did she take me straight to that little flat in Drumcondra, where the chemist shop beneath would have been closed and dark, with no customers, no neighbours, either, to see her arrive carrying a small child, who might have been crying? Did we walk all the way? Such a long way on a cold winter night. And when did I stop being Ailish, forget I had a real mother and father and a sister and brothers, and become Louise?

'It's all right,' Nora is saying. 'I'll help you. I'll come over and we'll sit down and I'll tell you everything I remember, and we'll get to know each other again. I thought you were gone forever. I knew about the cards my mother got in the post every year and I used to believe what they said, that you were all right and that you were happy. But then they stopped coming and we all stopped believing. Except my mother.'

'Tell me about her. Tell me about things that happened, that I might remember.'

Nora inclines her head and shifts the focus of her eyes towards somewhere I cannot see. She's thinking, rummaging among her own memories.

'Do you remember we used to grow cabbages and spuds and carrots at the back of the garden?'

'Vaguely . . . '

'Well, one day, there was a knock at the front door and, when Mammy opened it, there was one of the local lads standing there with a load of cabbages in a wheelbarrow. 'Look at these lovely cabbages, missus,' he said. 'Look at the lovely big heads on them. I'll do ye a good deal.' 'Ah, no,

sure, I have me own cabbages out the back,'
Mammy said.'

'Except these were her own cabbages.'

'You remember?'

'No, but I had an idea where the story might
be going. It's funny, though.'

'To tell the truth, I don't really remember it
very well myself, but Mammy used to laugh
about it every time she saw that lad. She was
lovely. She was the kindest person you could
imagine. She used to bring tramps into the
house and give them tea and sandwiches. Da
used to go mad. He used to tell her she'd end up
being murdered.'

'I remember her how she was on the night I
was taken. I remember her putting out the light
and telling us to be quiet and go to sleep. You did
what you were told, but I didn't. I wish . . . I'm
sorry.'

'You don't have to be sorry. It's not your fault.'

'I used to wish I had a sister. I used to imagine
what it would be like. Maybe I was remembering
without realising it.'

'Maybe you were. I used to think about you all
the time. I didn't understand it all at first. And
then it was as if I'd lost part of myself.'

Nora asks me what Marjorie was like and I
answer carefully, saying that she had been good
to me and that I had no idea I had been
abducted. I tell her that she died only a few
months ago.

'And were you happy, as the cards said? Did
you love her?' she asks.

I haven't expected this question and I have to

wait for several seconds before answering.

'Yes.'

What else can I say? It's the truth.

And even as I look at Nora, take in her creamy skin, the rich auburn of her hair, her vivid green-grey eyes, I'm aware of a thought forming in my brain. It says, My sister is a beauty, but I was the one my mother chose.

35

We get to know each other in the days that follow, Liam and I walking and talking, making video calls to New York. Sometimes Liam leaves Nora and me to chat alone. She's managed to cancel several weeks of singing engagements and has booked a flight to Shannon. She's going to be here in less than a week's time.

It's Imelda who breaks the spell. 'We'll have to tell the Guards,' she says.

Telling the Gardaí is something that hasn't entered my head, so immersed have I been in this strange new family, in having a brother and a sister and a whole world that I knew nothing about until just a few days ago.

Once we go to the police, nothing will be left unexposed. There will be media interest, not only in me and Liam and Nora, but also in Richard and David Prescott. And maybe even in Sandy.

I want to protect all of them from the imminent and inevitable intrusion into their lives. But, most of all, I want to protect my mother — Marjorie, the woman I still think of as my mother. The press will crucify her and she won't be able to defend herself. It will be up to me to defend her, and yet how can I say anything good about her without hurting Liam and Nora?

Some things start to make sense, including my mother's insistence that I go to London to study.

I hadn't really wanted to leave and I was homesick for months, almost bursting into tears every time I heard an Irish accent on the Tube or a piece of music from home. But my mother had convinced me that I had to go to London. Now I know she never really thought I was going to have the big career as a singer she had made me believe in. I was never going to be good enough for that. But, had I stayed in Ireland, been content to perform in concerts, oratorio and the occasional opera, there might have been photographs and interviews in Irish newspapers, and they might have led to someone spotting a resemblance to the O'Connors and starting to ask questions.

Yes, all of this makes sense. But there are other things that don't. Why had she taken the risk, all those years ago, of remaining in Dublin with a stolen child who could have been recognised? Taking her to cafés, like Bewley's, even sending her to school, although it wasn't a national school, but a private school, nowhere near Crumlin.

Was she mad? I ask myself this question several times a day. But that would make what she did too easy to explain away. She had loved me, there was no doubt about that, and had given me a wonderful childhood. She had also sought to reassure Mary O'Connor that I was safe and well, that I wasn't dead. She wasn't the monster that the papers will make her out to have been.

And I think back now to that last night in the hospital, when she made that strange shushing sound, and wonder whether, in some final moment of lucidity, she was trying to tell me at last what she'd done. Was she trying to say *Ailish*?

Tomorrow I will drive to the little airport at Farranfore, between Killarney and Tralee, to pick Sandy up. It was Nora who pushed me, over and over again, to invite him.

'I've mentioned it to Liam and Imelda, and they agree with me,' she said.

'But, Nora, this has nothing to do with Sandy.'

'It has everything to do with him. This — everything that has happened — is the biggest thing in your life, in our lives, even in Sandy's life. You've just found out you're not who you thought you were and he's just found out that the woman he married, thinking her name was Louise Redmond, is someone else entirely. You're Ailish O'Connor now. You have to make something good out of all the damage that was caused. You've got us, but you can have Sandy, too. At least give him one more chance. And, anyway, I'd like to meet him because he's been part of your life for so long. We all would.'

Sandy has been in my mind a lot over the past few days. Despite the joy and excitement I feel about discovering the family I never knew existed, I keep hearing the hurt in his voice when I told him not to come. And I remember that previous conversation, when he said he had felt as if he wasn't enough for me, as if he didn't matter. *We'd stopped being the way we used to be.* And we had. I had blamed everything on him, but now I realise I had been pushing him away for a long time. Maybe I had been keeping him at arm's length all along.

I called him.

'Sandy, will you come? I need you.'

The lightness in his voice told me everything I needed to hear.

'I'll be there tomorrow.'

I haven't spoken to Richard or David since I left Drogheda, and I plead with Imelda and Liam to leave it for just another few days before calling the Gardaí.

'What harm can it do to hold off for a bit? What difference will it make, after so many years? Look, I'll call them both today. And Sandy is arriving tomorrow. Can't we wait?'

Imelda defers to Liam, who, I can tell, is relieved to have the prospect of a few more days of privacy before his life is put on display to the world.

'I think we should wait until Nora is here,' he says. 'Ailish, those calls you have to make — do you feel up to them? I can do them with you, if you want.'

Ailish. My name. It's what Liam and Nora and Imelda call me, and I'm still getting used to it. Louise has been my identity for most of my life and now I know that everything about that identity was false. But I'm not yet ready to become Ailish. I will have to grow into her, learn more about her and who she was, and reconcile her memories with mine. I've spent hours in that little room, unfolding her clothes, staring at them, willing them to tell me the story of my childhood. But they sit limply in my hands,

320

keeping their stories to themselves.

'Thanks, but I'm fine. I'll make the calls now, get them out of the way.'

Liam and Imelda leave me by myself.

David first. He listens quietly as I tell him that my mother, still grieving for their daughter, abducted another woman's child and brought her up as her own.

I tell him that Mary O'Connor had twin girls of roughly the same age Louise would have been and that Marjorie took one of them. She probably never intended to do such a thing, I tell him. Maybe she had known their mother from her time at Tennyson's and, back in Ireland, had become obsessed with the two little girls, secretly watching them, aching for a glimpse of them. And then, maybe, on that dark and cold evening, on Louise's birthday, she took one of them in a moment of emotional madness.

I don't tell him about the other thought that refuses to go away, that she had always intended to take one of those children and had opted for the plainer, dark-haired child rather than the red-haired one who might have been more easily recognised. I don't tell him because I know it can't be true.

And then I hear a sound I don't immediately recognise. It's the sound of an old man crying.

'Are you all right, David?' I ask, when his quiet weeping subsides.

'I'm fine. I'm fine,' he says. 'It's just the shock of it all, the thought of how desperate, how desolate Marjorie must have been. I shouldn't have taken her at her word when she left. I should have pursued her. If I had . . . '

His voice trails off, but the ghost of what he was going to say hangs in the air: that, if he had pursued my mother, she wouldn't have stolen me from the O'Connors.

'Oh, David. Don't do this to yourself. You knew my mother. You couldn't have made any difference whatsoever.'

'Will you come and see me soon?' he asks.

'Of course,' I say. 'Very soon.'

I'm more nervous about making the call to Richard. I should tell him in person, I think, sit with him and comfort him as I tell him the appalling truth of my mother's actions. But I don't have time to make the journey to Dublin and return in time to meet Sandy at Farranfore. And I don't want to leave my brother, my new family, even for a day.

So I pick up the phone and dial the number slowly. I've rehearsed what I'm going to say to him, but as the phone starts to ring at the other end, I find I've forgotten all the careful sentences I've planned in my head. When he answers, I don't even say hello. I just launch into what I have to tell him. And what's really odd, really surprising, is that he doesn't even react. Maybe he's in shock. Or maybe . . .

'Richard, say something! Speak to me!' I shout into the phone.

His voice comes back, weary and barely audible.

'I-I don't know what to say. I tried to tell her, tried to make her see sense, but she wouldn't listen. I'm sorry you had to find out this way.'

Christ. What is he saying?

'You knew? You knew all along and you did nothing about it?'

'No, not all along. Not until late last year, shortly before she died. She hadn't been feeling well, but wouldn't go to the doctor. She said there was no point. I think she knew then that there was something seriously wrong with her. She came here and told me the whole story.'

'She told you that the real Louise had died and that I was a child she had stolen?'

'Yes.'

'Did she tell you why?'

'She was in despair after her child died. She didn't try to make excuses for what she did.'

'Did she say she regretted it?'

'Not in so many words . . . but I could tell from the way she spoke and the way she looked . . . '

'I can almost — only almost — understand why she did it. What I can't understand is why she didn't come to her senses and put things right. She could have done that. She could have left me in Clerys or the GPO with a note pinned to my coat and run off. I wouldn't have been able to identify her. There was no CCTV all over the place in those days.'

'I think perhaps she felt that, once she'd taken you, there was no going back.'

'Is that what she told you?'

'Not exactly. Louise, I'm so sorry about it all.'

'But why didn't you tell me? Why did you tell me all those lies when you knew so much? I trusted you, Richard. I really did.'

'Marjorie gave me permission to tell you the truth if I thought you could handle it. I would have told you eventually, but not then. Not when you were going through such a difficult time.'

'No, Richard, I don't think you would have got round to telling me. I think that, for whatever reason — maybe the spotlight that would come down on your own family — you would have gone on letting me think I was a Redmond. And now there are going to be reporters crawling all over your family, talking to your neighbours, asking if they remember my mother, talking to your son — '

'Reporters? You're not going to talk to the press, are you?' He sounds panicky now.

'We have no intention of talking to the press. But we have to tell the Gardaí. My mother — your sister — committed a crime. And it turns out that you've known about it for a long time, but haven't said a word. We can't pretend it didn't happen. Things have to be cleared up legally and, when that happens, the press will be all over it. And what you've done amounts to perverting the course of justice.'

'Oh, my God . . . '

I can imagine all too well how Richard's life will come under scrutiny. The fact that another man fathered his son may be exposed. Journalists will write about his background, his parents and their privileged lives in a village where houses now cost millions. They may even speculate as to whether he colluded with his sister in the abduction of a child from a working-class family that his own parents would never have had contact with.

I can't put him through that. Not when I think about how my mother used him, placing the responsibility for putting right what she had done wrong on to him.

'Listen, Richard, here's what we'll do. I'm not going to tell anyone that you knew anything. It was horrible of my mother to tell you what she did and then dump the responsibility for telling me on to you. Maybe you would have told me, as you say, and that's what I'm going to try to believe. So, when the Gardaí ask you whether you knew anything, just tell them you didn't. It's better that way. For all of us.'

I hear him exhale, a long slow breath.

But I haven't finished.

'I think you should come down here and meet my brother. You don't have to tell him what you've just told me, but you have to talk to him. I'm going to give you the address and you can work out where to stay. I don't think it would be appropriate for you to stay with Liam. There are hotels in Kenmare.'

He takes down the address and says he will think about coming down in the next few days.

'Thank you, Louise,' he says. 'For . . . under-standing.'

'I'm not Louise, Richard,' I say. 'My name is Ailish.'

36

I watch him come down the steps of the plane and, a few minutes later, he's striding into the lounge towards me.

'Louise!' he says, wrapping his arms around me and holding me tight, until I think I'm going to suffocate. But I don't stop him.

'You look good. You look happy. Happy and beautiful,' he says.

'You look good, too.'

Just a few words, but they feel like the best words I've heard and said in a long time.

When I drove from Kenmare to Kerry Airport, I took the most direct route, avoiding the mountains. But this time I take the road through the National Park because I want to show Sandy the spectacular landscape of the county in which my brother lives, and because we need this time together before he meets the family that will become his, too. If we can get our marriage to work again.

'I have to tell you something,' I say, 'and I'm afraid you'll hate me for it.'

'I could never hate you. You know that.'

But as I tell him about the abortion, I think I see a hundred thoughts fly across his face. His eyes seem to have dulled a bit, become wearier. What is he thinking about, I wonder, every time I glance across at him. Is he seeing a fast-moving set of images telling the story of a child that was never born, or maybe another child never conceived that could have been his? Ours.

'It's all right, hen,' he says finally. 'What could you have done? You were only a kid. You didn't have the wherewithal to stand up to your mother. And Marjorie must have thought she was doing the right thing.'

We drive on in silence for a while. There's something else I'm struggling with. I'm afraid to tell him about the miscarriage that I kept secret from him. How can he forgive me for concealing something like that? And do I have to tell him? Won't it be better for us and our future together if I don't? If I tell him, I may lose him all over again, and I don't think I can bear that. But when I look at him and he turns his head slightly to catch my gaze and smiles at me, I know I have to risk telling him what may drive us apart for good.

So I steel myself and start to speak. 'There's something else . . . '

I pull over and stop the car. I want to look down at my hands, protect myself from the look in his face that starts as one of mild enquiry, but will shift to appalled disbelief and then maybe even hatred as I tell the story of how deep my deception went. But I look straight at him and I don't falter, even as I see the light leave his eyes and he looks away from me and out of the car window.

'I'm sorry, Sandy. I'm so sorry.'

'I have to get out.'

He walks away from the car. I watch him until

he disappears from sight and I'm seized by a fear that he won't come back. But I've done the right thing, even if I lose him for ever.

He comes back after what seems like a very long time and gets into the car.

'Is there more? Or was that it?'

I could tell him about my recent affair with Declan, but I'm not going to. What happened between Declan and me this summer isn't part of the truth that needed telling. So I say, 'No, there's nothing more,' and wait for Sandy to tell me that this is too much and that our marriage is over.

He doesn't, though.

'I'm not going to say I'm not upset. You've driven a fucking stake through my heart, Louise. You were pregnant and didn't tell me. You had a miscarriage and didn't tell me. So I'm mightily upset. But I'm not walking away, because I think and I hope we're at a point where there's nothing secret any more.'

Relief and hope sweep over me and I close my eyes in a futile effort to stop the tears that are welling up and streaming down my face. And then I'm aware of Sandy's arms around me and his voice saying, 'Come here, hen, it's all right,' and I feel as if everything has come full circle. I feel reborn.

We switch seats and he takes over the driving, occasionally putting his hand on my knee in reassurance. We have just a few miles left of our journey, and I have something to say.

'Sandy, I've been thinking . . . ' I say, tentatively, not quite sure how to put it into words. 'I know I'm nearly forty-four now, but maybe we could still think about a baby . . . We could do IVF or maybe we could adopt.'

He leans over and leaves the lightest of kisses on my cheek.

'We can do either of those things, but we don't have to. We can be fine as we are,' he says, putting his hand on my knee and leaving it there. 'And we're fine. Very fine indeed.'

We drive through Kenmare and out towards Liam's house.

'Maybe we can buy a place down here, near your brother,' Sandy says.

'Maybe we can,' I say, quietly happy that he's thinking of a future that embraces my new family.

'And in the meantime,' he says, 'what should I call you?'

'Ailish, I suppose. But, to tell you the truth . . . '

We look at each other and start laughing.

★   ★   ★

Liam and Imelda are waiting for us outside the house. My brother stretches out his hand to my husband. They're both nervous of each other. And then Sandy opens his arms wide and hugs Liam, and I feel as if my heart is going to burst with happiness.

It's so different from that first time I took him to meet my mother and Dermot, all those years ago. I remember how my heart began to race as we neared the house.

'I'm a bit nervous about this,' I admitted to Sandy.

'As if I hadn't guessed already. You've been wired up to a brick for the past week.'

'You don't know my mother. She can be . . . '

'A pain in the backside?'

'I was going to say 'difficult'.'

'She probably thinks I'm not good enough for you.'

'It's not that. She's used to being the one who makes all the decisions and now I've made a decision to get married to someone she's never laid eyes on. She can be a bit omnipotent. Don't be surprised if she's a bit standoffish with you.'

'Och, dinnae fret, hen,' he said, going all Scottish. 'I'll be as charming as the Bonnie Prince himself. She'll be mad about me.'

I wouldn't be too sure about that, I thought to myself.

Minutes later, we were beyond the town and in the lane that led to the house, and Sandy whistled as he took in the view out over the estuary. My own breath escaped as it always did when I saw the way the light came off the water and heard the sounds the seabirds made, sounds that seemed to float on the wind. Time always seemed to stop for me when I looked out over those flat channels and had the sense that everything else might change, but the estuary would stay the same, except for the constantly shifting light.

The gate was open and, as we turned into the drive, Dermot was already coming out of the house.

'Come in, come in,' he said, giving me a hug and Sandy a vigorous handshake. He was still a fine-looking man and a healthy one, but he was old now and I couldn't help but feel a stab of sorrow at the thought that he probably didn't have many years left.

'Where's Mamma, Dermot?' I asked as Sandy got our bags out of the car.

'Ah, she'll be back any minute. She's gone for a walk with Molly. We weren't sure what time you'd be here.'

I looked at Dermot, lifting my eyebrows and inclining my head in a conspiratorial gesture that he returned. The man's a saint, I thought. And yet, even though I knew my mother was pulling a stunt, I ached to see her.

She made her grand entrance about half an hour later, when Dermot, Sandy and I were sitting, drinking glasses of whiskey by the fire they always lit in the evening, winter and summer. We heard the dog first, barking in excitement as the sight of the strange car told her there were visitors in the house. Then Mamma swept in. She was in her sixties, but looked much younger. She had changed her style over the years and at that time favoured loose cashmeres and linens that gave her a different kind of elegance, made her look ageless. She no longer wore her hair long, but had had it cut into a simple straight bob that she pushed back behind her ears. Her hair was white, but her eyebrows were still dark and her eyes still deep blue, almost navy.

She looked like something from an upmarket fashion catalogue, dressed in a long, dark grey jumper over jeans and plimsolls, a long silk scarf wound several times around her neck.

'Oh, Louise, I am so sorry not to have been here when you arrived, but Molly needed a walk and I really didn't think you'd make it down so quickly,' she said, opening her arms to me.

She turned her attention to Sandy then, bathing him in the aura of munificence that radiated from her. She was on top form and I was relieved, but I wasn't ruling out a change of mood at some point during the visit.

'So you're taking my daughter on, Sandy,' she said, beaming at him as if he were rescuing me from an otherwise unavoidable spinsterhood.

He beamed back. 'Aye, if she'll have me.'

For the rest of the evening, I veered between relief that they seemed to be getting on and annoyance that she had managed to captivate him with no trouble at all.

'So. What do you think of my mother?' I asked him later, when we went to bed in my old room.

'Magnificent,' he said.

'Ah, so she's reeled you in like all the other fishy-wishies,' I said, throwing a pillow at him.

He laughed and threw it back at me. 'You're just jealous.'

'She's been doing a number all evening, you know,' I said. 'She made sure she was going to be out of the house when we arrived.'

'I'd kind of figured that out. But maybe she was as anxious as you were and needed to grab a bit of control for herself. It's only for a few days. Just relax.'

So I relaxed and the days we spent with my

332

mother and Dermot were good ones. She was on top form, organising trips to Newgrange and Mellifont, cooking, entertaining. She couldn't do enough for Sandy. There were no moods. She didn't criticise Sandy behind his back, didn't refer to his divorce.

When we left to return to London, I kept looking back at Mamma and Dermot standing outside the house, waving us off. Maybe it was my imagination, but as we began the turn into the lane, I thought I saw her body shrink a little, become smaller and older, and I felt the old familiar tears flood into my eyes.

'It's all right, hen,' Sandy said, putting his hand on my knee.

He understood. He always has.

* * *

We're having breakfast, the four of us, when the postman arrives with a registered package addressed to me. I tear it open to find a short note from Richard and a bulky sealed envelope with my name on it, in my mother's handwriting. I get up from the table without speaking, signalling with my raised hand that I need to be on my own for this. Words are beyond me. I feel as if I'm choking.

I walk down to the bottom of the garden and sit on the grass that still has drops of dew on it despite the early warmth of the sun. The note from Richard has only a few words on it.

Marjorie left this with me for you. I have read it.

Forgive me for not having told you about it straight away, but she said it would be up to me to decide whether it was necessary. I foolishly hoped that everything would just settle and I would never have to give it to you. I am so sorry. And I'm sorry for being a coward, but I cannot face meeting your real family and having to explain myself to them. Not yet. I will some day.

I start to open the sealed envelope, but my hands are shaking so badly that it drops through my fingers. I stare at it, unable to move. And then Sandy is kneeling down beside me and saying something, but I don't hear him because my ears don't seem to be working properly, either. I watch as he picks up the envelope and slides his finger along the sealed edge. It all seems to be happening in slow motion. He holds out the letter to me and I'm almost afraid to take it, in case it slips through my fingers again.

I'm afraid of what I will read.

'Would you like me to read it out to you?' Sandy asks.

I open my mouth to say yes, but the word won't come out, so I nod my head up and down and watch as he unfolds the letter and starts to read.

'My darling daughter, I write this letter not knowing how much, if anything, Richard will have told you. I suspect that he hasn't told you very much at all, so I am going to start at the beginning, before you came along.

'The beginning was the birth of another little girl, a baby I hadn't planned or wanted. David

334

Prescott was her father. He was my boss and he was already married. I was a little in love with him from the moment I met him. The affair suited me. It was illicit and exciting. It wasn't meant to go on for several years, but it did and then the inevitable happened. I became pregnant. I panicked. A baby was the last thing I wanted. I thought about going to England to get rid of it. I drank gin in scalding hot baths. I made myself tumble down the stairs. But the baby survived and so I told my parents. The plan was to have it adopted. But when I held my daughter for the first time, my heart burst with feelings I never expected to have. I could no more have given her away than I could have taken my own life.

'David was eventually transferred back to England and I went with him, although not immediately. Once he and his wife had settled into their house, he found a house for me and my daughter. It was a little bit lonely. He came every day to see us, but he went home every night, except for one night.

'My daughter had been hot and feverish all day and, by the time David came after work, she was much worse. We took her to the hospital, where we were told she had meningitis and was unlikely to survive. I don't know whether you can imagine how we felt. We were desperate for her to live and yet, at the same time, already grieving for her.

'Sometimes when a child dies, the love between its parents dies too. That is what happened between David and me. I know he lost something precious too, but I couldn't bear to be near him because he was a constant reminder of what I had lost. I left and returned to Dublin. I left my daughter's ashes with David. I didn't need a grave to visit or an urn to keep on the mantelpiece to remind me of her.

'During those first few months after my daughter's death, I lived in a permanent state of anguish. Dublin seemed to be full of children. I couldn't bear to look at them. Whenever I saw small children, I walked the other way. And then something changed and I still cannot explain it. I was waiting for a bus one day and recognised a woman whose husband worked where I had worked. Her twins were born a month or two before my daughter. She didn't notice me because she was trying to keep the girls under control. When her bus came along, I got on as well, and when she and the twins got off, I got off too.

'I just wanted to watch the twins playing. They made me laugh with their high spirits. They gave me hope. I think I had a vague notion that I could become friends with the family, but I probably knew deep down that they would find it odd that someone of my class would want to be involved with them.

'Believe me when I tell you that I had no intention, no plan, and that what happened was something I had no control over. On the day my daughter would have been four years old, I found myself wandering around the area where I used to work and where this woman and her girls lived. It was cold and dark, a couple of weeks before Christmas, but some houses already had Christmas trees lit in the windows of their front rooms.

'When I saw the little girl, one of the twins, running along the pavement, my first thought was about how cold she must be, because she wasn't wearing a coat. She stopped at a green pillar box and was jumping up and down, trying to put a letter into it, but couldn't reach it. I went to help her. I was going to put the letter into the box and then I was going to take her home to her family and tell them to take better care of her and not let her wander around in the dark and cold without a coat.

'But I didn't, and I still cannot explain what happened in my mind to make me do what I did. I took her with me. I can't remember very much about those first few days and weeks, but after a while it was as if I had my daughter back, as if I had been given another chance to keep her alive.

'Now, I am giving you the opportunity to find the family into which you were born. Their name is O'Connor and they lived at 10 Walter Square, in Crumlin. They may not be there any longer, so you may need the help of the Gardaí to trace them. Dermot, by the way, knew nothing of what I did, so please do not think of him with anything but affection.

'I have often thought of talking to Sandy about all of this, knowing that whatever he did would be in your best interest. It's true that I was doubtful about him at first, and that our personalities did clash. How could any man love you as much as I did? But Sandy did, and I liked to think he might have been able to help bring this story to some kind of conclusion that might have saved everyone heartache. But I never did talk to him because I knew that it was wishful thinking on my part that everything could be put right. And, in any case, how can you repair the heart of a mother who has lost her child?

'There isn't much more to tell. The other part of your story is something you will have to discover for yourself. Perhaps, as you read this, you are wondering what our life together was all about. But let me tell you that you have been the light of my life, the star that burned brightly when I thought all the others had gone out. I wasn't always a good mother. Sometimes I acted in ways that left you hurt and confused, and I took decisions that you may still not understand, even when you have read this letter. I will not make excuses for myself. I did something that some would say is beyond forgiveness. But I dare to hope that, even when you come to hate me for what I did, you will also remember everything that was great and wonderful between us.'

Sandy stops. 'That's it,' he says.

'Did she sign it?'

'Yes,' he says, holding it out to me.

I take it from him and read.

From the mother who loved you best.

There's one more thing I have to do before I go back to London.

I weave through the paths among the graves behind Liam, the mountains around us and the

338

Atlantic beside us. We stop in front of a grave. My real parents are buried here, under a plain headstone that lists their names and the dates on which they died.

'This is it,' Liam says.

He stands, head bowed, and I can tell that he's praying quietly. I wish I could pray, too.

I've stared at photographs of my real mother, Mary O'Connor, who never gave up on the possibility that her missing child would be found, who kept all those little clothes and toys for her, just in case, by a miracle, she came home one day. I can imagine her pain, just as I'd be able to feel for any woman dealt such a tragedy. But I can't yet think of her as my mother.

The deepest pain I feel is for the woman I still think of as my mother, racked by grief over the death of her child, tortured and demented to the point of stealing another woman's child.

Some day, I'll grieve properly for Mary O'Connor, the way she must have grieved for me. But now, as I look out beyond the graves to the sea, the tears that stream down my face are for the woman who stole the childhood I should have had, who stole even my memories.

I see her in the hospital, becoming smaller and smaller in the bed, shrinking before my eyes. Her eyes are closed most of the time and, when she opens them, there are only glimmers of lucidity. And now I feel sure that, in those last hours of her life, she wanted to talk to me about what she'd done, to try to explain the inexplicable. Did she remember, every time her eyes opened, that she'd left behind her all the secrets she'd kept from me and which would hurt me? Did she want to prepare me for the terrible discoveries I would make?

In my mind, I hear that *ssshhh* sound she made as she lay dying. Only now it becomes *Ailish*, over and over again. *Ailish*.

Oh, Mamma! What I would give to be able to turn the clock back, all the clocks, but especially the one that counted down to the death of your little girl. Because then things would have been so very different for all of us.

37

Autumn is on its last legs. Most of the leaves have fallen and the temperatures are dipping low at night. I stayed several weeks in Kerry with Liam and Nora and Imelda, and now Nora is in London with Sandy and me. Now that I know her, I can't bear the thought of not being near her. I want her to think about moving here, or to Ireland. There's nothing keeping her in New York, she says. She can write and sing anywhere. She'll give it some thought.

Sandy and I are still thinking about whether he should take the Dublin job he has been offered, but I have a feeling we both know that neither of us will be leaving London. It's our home. And there's another reason we will probably stay here. We're going to try to have a baby. I'm still a little afraid, but I'm not terrified.

Nora loves Ursula. They're birds of a feather and I feel almost jealous when I look at the two of them together, their auburn heads moving enthusiastically as they become involved in some vivid discussion. They look more like sisters than Nora and I do. I take Nora to meet Sheila, whom I'll continue to see because I know I'm going to need her in the months ahead as I swing between loyalty to my mother, my not-real mother, and disgust at what she did.

'You're in good hands, there,' Nora says as we leave. 'Maybe I'll get myself a shrink, too.'

341

But I don't take her with me to Northampton-shire. The visit I promised David is long overdue and I want to see him by myself.

He looks frail, older than when I saw him just a few months ago. We've been through so much together that I feel a responsibility towards him. I will be the nearest thing to a daughter he can have. If he were my father, I would be proud.

We sit on old striped deckchairs in his autumn garden, where the sun still bathes the remaining flowers and plants. Wrapped up in jumpers and scarves, we drink tea and I tell him about the family I'm growing to love.

He listens quietly, and sometimes he bends his head and lifts a hand to his eye, and I wonder who his tears are for. Perhaps they're for everyone — for his daughter, for Marjorie, for himself and for me.

Eventually, when there's no longer any warmth from the sun, he stands up and we start moving back towards the house. I notice that he shuffles, that he's slower than he was just a few months ago.

'I'd like to play something for you,' David says, taking a vinyl record and placing it on an old turntable, carefully lowering the stylus on to the track he wants me to hear.

I close my eyes as I hear the crackly old recording, well worn from frequent use, burst into life. I've sung these words often and have never failed to be moved by them. And now, because I know David's story and because there's no happy ending for him, I feel as if my heart is going to break all over again as I listen.

Do not go, my love, without asking my leave.
I have watched all night,
and now my eyes are heavy with sleep.
I fear lest I lose you when I am sleeping.
Do not go, my love, without asking my leave.
I start up and stretch my hands to touch you.
I ask myself, 'Is it a dream?'
Could I but entangle your feet with my heart
And hold them fast to my breast!
Do not go, my love, without asking my leave.

Perhaps he's thinking of that night, long ago, when he watched his child die, begging her not to go, staying awake through the long hours as she slipped away. Or maybe he's thinking of my mother, wishing he had been able to keep her near him. I open my eyes. He's gazing out towards the garden. We both sit quietly until the music ends.

'It gives me comfort,' he says.

The song has stirred up my own thoughts, thoughts I will never talk about to Liam and Nora. I am sitting by my mother's hospital bed, waiting for her to die, talking quietly to her and hoping she can hear me tell her how much I love her. I see her bedroom in that little flat of my childhood, the bedspread startlingly red against the dark floorboards and wardrobe. On the dressing table, I see her Coty lipstick and Max Factor powder compact, her necklaces and bracelets, the silver cigarette holder that she was never without. And I close my eyes and wait for a few moments, knowing it will come, the woody, citrusy scent of Calèche that lingered in the air long after she had passed.

Acknowledgements

Special thanks to three brilliant and lovely people, from whom I've learned so much — my agent, Nicola Barr at Greene & Heaton, and my editors at Quercus, Stef Bierwerth and Kathryn Taussig.

Thanks to Nikki Dupin for a cover design I loved the moment I saw it, to Penny Price for her great copy edit and to all the Quercus team.

Thanks also to Richard Skinner of Faber Academy, a most generous writer and teacher, and to my fellow writers on the 2013 course.

And thanks to all those — family and friends — who found the time to read that very first draft and encouraged me to keep writing.

We do hope that you have enjoyed reading this large print book.

Did you know that all of our titles are available for purchase?

We publish a wide range of high quality large print books including:
Romances, Mysteries, Classics
General Fiction
Non Fiction and Westerns

Special interest titles available in large print are:
The Little Oxford Dictionary
Music Book
Song Book
Hymn Book
Service Book

Also available from us courtesy of Oxford University Press:
Young Readers' Dictionary
(large print edition)
Young Readers' Thesaurus
(large print edition)

For further information or a free brochure, please contact us at:
Ulverscroft Large Print Books Ltd.,
The Green, Bradgate Road, Anstey,
Leicester, LE7 7FU, England.
Tel: (00 44) 0116 236 4325
Fax: (00 44) 0116 234 0205

Other titles published by Ulverscroft:

PARADISE LODGE

Nina Stibbe

It's 1977, and fifteen-year-old Lizzie Vogel is working in an old people's home. The place is in chaos, and it's not really a suitable job for a schoolgirl — she'd only gone for the job because it seemed too exhausting to commit to being a full-time girlfriend or a punk. She's also distracted by her family's financial troubles, keeping up with schoolwork, and deciding which brand of shampoo to use. When a rival old people's home opens, offering better parking and daily 'chairobics', business at Paradise Lodge takes a turn for the worse, and everyone must chip in to save the home before it's too late — from the crazed Matron, to the assertively shy nurse who only communicates via little grunts, to the very attractive son of the Chinese takeaway manager . . .